SOMETHING CHEEKY

Also by Thien-Kim Lam

Happy Endings
Full Exposure

THIEN-KIM LAM

SOMETHING CHEEKY

A NOVEL

AVON

An Imprint of HarperCollins*Publishers*

SOMETHING CHEEKY. Copyright © 2025 by Thien-Kim Lam. All rights reserved. Printed in the United States of America. No part of this book may be used or reproduced in any manner whatsoever without written permission except in the case of brief quotations embodied in critical articles and reviews. For information, address HarperCollins Publishers, 195 Broadway, New York, NY 10007.

HarperCollins books may be purchased for educational, business, or sales promotional use. For information, please email the Special Markets Department at SPsales@harpercollins.com.

Avon, Avon & logo, and Avon Books & logo are registered trademarks of HarperCollins Publishers in the United States of America and other countries.

FIRST EDITION

Interior text design by Diahann Sturge-Campbell

Library of Congress Cataloging-in-Publication Data has been applied for.

ISBN 978-0-06-323738-4

24 25 26 27 28 LBC 5 4 3 2 1

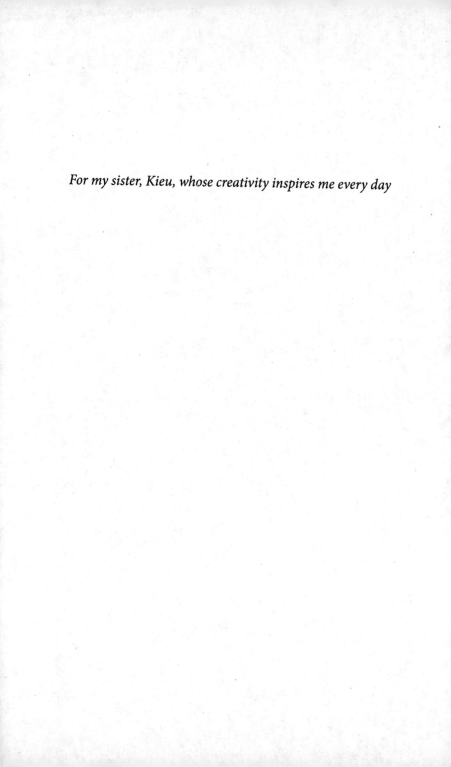

For my sister, Kieu, whose creativity inspires me every day

ACKNOWLEDGMENTS

Something Cheeky took much longer to write than I expected. It was partly due to personal and family illnesses, but mostly because both Zoe and Derek embodied so much of myself that it was challenging to write their story. There were times when I wasn't sure if I could pull off this novel, but I wasn't ready to give up on it or myself.

So in the words of Niecy Nash, "I want to thank me. For believing in me."

I actually finished this book and I'm damned proud to share it with you. Kidding aside, *Something Cheeky* wouldn't be here without the support of many people.

Thank you to my editors, Erika Tsang and Madelyn Blaney. You gave me and this book so much care (and patience). This novel wouldn't be in readers' hands if it weren't for Erika's love of theater. Thanks to my agent, Tara Gelsomino, continually checking in on me and making sure I prioritized my health.

I'm incredibly grateful to my fellow writers who offered their time, energy, and shoulders to cry on as I worked on this book. Donyae Coles, who's seen me at my best and my worst—writing life is less lonely with your company. Deborah Wilde and Heather Novak (whom the novel's stage manager is named after) talked me through the plot whenever I got stuck. Cathy Yardley, I'm doing my best to embrace your "be weird" advice. Mary Robinette

Kowal, your gentle guidance in your Patreon class on writing through stress and fatigue was invaluable.

Even though I worked in theater for many years, there's so much I don't know about the non-costuming side of things. Molly Smith, former artistic director, and Edgar Dobie, executive producer, of DC's Arena Stage took time out of their very busy schedules to answer my questions about what it takes to produce a big show. Major thanks to them. Anything about the theater world that's incorrect is all my fault. (Note: *Something Cheeky*'s Prestige Repertory is in no shape or form based on Arena Stage.)

To my real-life Boss Babes Jennifer Seneca, Leticia Barr, and Lisa Frame: thanks for checking on me while I was in my writing cave. I apologize for my many bouts of radio silence. You always welcomed me back with open arms. I'm not sure how I won the friend lottery with y'all.

If it weren't for the theater, I wouldn't have met my husband. He's my biggest cheerleader in this thing called life. He also secretly loves how I include easter eggs from our relationship in my novels. Your love for me inspires every hero that I write. Thank you also to my teenagers, who listened to me talk about the characters as if they were real people. That made for entertaining dinner conversations!

To my favorite (and only) sister, Thien-Kieu Lam: your creativity has inspired me ever since you brought home your first watercolor set. As kids we fell in love with the story of *Tấm Cám* and look at it now! You've encouraged and supported all my wild ideas and endeavors while quietly working on yours. I wish I was a knitter so I could create all of your thoughtful, beautiful patterns. I don't say it enough, but I love you. (If you're a knitter, check out @kieurious on IG and Ravelry!)

SOMETHING CHEEKY

CHAPTER 1

"M y ex's wedding is in three hours," Zoe Tran's customer cried out. "I need my assets to look so perky that he'll get a boner the moment he sees me. And jealous of my date."

The Latina pulled her shoulders back to accentuate her ample breasts and full hips and wiggled her body sensually.

Zoe laughed in delight. Her quiet Saturday afternoon in Eden Center had finally become exciting. She thrived on helping customers like this woman in her plus-size lingerie boutique.

"Welcome. I'm Zoe, the owner of Something Cheeky. Yes, I can definitely make your ex *and* your date rise to the occasion."

Her customer giggled. "I like you already, Zoe. I'm Tiff."

"Is that the dress?" Zoe pointed to the NPR tote bag in Tiff's hand. A shimmery teal chiffon fabric peeked out of it.

"I need a strapless bra for it. Sorry it's so crumpled." She cringed in embarrassment as she handed it to Zoe.

"I've got a steamer in our workroom that performs miracles." Zoe smiled reassuringly. "We'll find the perfect bra for you and this dress."

Twenty minutes later, Tiff stepped out of the fitting room wearing her perfectly de-wrinkled dress and the correct size bra under it.

"How do I look?" she said shyly as she stepped in front of the three-way mirror.

"Stunning!" Zoe exclaimed truthfully.

"I feel like a princess." Tiff beamed and twirled, letting the chiffon skirt swoosh around her ankles.

Zoe put her hand on her hip and studied the woman's reflection. Something wasn't quite right with the dress's fit.

"Wait here." She ran to the counter and grabbed some pins and her scissors. "What if we take in the waist a little?"

Zoe demonstrated by pinching the fabric at her sides.

"Whoa." The woman's eyes grew wide.

"Now imagine this slide slit goes up mid-thigh instead of to the knee." Zoe pulled up the skirt to illustrate.

"Hot damn, that's sexy." Tiff's smile disappeared as she pressed her lips together in worry. "But we don't have time for that."

"Will you let me be your fairy godmother?" Zoe checked her phone. "It'll take me thirty minutes—forty-five minutes tops—to alter the dress for you."

"I've always wanted a fairy godmother." Tiff nodded vigorously and ran back to the fitting room to take off her dress so Zoe could make the suggested changes.

Forty minutes later, Zoe handed her customer a garment bag with the newly altered dress. Tiff had decided to wear one of her new bras right away. She gleefully flung the one she'd worn into the store into the trash.

That one small change in her undergarments buoyed her confidence. She stood straighter now that her chest was more supported. There was even an extra spring in her step as they made their way to the front counter.

"You're a bra whisperer," Tiff declared as she paid for her purchases. "I've never worn a strapless that felt so comfortable."

"It's my calling." Zoe grinned so widely that her cheeks hurt. "I hope you'll leave us a review online and tell your friends about Something Cheeky."

"I'd give more than five stars if I could. This has been the best bra-shopping experience I've ever had."

"You're going to be fabulous at the wedding. I want to see pictures next time you come in here," said Zoe as she wrapped up Tiff's other purchases.

"Is that a costume from Prestige Rep's *Lysistrata* displayed in your window?" Tiff pointed to a sequined dress with a long marabou feather train.

"It's my favorite from the production. We sewed some of the costumes for it."

"That's so cool! I went to a performance two weeks ago. Your costume designs were gorgeous."

"Oh, I didn't design them. My team and I constructed them based on the designer's sketches." Zoe handed Tiff a lilac bag with her new bras inside. "You did purchase a couple of Zoe Tran original designs today."

"Wait, you designed everything here?" The woman spun around as if seeing the store with fresh eyes.

"I love designing for plus-size folks like us." Zoe's chest puffed out proudly. She'd worked hard to launch and grow her boutique.

"I'm coming back and bringing friends so they can get Zoe originals." Tiff blew her a kiss and breezed out the door with her freshly steamed dress and a rack that was ready to knock people's socks off.

Zoe's entire body was buzzing. She danced around the empty store as she cleaned the fitting room and put away the items that hadn't worked for her customers. People like Tiff were the reason she'd become a lingerie designer. Fat women like them deserved undergarments that made them feel sexy *and* supported.

She'd dedicated the past six years to doing that with her designs and Something Cheeky. Most women would be thrilled to have achieved what she had at the age of twenty-seven. Yet today proved that she needed more to keep her fulfilled creatively.

Maybe it was time to dig out her sketches and launch the Vietnamese-inspired clothing line she'd only dreamed about. The idea scared her. Was DC ready for something like that? Even if it was, she'd have to invest a significant amount of time and money into a completely different line.

The idea terrified her. Something Cheeky was a well-oiled machine that she didn't want to break. It was better to focus on her already successful lingerie collections. The endorphin rush from helping Tiff faded.

Zoe shook her head to clear it of what should be only a fantasy. Thinking about what could've been if she hadn't quit her theater major was pointless. She knew exactly what would keep her spirits up.

CHAPTER 2

"Hey, Zoe! You want your usual?" TJ Nguyen greeted her from behind the counter of Pop Boba.

She could barely hear him over the V-pop blasting in her favorite bubble tea shop. Waving at her friend, she scooted around the packed tables of high schoolers. As one of the few non-chain shops near her, Pop Boba wasn't known for its ambience but was highly photogenic for social media. If Pearl River Mart and the floral section of Michaels craft store had a baby, it would look exactly like this.

Thanks to the shop's music tastes and the plastic ivy climbing the bamboo slats lining the walls, the place was a magnet for teenagers, who found the cheesy decor funny-cool. A couple of them were posing for selfies under a neon sign that read SUCK MY BALLS.

"Bobarista, I'm in the mood—"

"Call me that one more time and you'll have to start paying for your drinks," TJ threatened, then rolled his eyes. "They make me wear this shirt because we're supposed to push the merch."

Zoe smirked at his bluff. TJ gave away freebies as a way to stick it to his boss. And flirt with customers.

"It looks good on you."

He'd knotted the BOBARISTA shirt to turn it into a crop top and paired it with white skinny jeans and white slip-on sneakers. A daring choice for a job that was prone to spills, but he had the confidence to pull it off. And Zoe had to admit that the white looked good against his tan complexion.

"Thanks, babe." He curtseyed. "Now, what shall I whip up for you?"

"I'm in the mood for something new," Zoe continued. She'd never given the menu above the counter more than a cursory glance before now. She rarely deviated from her usual drink.

"Oooh, someone's feeling frisky today." TJ's eyes narrowed as he cocked his hip. "Is something wrong?"

"Why would something have to be wrong for me to switch my order?"

"For the six months I've worked here, you've always ordered a large Viet coffee, full sweet with tapioca and extra ice. Even in the dead of winter." TJ drew out his last sentence dramatically and shuddered.

"I always crave icy drinks when there's snow on the ground. Or when temps hit below freezing." She'd been disappointed by the lack of snow this past winter.

"Weirdo. I hate snow with a passion. It's hard to look cute when you're stuffed under five layers and a giant coat. But you do you." He shrugged.

"Let's try a mango slush with lychee jelly. Full sweet, of course."

"You sure?" TJ asked.

"Yes. I'm allowed to try—"

"I'll make it and your usual. Just in case." He winked as he grabbed the ingredients to mix her drinks. "Don't tell my boss, okay?"

Zoe mimed zipping her lips. She'd discovered Pop Boba and TJ when a sudden thunderstorm made it impossible to see farther than a few yards in front of her. The shop's sign was a glowing beacon so she turned into its parking lot. She and TJ hit it off as she waited out the storm.

"Also, we didn't even get enough snow this winter for the plows to run. I don't know what you're complaining about," she reminded him over the whir of the blender.

"I can't wait until I move somewhere warmer."

"Wait, does that mean you're leaving the DMV soon?" Zoe asked, using the locals' abbreviation for DC and the two states surrounding it.

"Not yet, but as soon as I have enough saved, I'm moving to Vegas. Audition for somewhere I can dance all night. Is there a drag version of Thunder from Down Under?" TJ dreamed of doing drag full time and not as a side hustle.

"Maybe I'll go with you."

"And leave your gorgeous shop behind?" He gasped.

For half a second she imagined being surrounded by sequins and feathers as showgirls (or boys) ran around backstage as the stage manager yelled instructions. Her stomach clenched at the idea and she frowned.

"You're right. Vegas sounds stressful. I love my shop and I love being my own boss even more."

"Speaking of showgirls, thanks for the tickets to *Lysistrata* last weekend. Your costumes were fire."

"You're welcome. Technically they're not mine. My team and I only constructed them." Zoe was thrilled that Prestige Rep had outsourced their work to her. Not only did it pay well, it was a refreshing change to work with rhinestones, tulle, and spandex. They weren't the easiest fabrics to sew, but she'd worked with them in college.

"Don't sell yourself short. I saw the designer's sketches—if you can call washes of color and vague lines sketches."

"They were pretty."

"With plenty of room for interpretation. It takes talent to turn them into three-dimensional works of art."

Zoe stood taller. She was proud of her team. They'd put in overtime to get the garments ready for tech week. She'd even done a few all-nighters of her own. That hadn't been so different from the late nights in her college costume shop. A couple of super-strong coffee bobas had given her the caffeine kick she'd needed.

She remembered how much she enjoyed making over-the-top costumes. Lingerie wasn't boring, but her clients preferred the same silhouettes. Every season was the same basic pattern with minor tweaks made in different colors or different fabric combinations. The few times she'd tried to introduce an innovative design, it didn't sell well.

"I've always been good at draping and patterning. Helps to be good at math."

TJ nodded as he slipped the cups into the machine to apply the film on tops of the drinks.

"I appreciate your feedback on the linings and undergarments," she added.

"Anytime, babe. Thanks for letting me borrow your machine to work on my drag brunch outfits. Lady Sriracha-cha has never looked so good." He held out the finished drinks and shimmied.

Zoe chuckled absentmindedly at TJ as she reconsidered her idea of a fashion line that included items that weren't undergarments or relegated to the bedroom. Maybe that was the answer to this restlessness inside her. The same one that made her order the mango slush.

TJ handed Zoe her new order. She shook it hard to distribute the lychee jelly before stabbing the plastic film with her neon green plastic straw.

"O-M-G!" TJ exclaimed. "Don't turn around, but there's a tasty snack standing outside."

She reflexively turned her head, but TJ grabbed her arm.

"Didn't I say don't look?" He tsked. "Let's play Your Team or Mine."

Zoe smiled indulgently at the mention of his favorite game to play whenever she stopped in the shop. When things were slow, they checked out cute guys together and made up life stories for them. TJ also recounted his many sexcapades—all of which ended after the third date because he couldn't possibly ask someone to commit if he was planning to leave for Las Vegas if the audition of a lifetime presented itself. She had yet to meet someone she wanted to date, but enjoyed living vicariously through his stories.

"Okay, he's tall, maybe five-nine or five-ten. Looks Vietnamese, though clueless about good boba if he decides to come in here."

"Hey! I like the drinks here."

"That's because you get my secret recipe. He's got longish hair that looks like it's been cut recently. Round glasses with thin frames give him a cute nerdy look. He's wearing all black, even though it's almost a hundred degrees out."

Zoe huffed. Nothing TJ had described gave any indication of the person's orientation.

"Give me details on his clothes. Do they look stylish or just thrown together?"

"Hmm, it's hard to tell." TJ craned his neck for a better view.

Zoe growled in frustration. She spun around so she could play their game using her own eyes.

Hot damn.

If she were the type to be attracted to someone merely based on looks, this man hit all the marks. Mystery Man was looking at his phone, but she could still make out the high cheekbones where his wire-rimmed glasses rested and a strong, angular jaw. Even his lips were perfect. His sateen cotton button-down shirt was neatly tucked into his jeans, which could come off as uptight. But a pair of black Chucks kept his vibe stylish yet casual.

"Close your mouth," TJ teased. "Or don't—wait until he looks back up so you can see his entire face. Beautiful."

Maybe she'd stared too hard through the glass, because Mystery Man looked up from his phone and straight into Pop Boba.

Zoe froze. It couldn't be. Her entire body broke out in a cold sweat. He was supposed to be in New York doing his directing thing. Maybe he wouldn't recognize her. Her foot twitched and she turned quickly around to face TJ instead of the door.

"That's Derek, my best friend from college," she whispered to TJ, even though Derek couldn't hear them from ten feet away *and* through glass doors. "Oh God, I can't believe I just lusted over my friend."

"Wait, you've known this guy for years and never dated? Spill the tea."

Zoe's cheeks burned as she covered her eyes with her hand. They'd made a pact freshman year that they'd keep things platonic. Yet here she stood, lusting over her best friend—technically, ex–best friend. It felt so wrong and weird, even though she hadn't realized it was Derek at the time.

"We made a promise to never date each other. I haven't talked to him in six years because, well, because." Zoe waved her hand dismissively. She wasn't in the mood to rehash their drama from undergrad. "Do you think he recognized me?"

"Whatever happened between you two must be bad if you're avoiding a guy who looks like that." TJ smacked his lips in appreciation. "You're safe. He's looking at his phone again."

She sighed in relief and sipped her drink to cool down. Her body wasn't flushed from the heat because Pop Boba's air conditioning was on full blast. Bright, sweet flavors danced on her tongue. Had TJ put fresh mango in it? She hadn't paid attention to how he had made it. The lychee jelly wasn't overly chewy, though she missed the texture of the tapioca pearls. Maybe it'd grow on her after a few more sips.

"Oh shit, he's coming into the café!"

"What? No!" She searched for an open seat to escape to. The teens had taken every single space.

Zoe scooted from the ordering side of the counter to the pick-up area even though they were barely a foot apart. She hunched over her drink to shrink herself as much as possible. Except Derek would need to be completely oblivious if he missed a size twenty-two woman standing right in front of the order counter. It was too late for anything else, so she had to commit. She'd only call more attention to herself if she ran out of the café.

"What are you doing?" TJ asked.

"Trying to hide! We stopped talking after a big fight and—"

"Girl, you can't hide in front of the counter. Come back here and pretend you're working."

He tossed an apron at her as she ran behind the counter. She placed it over her head and tried to tie it behind her back but the straps weren't long enough. Of course they weren't. This world was made for skinny people and she only lived in it.

"How do I look?" She ran her hands through her hair and tried to smooth out her clothes.

"Seriously? You're avoiding the guy but want to look good?" TJ chuckled but gave her a thumbs-up. "But maybe put this on, too."

If she had to wear a dumb BOBARISTA cap to avoid talking to Derek, then so be it. At least she'd already taken a selfie earlier to document her good hair day.

"I'm a complicated person, okay?" she tossed back a bit too harshly. "Sorry."

Even if Derek didn't recognize her, she had to look put together. Or maybe he'd check her out, too. What the hell was she even thinking? They had been platonic friends. Panic had forced all common sense out of her.

"Stand over there and pretend you're, um, tasting new boba flavors or something." TJ pointed to a spot behind him near the blenders.

She nodded and did as he instructed. They fell silent as the door opened. Derek's footsteps grew louder as he made his way through the shop. Zoe's heart pounded harder with each step.

"What's happening?" she whispered as she moved some cups around on the counter.

"He's looking around the shop and has a WTF expression."

"At me?"

"No. Everyone has that expression when they walk in here. Chill, okay? He didn't see you."

She took a larger sip of her drink both to hide her face and to force herself to calm down. Chewing the lychee gave her nervousness an outlet.

"Excuse me," said a deep voice she'd hadn't heard in more than six years.

She snuck a glance at the man standing at the counter while he was focused on TJ. Zoe swallowed hard.

Her nerdy best friend from college had become more handsome since she'd ghosted him years ago.

CHAPTER 3

Derek pocketed his phone and stared at the menu without really reading it. After driving in what felt like several circles of hell, he finally admitted that he had no idea where he was going. For the past two hours, he'd resisted the urge to toss his phone out the window whenever the super perky British voice instructed him to make a U-turn. Hopefully someone here was more helpful.

Or maybe not. The place looked like social media threw up in it. Every loudly decorated wall was a potential selfie background. Did that neon sign read SUCK MY— He sighed.

He was hungry, thirsty, and tired of being lost. As a New Yorker, he was a bit rusty behind the wheel. It didn't help that DC drivers were awful. This place was as good as any for a break before heading back on the road. If this place didn't pan out, he could still grab a sandwich from the bánh mì place next door.

"Excuse me," he said as he approached the counter. Derek was surprised there wasn't a line considering how packed the tables were.

"You look like a matcha slush with brown balls kinda guy," announced the employee. The woman working the back area snorted.

"Sorry?" Derek squinted at the employee's name tag. "Hi, TJ, maybe you can help me with some directions. I'm a bit lost."

"As long as you order something, I'm here to serve." TJ winked and pointed to the menu over his head.

TJ's coworker cleared her throat loudly.

"Is she okay?"

"Don't worry about her," said TJ. "She's reminding me that we gotta keep our boss happy and sell drinks."

"Gotcha. First, can you tell me how to get to Something Cheeky?" Derek asked.

The woman behind the counter gasped. Suddenly she dropped her drink and coughed. Her face was hidden behind a cap, but it was obvious she was in distress. He had to do something.

"I know how to do the Heimlich," Derek offered loudly so she could hear him over her coughing and the din of the café.

His head swiveled from TJ to the choking woman, who put her hand up. Was she telling him to stop or reaching out for help?

He turned back to TJ, who seemed only mildly concerned. The man shook his head at Derek and pointed to a laminated poster near them with basic first-aid diagrams. Right, if someone was coughing, they didn't need assistance.

The woman's choking turned into harsh coughs, and then a piece of food flew out of her mouth onto the floor. Her face was red from the exertion.

"Get her some water!" Derek barked at TJ.

"You good?" TJ asked as he grabbed a bottle from the display behind him and handed her the water.

She nodded but her eyes were still obscured by her cap.

"See, you should've gotten your regular," TJ teased and handed her a dark brown drink with boba.

"That's not"—she coughed and pulled off her cap to fan her face—"funny."

What the hell? Derek leaned over the counter. It couldn't be.

"Z?"

She turned around fully. Derek froze. He'd rehearsed all the different ways he'd greet her after six years of not talking. Finding her choking on bubble tea wasn't one of them.

"Zoe, is it really you?" he said, mostly making sure he wasn't dreaming.

She nodded as she rubbed her chest with her hand. Zoe took a deep breath and her lips quirked into a familiar crooked smile.

"Hey! Funny seeing you here, Derek," she said brightly as she pulled the apron over her head and rolled it into a ball.

Derek's heart pounded. Zoe in real life was more stunning than the Zoe of his memories. Her previously long black hair had lavender tips that hit below her shoulders. She wore a loose, stylish top in lilac, her favorite color. And her pants hugged her hips in the most delicious way.

He blew out a breath. *Don't get distracted.* He'd come here to invite her to work on his project with him. Once he got that out of the way, he'd figure out how to tell her the truth. He gave her his best smile, the one he used to impress producers when he pitched plays to them.

"Talk about fate," Derek said. "I swear I've driven across the entire state of Virginia looking for your shop."

"Surprise . . ." Zoe's voice trailed off. She bit her lip before adding, "You found me. Making an idiot of myself, but here I am."

"You're too pretty and way too smart to be an idiot," Derek said softly, then clamped his mouth shut. Way to make things even weirder.

"Come on, choking on a piece of lychee jelly is the dumbest way to die," Zoe joked, but her cheeks were flushed.

She bit her lip as he stared at her. He couldn't remember the lines he'd prepared for their meeting. All those years onstage and he'd forgotten everything he'd learned about composure in her presence.

"Her shop is about half a mile down the road that way," TJ offered, coming to their rescue. He pointed north. Or was it south?

Derek had lost all sense of direction. He shook his head and shrugged.

"I think I took a wrong turn at Seven Corners. Why is it even called that? There are no corners. It's the worse intersection I've ever driven through!" Derek tossed his hands in the air.

"I've lived in the DMV for almost a year and still can't remember which side of the Beltway is the outer loop and the inner loop." TJ drew a circle with his finger and then reversed direction while shaking his head.

Derek nodded in solidarity, even though he had no idea what TJ was talking about.

"Stop, you don't even drive!" Zoe stepped out from behind the counter. "Don't get him started on the drivers here."

TJ shrugged. "Rideshares count."

The two of them were too familiar with each other to just be co-workers. Derek was suddenly jealous that TJ knew Zoe better than he did. He had no clue if she still liked the same foods or movies from when they were in undergrad together.

"He claims people are nicer drivers in North Carolina, where he grew up. But there's way fewer people there," she continued.

Were they dating? No way.

"So, handsome, you must be parched after all that driving," said TJ as he batted his eyes at Derek.

Derek sighed in relief. The two were only friends. So he still had a chance with Zoe.

"Yes. I'll have a Vietnamese coffee, please, half sweet with, uh. . ." Derek paused as he studied the menu.

"Coffee popping bubbles," Zoe finished for him.

"Yes, what Z said. It's my favorite but not everyone carries it."

TJ raised his eyebrows at Zoe before turning to make the drink.

"Go sit. I'll bring your drink to you." TJ pointed to a tiny table in the corner that was miraculously unoccupied.

Before they could claim it, two teen girls holding hands grabbed it.

"Young love is so cute," Zoe said, "until they hog all the tables."

"I don't mind standing. I need to stretch my legs after sitting in that tiny car for hours." Derek's shoulders finally relaxed after being stuck in the rental car. His favorite boba was what he needed to fuel up before the second most important conversation of his life.

"Derek, shouldn't you be in New York directing a show?" Zoe asked.

"Trying to get rid of me already?"

"No, it's— Didn't you just open a play off-Broadway? I thought you were supposed to hang out for a few days after."

"Nah. That's what stage managers are for. A good SM is—"

"Worth their weight in gold," Zoe finished.

They laughed.

"You still remember that from school."

"How could I not? They drilled that into our heads for four years."

"Never, ever"—Derek deepened his voice to imitate one of their professors—"piss off the stage manager. They'll make your life hell."

"That was perfect!" Zoe clapped her hands.

"How could I forget our technical director and his weird stories."

"One time during a performance of *Clue*," Zoe said in a deep voice, "I had to hold up a broken door for ten minutes while—"

"Standing behind it onstage," Derek finished.

"It's the equivalent of those stories about walking to school in the snow uphill both ways," Zoe said in her normal voice.

"You're still terrible at accents," he teased.

"Shut up!" But she chuckled. "That's why I wasn't an acting major."

"You had terrible stage fright during our New Faces rehearsal."

Derek recalled the first time they met. He didn't know anyone at the freshman show, but his classmates were already laughing and joking with one another. He later learned that they'd arrived at school early for orientation. It hadn't been mandatory, so he'd stayed in his hometown to work and save money. The professor had partnered him with Zoe because they were the only Asian students that year.

That microaggression gave them something to bond over. The two of them were inseparable for the next four years. Technically three and a half because the last semester—

"Here's your boba," TJ said, interrupting Derek's foray down memory lane. "I made you a fresh one, too, Zoe."

Derek turned his attention back to Zoe, whose eyes were dark. Had she been recalling the same memories he was? He dug out his wallet without looking away from her.

"Nope. My treat since you two are old friends." TJ pushed Derek's hand back.

"Thanks." Derek grabbed a ten-dollar bill from his wallet and stuffed it in the half-empty tip jar.

TJ nodded approvingly.

"If you're still looking for Something Cheeky, I can write down directions for you," TJ offered. "Along with my phone number in case you get lost again."

"I don't need them anymore." Derek turned back to Zoe. "I found who I was looking for."

CHAPTER 4

Derek's stomach swirled. He meant to let TJ down gently. He was here for Zoe and no one else. She was why he'd taken an unintended scenic tour of northern Virginia. Instead he sounded like he was stalking Zoe.

He ignored the heat creeping to his cheeks and flashed Zoe a *save me* look. She bit her lip to hide a smile as if she found joy in his discomfort.

"Oh la la," TJ trilled. "I know when I've been dismissed."

"Look! A table opened up." Zoe pointed and grabbed Derek's arm.

Derek happily let her pull him to a corner near the front of the café. Once they arrived at the table, it was obvious why it was unoccupied. It was barely big enough to be a plant stand. Not only was it tiny, but someone had taken the chairs. At least the corner provided some privacy.

"This is weird, Derek," Zoe said as she maneuvered herself next to the wall.

"No weirder than you ghosting me after graduation." He slid in opposite her, their bodies only a couple feet apart. A whiff of her lavender-and-honey perfume transported him back to their late-night rooftop conversations during college.

"You could've tried harder," she said, avoiding his eyes.

Derek took a step back to clear his nose of her sweet, intoxicating scent. A half-step was all the space allowed. He couldn't believe she was still wearing the same perfume after all this time. He wanted to tell her everything about their time apart. But he had six weeks in DC. It was more than enough time to catch up.

"I did. I texted you every day during my first month in New York." He bit his lip. Did he sound lonely or, worse, desperate for her attention? But that first month *had* been lonely. Everything he'd done for the first time in the city reminded him that she was supposed to be there with him.

"Sorry," she mumbled. "I swear I read all of them, but I was working nights at my parents' restaurant. By the time I remembered to respond to them . . ."

"It felt too awkward?" he finished for her.

"I'm a terrible friend." Zoe grimaced in embarrassment. "I really meant to text you back, but after you stopped I thought you were mad at me."

"Oh." Relief flooded his body. She hadn't completely abandoned him after all.

"You weren't the only person I did that to," she confessed. "I was burned out after school and it seemed like a good time to disconnect from everything. Everyone."

"Even me?" He couldn't hide the hurt in his voice.

"I hoped that you were killing it in New York. Which you are." She smiled hopefully.

"I thought you were mad at me," he said bluntly. "I wrote you that long email."

"No, *you* were mad with *me*," Zoe said adamantly.

"Maybe a little," he lied, but changed his mind. "I was angry. We were supposed to go to New York together. Start our careers together."

"I'm sorry I let you down." She looked straight into his eyes. "I felt horrible about ruining your plans and it was hard to face you. But I saved your long email."

Derek studied her as her words sank in. All this time, he had felt guilty about pushing her to do something she wasn't ready to do. It turned out they'd been so worried about their postgraduation plans that they'd failed to really listen to each other.

"I should've supported you better when you changed majors," he finally said. "I was a jerk."

"We were both jerks to each other. Senior year was hard." She shrugged. "That's in the past. I'm happy with my boutique."

"I'm glad. You're meant to do great things."

"I don't know about that, but I'm helping people." Zoe shrugged.

Derek pushed his glasses up and stuck his hands in his pockets to keep himself from giving her a bear hug. He'd apologized and she'd done the same. Now they could try to mend their friendship. Maybe he'd convince her to let it grow into something more.

"How about we leave the past behind us and try again?" he suggested.

"I'd like that." She smiled and nodded. "Now back to my question. What are you doing in DC?"

"Z, you haven't changed. You look fantastic," he noted, avoiding her question. The tingling of nerves crept back across his body again. He didn't want her to think he'd only come here to ask her to work with him.

"You know Asian don't raisin." She placed her hands under her chin, kicked up her back leg like an anime character, and batted her eyelashes. Or at least as much as she could crunched into the corner.

Derek shook his head at her bad joke. Could she be any more fucking adorable?

"You look really good, too." Zoe gestured at his head down to his legs. "Glad to see your fashion sense has improved."

"Damn right. Everybody looks good in black." Derek did a very tiny shuffle hop step and narrowly avoided kicking over the table.

"You still got the moves," Zoe said, chuckling. "After all this time."

"I'm a bit rusty, but a man's gotta stay in shape somehow." He patted his flat stomach.

"Still scarfing down late-night Taco Bell Nachos Bellgrande?"

"Don't forget the cinnamon twists. Bring on the crunchy snacks." He grinned.

"Mr. Big Director still orders off the value menu," she teased.

"Old college habits die hard. After twelve-hour days during tech week hell, my body demands comfort food," he reminded her.

"Junk food, you mean," she shot back, the same way she used to during college.

"So Cheetos aren't junk if you use chopsticks to eat them?"

"Orange cheese dust on Hamlet's costume didn't work with his emo vibes." She raised an eyebrow, as if daring him to counter her.

"Fine. You win this one." He conceded with a dramatic tight bow.

His anxiety from earlier had dissipated with their playful banter and laughter. He and Zoe had been inseparable in college for a reason. And they'd picked right back up as if no time had passed.

They'd taken different paths since finishing their undergrad theater program six years ago. She'd gone home to DC, and he'd packed his bags to couch surf in New York City, hoping for his big break.

His first year had been rough, especially without his best friend cheering him on. He'd taken whatever gigs he could, even if he was playing nerds or gang members. He even had a couple of roles as extras on whatever *Law & Order* show was filming at the time.

He did everything and anything to pad his résumé and get his name out. Lucky for him, it took only a year to land a decent role. That same job was where he'd met his mentor, who gave Derek his first job as assistant director. Fast-forward to today, and he had his choice of directing gigs across the country.

Which was what led to his standing in the corner of a wacky boba café in front of the woman he loved. Except she didn't know he loved her, because he'd been too chickenshit to tell her.

Derek rubbed the side of his thigh. *Spit it out and get it over with.* He wasn't a stranger to rejection, but he'd be crushed if she turned down his offer.

"I want you to design costumes for my new musical," he blurted.

CHAPTER 5

You what?" Zoe's brown eyes widened in confusion. "Did you say new musical?"

"Yes. And I want you to design the costumes," he repeated slowly, as if she hadn't heard him correctly the first time.

"What does a big-shot director want with a lingerie designer?"

"You're more than a lingerie designer. And I'm not a big shot. Not yet anyway." He shrugged as if he hadn't received rave reviews in the *Los Angeles Times* and the *New York Times* for his work.

"You'll be on Broadway soon enough," Zoe said with conviction. She believed this because she had been following his career even though she'd actively avoided him since graduation. It'd been easier to ignore Derek's texts when she'd been so raw and vulnerable after changing majors at the last minute and barely graduating on time.

"So you're still keeping tabs on me." He couldn't keep a wide smile from forming on his face. She hadn't forgotten about him all these years or given up on theater.

"My mom keeps me apprised of your accomplishments," Zoe replied nonchalantly, but the corner of her lips curved up in a half-smile. "I swear she has a Google alert set up for you."

"Seriously? How are Cô Hồng and Chú Minh?"

"Same. Loud and nosy as ever."

They laughed. He'd defended himself from her mom's onslaught of questions whenever he'd come to DC during school breaks. No matter how much Zoe begged her to stop, her mom interrogated him about everything, from growing up with a single mom to how people in New York could work in all that snow.

"If you want to say hi, she's working in the restaurant today. I can give you directions."

"Z, you're killing me here. I'm not ready to get back in the car."

"If you can find Phở-Ever 75, then you can find Something Cheeky."

"That's right! You're in Eden Center now. What's it like working so close to your parents?"

"Mom and I have learned to give each other space. Literally and figuratively."

"So you picked a location on the opposite side of the shopping center on purpose?"

"It was the best space for my boutique, which just happened to be far away from my parents."

"How fortunate," he said and chuckled.

"I got a sweet deal on it thanks to a new pilot program there for AAPI business owners. We're trying to get it recognized as a historic site."

"Whoa. I wish my hometown had something like Eden Center. We had hole-in-the-wall places that catered to non-Asian taste-buds." Sadness flashed across his face so quickly that she almost missed it. "The program sounds super cool."

"But you're not here to talk about a strip mall's history. Tell me about this musical." Zoe sipped her new drink slowly. It'd be embarrassing if she choked on this one, too.

"It's brand-new and Prestige Repertory is producing the world premiere. Which was why I went looking for your award-winning shop."

"You're laying it on thick. How did you know?"

"You're not the only one whom your mom keeps informed."

"What did I tell you? Nosy *and* meddling." She smiled as she shook her head indulgently. "Between her and my aunts, they have my life figured out."

"You're lucky to have so many family members who care about you," he said wistfully.

She'd stuck her foot in her mouth. Derek's mom had raised him on her own. Whenever they watched movies with huge, loud Asian families, jealousy flared inside him. Every time he'd come with her to DC during school breaks, he'd handled all her aunts, uncles, and cousins with ease.

"I know." Zoe stirred her boba with the neon pink straw. "Sorry. I didn't mean to—"

"It's okay. I love my mom. And I have my theater family in the city. We misfits have to stick together."

"I'm sorry," Zoe said so softly he almost missed it. Her shoulders slumped. "I'm sorry I never tried to mend things between us."

"We're doing it now." He leaned in closer to her. Not that he had to move far in their tight space.

"I meant to text you once I had a handle on my life. But I was working long hours apprenticing with my fashion mentor and then I opened the boutique. The longer I went without, the worse I felt. Then you got famous." She clamped her mouth shut to stop babbling.

"Theater famous means not at all. Unless you're Lin-Manuel," he half-joked. "It's not like people recognize me on the subway."

"I didn't want you to think that I texted out of the blue because you're a big deal now. I'd never abuse our friendship in order to name-drop you."

"Z, I would never think that. Not after all we've been through in undergrad."

"I know that, but it'd feel like that to me."

"Would you feel better if we act out the scenario that's playing in your head? I can improv some not-so-pleasant feelings against you. Maybe if you stomp on my foot." He set his right foot in front of him.

"Still a Method actor, I see." She rolled her eyes. "I'm not going to hurt you to make myself feel better."

"Well, I found you first. Which means you're not taking advantage of me. Better?"

She shrugged but a smile crept on her face. He tapped her shoe with his until she looked up. Derek tapped her shoe again and stuck out his tongue.

"Stop it." Zoe laughed and lightly kicked him in return. "I've missed you."

"I've missed you—*us*. It's been too long. How about a hug?" Derek opened his arms.

Zoe had to take only a short step to fall into his hug. He wrapped his arm around her torso and lifted her off the ground with barely any effort.

"You're lucky we're not outside where I could spin you around," he whispered.

His low voice tickled her ear and a flutter ran through her abdomen. Zoe froze for a second but relaxed when he squeezed her harder. She only imagined that flutter.

"Put me down!" Zoe laughed. "You're nuts."

He gently set her back on the ground. His entire body tingled from their embrace.

Suddenly the corner felt too constricting, too small, for the two of them.

"Do you miss it?" he blurted out. "Theater."

Zoe opened her mouth and closed it. She pressed her lips together and shrugged. He didn't push her to answer. Instead he took a long swallow of his boba and chewed on his popping bubbles.

His glasses slid down his nose. She wrapped both hands around her drink to keep herself from pushing them back up.

"My team and I constructed the costumes for a production of *Lysistrata* last month," Zoe confessed. "I'd forgotten how much fun it was."

"That's perfect, because I'm working on a new production. From scratch." Derek's face brightened. "I'll finally have something I can call my own."

"That sounds really cool, Derek. It's here in the DMV?" She'd never seen him this excited about a production.

He opened his mouth but stopped when his phone buzzed. He held out a finger for her to wait before pulling out his phone.

"Crap. I'm sorry to cut this short, but I'm going to be late for an important meeting downtown." He slid his phone back into his pocket.

"Next time don't get lost," she teased.

"So there will be a next time." He flashed a grin. "How about dinner tomorrow so I can properly tell you about the show?"

"I'd love that. But don't leave me hanging until tomorrow. How about a hint?"

"Remember what we used to dream about out on the roof of our college apartment?"

"*Tấm Cám*?" Zoe whispered, as if speaking it too loudly would jinx it.

Whenever their theater classes felt too western or too white-centric, she and Derek would fantasize about their imaginary production of the Vietnamese fairy tale. But it'd been all talk. A fantasy that grounded them in who they were and where they came from.

"I'm doing it." He waved his hands excitedly. "We're doing a Vietnamese Cinderella rock musical."

"We?" Zoe's mouth hung open. "But it was a silly game we played."

"It's real, Z."

"Real," she whispered, wondering if she should pinch herself to make sure she'd heard him correctly.

"Yes." He grabbed her hand. "You didn't think I'd do it without you? I want you to design costumes for *our* musical."

"Me? Shouldn't you hire someone with actual experience?" Zoe shook her head quickly. "I've never designed anything outside of college. And you know how that went."

"Our professor was an ass," Derek replied a little too loudly. "He's a has-been actor who got off on his power."

Zoe nodded in agreement.

"Zoe, this is our time to shine." Derek grabbed both her shoulders and looked directly into her eyes.

His fingers twitched as a tremor ran through her body. The hairs on her arms stood up as goose bumps spread across it. As much as she was protesting, excitement pulsed through her body.

"You don't have to decide right this minute," he continued. "I'll fill you in tomorrow."

"Okay" was all she managed to say.

"Everything shall be revealed tomorrow night." He hugged her again. "If I don't leave now, I'll be late."

He left the café as abruptly as he'd reentered her life. But not before reawakening the dream she'd given up so long ago.

Zoe ignored TJ's attempt to get her attention as a multitude of feelings unspooled inside her. What if this was her second chance to become a real costume designer?

CHAPTER 6

"G reg, sorry I'm late," Derek said, slightly out of breath. After driving around the same three blocks multiple times, he'd dropped his car at the valet.

His mentor and Prestige Rep's artistic director grinned and gave him a firm handshake. To say the man had opened doors for Derek was not enough. Gregory A. Powers had changed the trajectory of Derek's career. They'd met when Greg guest directed an off-Broadway production. He'd cast Derek in a small role, which eventually turned into an assistant directing position.

"Derek, you made it! Have a seat." The fiftysomething white man spoke quickly and forcefully, like someone who knew without hesitation that people always listened to what he had to say.

For the five years that Derek had known Greg, the man was inundated with offers to direct shows. The man was practically an icon in the industry. Everyone knew the story of how he'd sold his car in order to finance his first production in some small midwestern town. After he'd moved on to bigger stages, his first board of directors named his first theater after him: the Gregory A. Powers Performing Arts Center.

"Let's get you a drink. What'll it be?" Greg flagged down a nearby waitress.

"Uh—" Derek scanned the menu that Greg slid across the white tablecloth. He could buy an entire bottle of decent bourbon for the price of a cocktail here. "Just iced tea, unsweetened."

"Are you sure? Dinner's on me. Actually, it's on Prestige." He winked and turned to the waitress. "I'll take another G and T."

"Maybe another time." Derek nodded a thank-you to the waitress, who left to get their drinks.

"Do you like the apartment we put you in? I told production to put you in the best one."

"I only dropped off my bags before driving to Falls Church to see an old friend. And got a little lost," Derek admitted. He stifled a yawn, regretting not taking a nap on the train down.

"Try to pace yourself while you're in DC." Greg tapped at the menu. "I took the liberty of ordering some appetizers for us."

"Greg, I'm so grateful that you're taking on my *Tấm Cám* musical."

Derek had pitched it to several theaters, but most would agree only to a staged reading. He'd worked too hard and too long on it for that. He needed to gather a design team and the actors and the dancers so they could breathe life into the show together.

This musical was his love letter to his Vietnamese community, and it deserved the full treatment.

"How could I say no to one of my favorite up-and-coming directors?" Greg finished off his gin and tonic.

"Honestly? I wasn't sure a big theater like yours would want to produce an all-Asian musical production." The other theaters that he'd approached had turned him down, citing how risky it was to take on such a new production the way Derek envisioned it.

Greg had been at the helm of DC's oldest theater for fifteen years and counting. As the largest one in the metro area, Prestige Rep contained multiple performance spaces and a gorgeous building in Southwest. It was a dream come true to launch his project there.

"I'll be honest with you then. It took some time to convince the board to invest in a brand-new musical from an unknown." Greg swirled the ice in his highball before setting it down.

"But—"

"Yes, I know you're making waves in New York, but these board members—they wouldn't know art if it smacked them in the face."

"Oh."

"They're old and out of touch. Fuddy-duddies." Greg winked. "Not young and innovative like us."

"Yeah." He wondered if the board members were as old as Greg implied.

"You and I both know that this will be groundbreaking. It's the first of its kind. I'll be known—I mean, Prestige Rep will be on the map for supporting marginalized artists."

"And I appreciate that." Derek's chest tightened; he was worried about where the conversation was headed.

"That's why we're premiering in May for Asian History Month."

Derek bit his lip at how Greg bastardized Asian Pacific Islander Heritage Month.

"My favorite month," joked Derek to hide how anxious the deadline made him. Six weeks until previews and another week and a half after that for opening night. It sounded like a lot of time on paper, but he and his cowriter still had to finish writing a couple of songs.

"I also told them they'd regret not producing your *Tấm Cám* because it has Broadway potential." Greg pronounced Tấm as in *Tammy* and Cám in *camera*.

Derek had tried numerous times to teach him the Vietnamese pronunciation but had given up. In his native tongue, the names were softer, more lyrical. The *T* in *Tấm* was similar to the English *th* sound, while the *ấm* sounded closer to *um* in umbrella. But he had to pick his battles and today wasn't the time.

"I hope so," Derek said cautiously. What theater director wouldn't want a show on Broadway? The possibility only put more pressure on him, so he tried not to think about it too much.

"I know so. And in the end the board understood that taking a show to Broadway means we get a cut of the profits. Which we can reinvest back into the theater."

"So it's all about the money." Derek's shoulders relaxed slightly. Producers' monetary motivations were predictable, which meant he could find ways to keep them happy.

"For the board, yes. Me? Your musical is art in the making. How lucky are we that I'm here to nurture your career?" The artistic director flashed him a smile.

"Greg, I appreciate all you've done for me over the years." Derek meant it, even though he didn't always enjoy socializing with Greg. He continued to meet the man for drinks whenever asked because Derek didn't want to burn his bridges.

The waitress brought their drinks and the appetizers that Greg had ordered.

"Damn, that looks amazing. Have you ever had bone marrow before?"

"Not like this." Derek shook his head. He'd slurped the beef bones that his mom simmered in her phở broth, but this looked entirely different. A long beef bone had been cut lengthwise to reveal the rich marrow inside.

"You probably can't afford this in New York on your budget."

"I prefer more casual restaurants." Derek ignored the dig. "The best food comes from hole-in-the-wall places, you know."

"You have to taste it at least. You scrape this unctuous fat out with the spoon and spread it on the toast like this. Add some of these herbs and a squeeze of lemon to balance out the richness." Greg demonstrated with glee, as if he savored the opportunity to show off his knowledge about upscale cuisine. He popped the toast in his mouth and groaned.

Derek shifted in his seat. He'd never seen his mentor lose his mind over food before. He resisted the urge to give Greg some privacy with his bone marrow.

"Try it," Greg said in between bites.

"Maybe in a little. I'm still full from the boba I had on the way here."

"Is that the funny-looking drink you have to chew?" Greg closed his eyes as he ate his toast.

"I don't think it's funny-looking, but yes, you chew the tapioca in it. It's a refreshing dessert in a cup." He'd been surprised how good the drink was considering the café's trendy decor.

But not as unexpected as running into the very woman he'd spent two hours searching for. He'd wanted to look her up for the past six years but hadn't been able to come up with a reason to visit Zoe. Until now. Until this musical.

"I know we talked about this before, but I want to be completely sure. I have full autonomy over who's on my creative team and in my cast?" Derek asked.

"Of course! As long as they're good at what they do, I don't care who they are."

"Thanks." Derek hid his relief behind his glass. Several people on his creative team were not as credentialed as Prestige Rep's past designers, but not for lack of trying. In this world, you had to know people to get the bigger gigs.

"Look, I have to tell you something. Just between you and me," Greg announced in a low, quieter voice. He wiped his mouth with his white linen napkin. His expression had gone from light to serious.

"Sure." Derek swallowed some tea to calm his nerves. The cold liquid sliding down his throat only spread his anxiety. Maybe Greg would tell him this was all a joke and the board had changed their minds about the musical.

"The board wants us to produce more shows by people of color. I agree with them."

"You've had only one show with a majority POC cast during the past three seasons. And zero POC directors." Derek had researched all the possible theaters before pitching his show. Prestige Rep was the only one that had said yes.

"Exactly! I tried to tell them that they can't support a majority POC show *and* expect to make a ton of money. But we do it because it's the right thing to do."

Derek opened his mouth to protest the self-fulfilling prophecy, but Greg put out his hand.

"The market's not ready for it. For you. But I've seen your work. I know that you've worked on enough productions at enough places across the country that you understand how important your musical is."

"I do. It's going to give Asian actors more jobs in roles that are written for them. Not jammed into a role that's been turned into a diverse one."

"Exactly. So if this musical fails, the board is less likely to invest in more productions with directors of color."

"Oh." Derek sat back in his seat. A lump formed in his stomach. "That's a lot of responsibility."

"It's a lot to take in, Derek, but I know one thing—mind if I finish this off?" He gestured at the plate.

"Go for it." Derek's appetite had disappeared.

Greg dug into the second piece of bone marrow.

"I know this"—Greg waved his spoon as he continued—"if anyone can do it, it's my mentee. I've trained you and taught you almost everything I know. You're going to knock it out of the park."

"I appreciate your confidence in me," Derek replied more brightly than he felt. Mounting a brand-new production would be hard enough. Now he had to worry about the fate of guest directors who would come after him.

CHAPTER 7

"M om." Derek sighed before continuing in Vietnamese. "Tap the circle made of two arrows."

Sometimes, if he was lucky, he'd catch a glimpse of his mom's face during their weekly Sunday morning calls. If only he had a sibling to abdicate his tech support duties to the way Zoe had with her brother, Eddie.

No matter how many times he'd shown her how to video chat, a good chunk of their calls gave him a clear view of the yellowed carpet of his childhood home. He could make out the stain where he'd knocked over a bottle of black nail polish during his emo phase.

His mom's place was the complete opposite of the shiny, modern apartment the theater had set up for him while he was in DC. It was swanky but generic, lacking warmth. He leaned back on the black couch and stuck one of the million pillows behind his head. He wondered how many famous directors had stayed here. Maybe they had left behind some of their creative energy.

"Sang." His mother drew out his Vietnamese middle name to bring his attention back from her lack of technical ability. "Where are you now?"

"In DC," he replied to the carpet. "Working on a new musical."

His mom's phone shook for a few seconds before he was rewarded with a close-up of her eye, her brow knitted in concentration.

"It's working!" She propped the phone against something on the coffee table and leaned back on the same IKEA couch they'd owned since moving in fifteen years ago. "Which cải lương is this?"

"It's not—" Derek laughed. He didn't know the Vietnamese word for *musical*, but this song-driven storytelling was similar to traditional folk operas. "It's a new rock musical that I'm writing with my friend Thảo. The one about Tấm and Cám."

"That's a kid's story," she scoffed. "Why would anyone want to see that?"

By *anyone*, she meant people who weren't Vietnamese.

"People love Cinderella stories. Our version is better. It's got everything: suspense, romance, and danger. Murder, too." Some of his favorite childhood moments had been when he curled up in bed with his mother while she embellished his favorite scenes from *Tấm Cám*.

Her eyes softened. Maybe she was recalling the same memories he was.

"You loved acting out all the parts, especially when Tấm sang to the magical fish."

"I became a storyteller because of you. That's what theater is for me. A chance to share our stories with the rest of the world."

Even though her lips were pressed together in slight disapproval, she nodded. The small glimpse of pride in her eyes gave him confidence to continue.

"Mẹ, if this show does well, mine could be a household name! People would celebrate our culture and myths. More importantly, it would create more jobs for Asian actors." Derek had fought for every acting and directing gig he'd gotten. It wasn't fair that he had to compete against his fellow Asian actors for a handful of roles. His musical could make a difference.

"And if it doesn't? Do you have a backup plan?" she countered.

Her question wasn't due to lack of confidence in his skills but to practicality. Raising a child on her own meant pragmaticism was her default. She always had backup plans for her backup plan, because she couldn't afford not to. She'd sacrificed her own needs for him.

"The world will be singing *Tấm Cám* songs by next year. I promise," he proclaimed emphatically. He didn't have a backup plan. "Then you can retire."

"Are you saying I'm too old to work?" She clicked her tongue and shook her head. "I like staying busy."

"No, but you could do something you enjoy instead of being the business manager of my old high school." She'd taken the job so his tuition could be waived, but the rest of his experience at the elite private school was best forgotten.

"And when you can't find your next job? Who will take care of you then?"

"We're workshopping the show in DC," he said, ignoring her questions about his future. "If I buy you a plane ticket, will you come to opening night? I have a guest room here."

"That sounds expensive." She shrugged. "I don't even know if I can take time off."

"Mẹ, please?" He didn't expect her to agree right away. She didn't like traveling, so he wanted to warm her up to the idea first. "This is the most important job I've ever had."

"I'll think about it."

His shoulders slumped in relief. That was a start. Two months was plenty of time to convince her.

"If it's that important, you should get back to work then." The tone in his mother's voice meant the discussion was over.

"I will."

"And don't work too hard," she reminded him. His mother's concern meant she cared and worried about him.

"I won't. I love you," he said quietly in English. Declarations of love were too awkward in his semi-fluent Vietnamese. Love was usually expressed through home-cooked meals or neatly folded laundry.

"Okay, make sure you eat. You look too skinny."

"I will." Derek smiled. He never expected her to say "I love you" in return, but that didn't stop him from saying it every time they spoke. "Bye, Mẹ."

She nodded and fumbled with the phone until it hung up.

Derek's work had kept him away from Auburn, New York, for too long. But he'd rather move his mother closer to him than return to the semi-rural town that barely tolerated their existence. Once the musical made it to Broadway—to rave reviews—he could finally take care of her instead of the other way around.

CHAPTER 8

"That breeze from the water. I need more of it." Zoe fanned her neck with her hand as she turned toward the Potomac River to catch the currents of air coming from it.

Today was slightly cooler than yesterday, but not by much. She'd spent the afternoon in her apartment trying on different outfits in front of her cat, Mr. Bobbins. What does someone wear to catch up with an old friend who was also offering her a job of a lifetime? She'd settled on a long, light dress with pockets.

"Let's eat by the water," Derek said, and pointed to an empty bench on the waterfront.

Zoe mostly came here for concerts and when she stopped by her friend's photography studio. Without the busy weekend crowds, the Wharf held a magical energy. Outdoor booths were shuttered for the day but their strings of lights gave them a soft glow. Most of the restaurants were closed or closing when they arrived, so they'd ordered takeout.

"Tell me about your boutique," he said as they settled down for an impromptu al fresco dinner.

"Something Cheeky was voted the DMV's best lingerie boutique. Two years running," Zoe said with pride.

Derek's forehead wrinkled in confusion.

"DMV is what we locals call the DC metro area. DC, Maryland,

and Virgina," she explained. "You're going to hear it a ton while you're here."

"That makes way more sense. How does it feel to create something that's all yours?" he asked.

Had she heard a tinge of envy in his voice?

"Something Cheeky saved me after what happened during senior year." She bit her lip and shook her head to rid herself of the feelings those memories brought up. "I'm proud of what I've accomplished."

Zoe's professor hadn't left her with any other option but to quit theater. Removing herself from the situation entirely had been the only way to escape the controlling and power-hungry man.

"You should stop by for a tour. My workroom is ten times swankier than our college costume shop."

"Anything is an improvement over that basement."

"No windows and it was freezing from November through April." Zoe shivered and frowned in surprise. Her body hadn't forgotten. "It's really hard to sew when you're wearing your winter coat and gloves."

"All that lake effect snow piling higher and higher after the plows came through?" He shuddered. "It gets cold in New York City but not like in Syracuse."

"Remember our first Halloween at CNY College? It snowed so hard I could barely see in front of me!"

"Don't remind me. We went to the party dressed as Mulan-Ping and Li Shang as a romantic couple. And I got trashed." He shook his head disapprovingly at his younger self.

"You also dared me to find our way back to our dorm in the snow." Zoe barely knew her way around Syracuse during her first semester in school. Derek didn't either, even though he'd grown up in a small rural town thirty miles away.

"Like I said, I was drunk," he reminded her. "You didn't have to accept the challenge."

"You knew I can't resist a dare. I got us back, didn't I?"

She wasn't sure how the habit of daring each other to do things started, but she could never turn down a dare from him. Growing up with an older brother and several older cousins had given her a competitive streak.

"Via the most roundabout way ever," he said, rolling his eyes. "What if we'd gotten frostbite?"

"So dramatic. If it weren't for me, you would've puked in the dorm stairwell and not in a random snowbank. I saved you the hundred-dollar cleaning fee." Zoe tossed him a smug smile.

"You win," he conceded. "Again."

"I always win." She didn't bother hiding her smirk.

"It's rude to gloat."

"Remember that the next time you do it," she teased, poking his arm.

Derek chewed on his bottom lip, a sign that he was overthinking something. She used to tell him girls fell for that nerdy, thoughtful look. But for some reason she didn't say it today. He'd forgiven her for ghosting him, but she wasn't sure if they were back to teasing each other about their love lives yet.

"How did it go last night?" Zoe changed the subject right as Derek shoved a pork belly taco into his mouth. Ever since Derek brought up the musical yesterday, she'd thought about it nonstop.

"Sorry," he mumbled. He chewed quickly and swallowed before adding, "Oh, this is so good."

He gestured for her to taste hers. She unwrapped her takeout order. Her stomach grumbled as the smoky, spicy smells hit her nose. They'd arrived at the Wharf right when everything was closing. On a Sunday night, their only remaining choices were either tacos or greasy burgers.

"I'm having regrets about not getting those." He pointed to her bulgogi with kimchi tacos. "I got these pork belly ones last night and couldn't stop thinking about them."

Zoe picked up one of her overflowing corn tortillas, but she couldn't take a bite. A nervous energy skated over her body like some sort of shield. Her brain needed more information to process instead of the crumb Derek had dropped in the boba café.

As much as she loved her boutique, a tiny part of her missed the creative chaos of a stage musical. It was magical how a group of people took words from a page and turned them into a beautiful, emotional production for complete strangers. Designing lingerie didn't fulfill her creative well in the same way.

"You okay?" Derek's face was shadowed with concern. "Eat. You won't regret it."

"Last night's meeting was about the show, right?" she tried again. Zoe's stomach did a tiny flip. She was afraid to say "Vietnamese musical" aloud as to not give it too much hope. She had no idea how far along in the process he was.

"This musical is going to blast the doors wide open for us." He threw his hands out. "*Tấm Cám* will change theater for all Asian Americans. Imagine our stories as part of household conversations."

Zoe bit her lip. It all sounded too good to be true.

"But I can't do this without you." He grabbed her hand. His eyes blazed with excitement. "Please tell me you'll design the costumes for *Tấm Cam*. I need you, Zoe."

The confidence Derek exuded now was different from back then. Was it because he wanted to change a system that wasn't created for them? Or was he hiding something?

She didn't know how to respond. Her stomach twisted. The idea of returning to theater excited and terrified her equally.

"I—I can't," she finally blurted. "I gave up that dream a long time ago."

And it hurt. She swallowed the words, but the regret caught in her throat. Regret that she'd allowed their professor to make her choose between her career and her morals. But her professor had been right. She didn't have what it took to make it in theater. Not if it meant compromising her values.

"What can I do to change your mind?"

"Nothing." She forced a wide smile to hide her uncertainty. "I'm happy with my boutique."

"Liar." His tone was light but it struck her hard.

She withdrew her hand and turned toward the water, where the boats at the marina swayed gently. He knew her too well. Both the good and the bad memories she'd didn't want to rehash.

"I'm not our professor. I'm not an old white man with tenure who cares only about what the donors want."

"I've moved on from that," she declared. If she repeated it enough, then she'd start to believe it. "I refuse to leave my fate in the hands of others. With my boutique, I'm in control of my career."

Derek sighed loudly and pressed his lips together.

"We should eat while the tacos are still hot," she said. She unwrapped her food loudly, as if it could drown out the disappointment emanating from him. Finally, she took a bite. The bold flavors were a welcome distraction from her mixed emotions. "Oh my God, this is amazing."

"Told you," Derek gloated.

"We should come back here and try out the full menu," she suggested, relieved that he had dropped his request.

The next few minutes were quiet as they savored their food. In any other circumstances, eating on a bench with a view of the Wharf would be romantic. She couldn't help but notice how the moonlight accentuated his strong, angular jaw and full lips. But this was Derek, her college best friend, and they were here to discuss his work.

What if this was her only opportunity for a do-over? Her fellow Boss Babes would berate her if she turned down the chance of a lifetime without at least hearing him out.

Zoe thought about her secret sketchbooks filled with *Tấm Cám* costume designs. She'd told herself they were only studies to keep her creative and drawing skills honed. Each set was drawn in a different style and genre, from Elizabethan to full-on Vietnamese traditional clothing. But she'd never imagined the story as a rock musical until running into Derek yesterday.

On the drive back home she'd mentally designed Viet-inspired rock costumes in her head. Zoe couldn't remember the last time her imagination had yelled so loudly for her to sketch out her ideas.

Maybe she missed theater. Just a little, tiny bit. Zoe swallowed her last bite of food and looked him in the eye.

"Okay, tell me more."

"Really?" Derek almost dropped his food. "You just said you were happy with your boutique."

"Don't make me change my mind," Zoe teased. "It's not fair for me to turn you down without hearing you out."

He nodded and finished his final taco in two bites. He chewed faster and faster and groaned in delight. The man still appreciated food no matter the cuisine.

"Slow down!" She laughed. "I promised to hear you out so don't speed run your dinner. One of us choking on our food this week-end is plenty."

He chuckled as his jaw visibly slowed down. Finally, Derek washed down his food with his soda. He took a deep breath.

"Thảo and I have been working on the musical on and off for a year now. She's my cowriter and composer. A few months ago, we came down and performed a private workshop for Prestige Rep's artistic director, executive producer, and a few of their board members."

"Wait, you were here once already and didn't tell me?" Zoe frowned. No, she wasn't allowed to be hurt that he didn't contact her. After all, she was the one who stopped texting him in the first place. He owed her nothing.

"I was afraid to tell anyone about it. You know, in case we bombed." Derek gave her an apologetic look. "I wasn't even here for twenty-four hours."

"But they loved it, right?" Zoe sat up straighter. Her body was tense in anticipation.

"It was the first time we'd shared the songs with anyone besides Greg, the artistic director. I was terrified they wouldn't get it. Or say it was too Asian to be marketable."

She nodded. Of course she understood his fear. They'd dealt with similar concerns during college and their summer theater gigs.

"But they loved the three songs we performed for them." He smiled broadly. "They wanted a complete first draft before investing in a full production. That took us several more months, but it's official. We've signed an agreement for Prestige Rep to produce it."

"Derek, I'm so proud of you!"

Zoe threw her arms around him. Without hesitation, he wrapped his arms around her. She closed her eyes as her body relaxed against his warm, muscular chest. The anxiety and nervousness from earlier completely disappeared.

As she breathed in his familiar scent, a tingle spread through her body. The kind that she didn't associate with Derek.

Zoe pulled away as quickly as she'd gone in for the hug. Her cheeks burned. In her excitement over his success, she'd wrinkled the boundaries they'd agreed on freshman year: friends only.

She cleared her throat. What the hell was she doing thinking about him in that way?

CHAPTER 9

T hank you. We worked hard to get here," Derek said. He crumpled up his now-empty wrappers to avoid eye contact with her.

Whatever that moment was, it ended too soon. For years, he'd
longed to hold her close. To inhale her lilac perfume mixed with
her warm, sweet scent and finally confess his love for her. But
she'd pulled away as if she'd been burned.

"So what happens next?" Zoe asked a little too brightly. Her
cheeks were pink and she shifted on the bench.

He took a deep breath to clear the roller coaster of emotions
he'd gone through in less than a minute. *Remember the plan.
Musical first, then personal.* A light breeze cooled the flush from
his face as he met Zoe's gaze.

"We have about six weeks until previews start. Six weeks until
a real live stage musical of *Tấm Cám*."

"No way," she whispered.

"Greg Powers—that's the artistic director—agreed that we
should do our best to form an all-Asian cast and creative team. He
fully supports my vision."

"All-Asian show," she responded in disbelief.

"I've pinched myself every morning since I arrived in DC.
We're set to open in May."

The waves broke against the pier as if applauding his monu-
mental achievement.

"So will you do it?" Derek asked quietly. He knew it wouldn't be personal if she turned down his offer. He wanted to be the reason she agreed to work with him.

"Why me when you can have your pick of New York folks to design your costumes? Or even big-name Asian American fashion designers."

"Because it's *our* dream, Zoe."

"It *was* our dream and only that," she reminded him.

"You *are* a big-name designer," he added. "You've won awards."

"For lingerie. In the DMV." Zoe crossed her arms and leaned back into her chair, creating distance between them. "I haven't done any costume design since college. I don't want to be the weakest link on your team."

"Designing lingerie is even harder than costumes. Not only that, but you've created clothing that people want to wear. Some people don't even want to take it off during sex!"

"You read my Yelp reviews?" Her eyes widened in surprise but a tiny smile crept to her lips.

He nodded. "I did my research."

"My favorite one-star review is the person who complained that my plus-size shop didn't carry anything smaller than an extra-large." Zoe rolled her eyes.

"Would you do it if I promise to help you however you need? Though you don't want me near a sewing machine," he added, referring to his disastrous attempt to learn to sew during his freshman-year tech rotation.

Derek was lucky that their costume shop foreperson allowed him to even use a seam ripper after he almost set a machine on fire.

"You stay away from my babies!" Zoe warned. She hadn't forgotten that incident either. "And no touching my fabric shears."

"Don't worry. I don't have a death wish," he added.

He'd missed this energy between them. He'd missed Zoe. He couldn't think of a better excuse to see her every day than working on their musical together. Eventually, he'd find the right time to tell her how he felt.

"I don't know," Zoe said after their laughter subsided. "I've put off launching my Viet-inspired formal collection long enough."

"Think of the possibilities. The recognition you'll get by designing costumes for the first musical to have an all-Asian cast and creative team. You'll get lots of love here as a local. If we make it to Broadway, this show will get you national recognition for your upcoming fashion line."

She gave a noncommittal huff.

"We're inviting all the famous Asian celebrities to previews and opening night. Can you imagine meeting Phillipa Soo or Kelly Marie Tran or Michelle Yeoh and how they could flaunt your designs on their next red carpet event?"

He was laying it on thick, but he'd already imagined himself greeting half the Asian who's who in New York and Hollywood. This was the show that would change both of their lives.

"Those are a lot of *ifs*." Zoe dragged her shoe across the ground.

"Dream big, Z. I've kept our vision alive for both of us until you were ready to dive back in. Here's your chance."

"It would be fun to finally turn our fantasy into real life." Zoe pursed her lips thoughtfully.

She was wavering. Derek almost had her. She'd always loved the challenge of designing for the stage back in college.

"Dip your toes back into my world. Nothing says you have to stay. Just one show, then you can focus on your shop," he pleaded. He didn't care if he sounded needy.

"Derek, I—"

"Zoe, we came up with the idea together. You and me, we're going to change the world." He swung his arms out dramatically for extra emphasis. The sleeve of his shirt snagged on the straw of his drink, flinging it toward Zoe.

She gasped and tried to block it with her purse, but it was too late. The plastic cup hit both her bag and Zoe. As if to insult him even further, the lid popped off and rolled away.

Zoe yelped and jumped off the bench. He groaned as his root beer transformed itself into a sweet, dark brown Rorschach mess on, well, everything. Not only was it all over the ground and bench, but Zoe was soaked. Her dress clung to the curve of her hips—he forced himself to look away.

"I'm so sorry!" Derek grabbed the flimsy paper napkins from their takeout bag and handed them to her. "Maybe there's a public restroom and— Shit."

He stood up and rubbed his forehead. She'd been seriously considering working with him and he fucking ruined the mood.

"I can't believe I did that. I'm so sorry," he repeated.

"Derek, stop. I'm not hurt." She grabbed his arm until he looked into her eyes. "It's only soda."

"I know, but—" Derek howled as she splashed the remainder of his root beer onto his shirt.

"Got you!" she yelled and backed away so she was out of reach. "Now we're even."

"Oh, that's evil, Z." He brushed off as much liquid as he could and flung droplets at her.

She squealed as they hit her in the face.

"Pure evil," he shouted playfully.

The laughter he heard was his. Zoe joined him. Their bodies shook until they collapsed on the bench. Neither cared that root beer was still dripping off it.

"Zoe?" he said as he tried to catch his breath.

"Yeah?"

"Is that your sketchbook in your bag? I think it got wet."

"Oh no!" She bolted and yanked her sketchbook out of her bag. The blue cover was soaked.

"I'd offer you my shirt to wipe it up, but someone threw a drink at me."

"You started it."

"Here—" He took it from her and used a dry section of his sleeve to dry it off. "I think only the cover got wet."

He flipped it open to shake out any liquid that hadn't been absorbed by the paper. Derek's heart pounded. Instead of lingerie or fashion sketches, he found something even better.

She'd drawn Tấm in various costumes. The initial one was soft and flowy to mark her naivete but the pieces fell away to reveal a harder, more confident woman. The pencil marks were light but drawn with assertive hands.

"Give it back," Zoe demanded. Her earlier lightness was gone. "That's private."

"Your sketches are exactly how I'd imagined the costumes would look." He blotted the sides of her sketchbook as much as he could. He ran his thumb across the edges of the pages. It took every ounce of self-control to keep from flipping through the rest of it. He held the sketchbook open to the drawing that had taken his breath away.

"Those were just for fun. To practice my drawing skills," Zoe replied with a forced smile.

He caught a hint of wistfulness underneath her superficial brightness.

"You never stopped dreaming about *Tấm Cám* either," he whispered. That meant she hadn't forgotten about him all this time.

"I—I haven't," Zoe admitted. Her eyes went soft and unfocused. Was she remembering those nights on the roof when they cast their dream show?

"Z, will you do this with me, please?" He immediately regretted his tone. Desperation wasn't a good look for anyone. His hands clenched around her sketchbook as he forced himself to breathe slowly.

Her eyes narrowed as she considered his request yet again. His stomach twisted. She was going to turn him down and this time she wouldn't change her mind.

"I'd have to postpone my formal wear collection if I did this. Can I think about it?"

She stuck her hand out for her sketchbook. He gave it back to her, but he couldn't erase her drawings from his mind. It was as if she had a direct link to his brain.

"You only came back into my life yesterday. I can't make a major decision in twenty-four hours." She held the book against her chest but remembered her clothes were soaked. Zoe tucked it back into her bag.

"I'm sorry. That's not fair of me." He stared at his shoes, which thankfully were still dry. "I panicked."

What he really meant to say was *Don't walk out of my life again.* That would definitely scare her away for good.

CHAPTER 10

Zoe examined her sketchbook for any spatter that Derek had missed as a way to avoid looking at him. The longing in his voice gutted her. He was trying so hard to mend their friendship. She had to make more of an effort because she was the one who'd kept her distance from him.

She missed her best friend.

The Boss Babes were also her best friends, but she'd known Derek the longest. They'd spent almost every waking hour together for four years. It took his coming back into her life to realize she'd had a Derek-shaped void.

Luckily the cover had done its job and protected the inside of the sketchbook. She flipped through the pages and tried to look at them with fresh eyes. With Derek's eyes.

"I guess these aren't so bad," she said as if speaking out loud instilled more confidence. She'd drawn them in a creative fog after running into Derek yesterday. The sketches were basic but she'd captured the character's energy and evolution. She needed to redraw them and add more detail and color, but deep down they felt right.

She knew this without reading Derek's script or hearing the music. They'd created this show from angst and frustration about their aspiring theater careers. She knew every scene they'd created by heart.

"Zoe, no one would believe that you drew those costumes without seeing our script," Derek said softly. "But I can. We lived and breathed *Tấm Cám* whenever we weren't working on stuff for class."

"Those nights on the roof were some of my favorite memories."

"Aha!" He grinned. "You haven't stopped thinking about it all these years."

"Well, it would be fun to design something out of the ordinary," Zoe conceded. To her surprise, she'd been bereft after turning in her *Lysistrata* commission.

"Lingerie is not ordinary. Give yourself credit."

"You know what I mean. Remember when my design professor gave me chicken wire, fabric scraps, and spray glue and told me to make a dragon headdress?" She flipped to a blank page in her sketchbook and tried to sketch it from memory.

"Oh God, for that weird play about dragons in space?" Derek groaned. "I know the point of the student playwriting showcase is to experiment, but that one was strange."

"I thrived on the challenge! Nothing like making costumes on a tiny budget." Zoe bit her lip as she tried to remember if it had a beard.

"You didn't have to play said dragon," he muttered.

"You were cute," she teased.

"I was supposed to be menacing. Villain, remember?" He mimed the choreography from the play and stopped mid-move. "You think I'm cute?"

"Stop! As if you didn't know half the underclassmen had crushes on you." After their run-in earlier, she finally understood why. He was adorkable.

He shrugged. "I was too focused on my classes to notice."

"How come you never dated anyone back then?" Zoe searched his eyes for clues, but he'd found some more napkins and wiped his shirt.

"Are we really going to talk about how uncool I was in college? I came here to discuss our future." He actually looked offended about his single status during undergrad.

"I was only curious." Zoe shrugged.

"You promised to hear me out, but why don't you read the script and watch the private showcase we did for Prestige Rep? But you can't show anyone."

"I'll lock my bedroom door before I watch it." Zoe crossed her heart and grinned.

"I'm serious," Derek said sternly. His eyebrows furrowed. "We can't have the news leak until we've assembled the rest of the creative team and cast. You know the media will judge us harder because of who we are."

"I swear on our secret handshake," she replied.

"Not the terrible handshake." Derek rolled his eyes. "I'm never going to live down that cast party, will I?"

"You can count on me to keep things quiet."

"Emailing it now." Derek pulled out his phone and tapped on it rapidly. "You can watch it at home after you change into some dry clothes."

"You don't want to be here while I watch?" Zoe's face fell. Dinner had been awkward but she wasn't ready for it to end. They had six years of catching up to do.

"No way. I'd be a nervous wreck hovering over your shoulder like Tấm's ghost did with the emperor."

"Cinderella's spirit was never anxious," she reminded him. "Besides, in our version she never dies."

"Maybe I need a fairy god and a magical singing fish to look over me." He closed his eyes and pretended to make a wish.

"Give me some chicken wire and a few hours."

They both laughed. Zoe was relieved that the weirdness between them had disappeared.

"Call me as soon as you finish reading and watching. Even if it's late."

Zoe shivered at the intensity in his eyes.

"Even if it's two in the morning?"

"Trust me, you'll want to talk about it." Derek began bagging up their trash. "There, as if it never happened."

Except for their soaked clothes. But no number of napkins could fix that.

"You really think our Cinderella will change Broadway?" Zoe had never in a million years thought their late-night ramblings would be turned into a musical. Yet here they were discussing costumes and musical numbers.

"I know it will if you're by my side," he said with so much confidence, it gave her chills.

AFTER A LONG shower with plenty of body wash, Zoe could no longer smell the root beer on her body. She wanted to watch Derek's video right away, but the soda had glued itself to her body. Instead of her usual evening routine of face creams and body butter, she grabbed her tablet.

"Mr. Bobbins, sorry I was out so late on a Sunday night," she apologized to her orange tabby.

The cat stood on the wide arm of her oversize fuchsia love seat and yowled. She patted her head as she debated grabbing her small tote of art supplies. Once she settled down in the plush cushions, it took too much willpower to get out of it. She'd learned the tough way that it was better to pull out everything she thought she'd want for the evening. Once Mr. Bobbins sat on her lap, she was stuck.

Not that she minded. The love seat was her favorite spot in the living room she shared with her roommate, Trixie Nguyen. It was the first piece of furniture she'd splurged on after moving out of her brother's place. After years of squeezing her hips into chairs, she'd wanted one big enough to curl up in to read or binge the latest fashion design competition.

"Wine. Yes, I need a glass," Zoe said to her cat.

She'd adopted Mr. Bobbins from a shelter after Trixie and her boyfriend got serious. Her roommate often spent the night at Andre's house, which made their cozy apartment feel too empty. The cat was finicky as cats tend to be, but he always knew when she needed a cuddle.

She pulled out a half-empty bottle of sauvignon blanc from the fridge. After setting it and a stemless wine glass on the coffee table next to her, she grabbed her sketchbook and bag of art supplies. Just in case she felt inspired after watching Derek's video.

"Well, Mr. Bobbins, I've stalled long enough." Zoe settled into her chair and tucked her legs under herself. The cat curled itself on her thighs and immediately fell asleep.

Her finger hovered over the email icon. What if the showcase was nothing like what they'd fantasized about back in college? Like how she could never capture the costume designs that she'd imagined in her mind. Maybe it was better to allow their version to be ethereal.

But Derek was so convinced they were on the same wavelength about the show—even after all this time apart.

"Don't be a wuss, Zoe," she said out loud. The cat stirred and mewed in his sleep. "Even Mr. Bobbins thinks I should get over myself and watch it."

The video automatically played after she downloaded the attachment. Derek and an Asian woman—she must be his cowriter—were on a small stage. She could make out shadows of people sitting in the fourth or fifth row. He introduced himself and Thảo, who was a composer.

Zoe sat up straighter. She'd never known of a Vietnamese composer. Of course they existed. Why wouldn't they?

Derek's brief summary of the story was *their* version. Then he nodded at Thảo, who played a few chords on the keyboard in front of her. He sang Tấm's part and soon Thảo joined him as Cám. The duet was haunting and beautiful. It was full of the love the stepsisters had for each other.

Even Mr. Bobbins approved by purring loudly.

Zoe's entire body was humming. Her chest was so full of excitement, she thought it might explode. The musical was everything she'd hoped for and more. She'd be an idiot to turn down the chance to design costumes for it.

But that would mean returning to a world that would always ask her to compromise her values. Every assignment she'd received from her professor had chipped away at her values little by little without her realizing it. Let's make this character more Asian, he'd said as he critiqued her drawings. He'd tell her to make the eyes smaller or comment on how she needed to make her figure drawings taller and skinnier.

By the time she had realized how little her designs reflected who she was, she didn't know how to fix it. Except walk away. She'd walked away from the theater program and eventually walked away from Derek.

When it came to lingerie and fashion, she trusted her instincts without hesitation. Her stomach twisted and her wine tasted sour. She didn't have the experience for this job. She had worked at summer theaters as an assistant but never had the chance to design a professional production on her own. She had no idea how much the industry had changed in the last six years.

Derek was hiring her because they were friends. Not because of her skill. There was no doubt this show would receive national media attention. If she failed this again, she'd take him down with her. Then both of their dreams would be shattered.

Zoe wouldn't do that to him. Theater was his life. At least she had Something Cheeky to give her purpose.

So why did it feel like she was giving up on herself all over again?

"Mr. Bobbins, want to watch the showcase again?" She scratched his chin, but the tabby only snored in response.

CHAPTER 11

Zoe, you look like shit. I hope you didn't drive here."

Reina Guidroz's sweet Southern accent did little to dull her bluntness. Her sass paired with her drive was how she'd built DC's best male burlesque club. Add that cheekiness to her auburn hair and creamy freckled skin and she was one of the DMV's most eligible bachelorettes.

Zoe didn't flinch at her friend's truthful observation. Reina had nothing on her mother's and aunt's brutal honesty about her body.

"I was responsible and took the train in from the Falls Church station," she mumbled. After staying up all night watching Derek's showcase on repeat, the only one who'd gotten any rest was Mr. Bobbins. She would never allow something like exhaustion to keep her from one of their Boss Babes' Monday brunches.

"Did you sleep at all last night?" Reina pointed at the dark circles under Zoe's eyes. "They're so big, you're going to have to pay to check them."

Zoe responded with a yawn so wide and long that her eyes watered. She dragged herself into their usual booth at Hazel's Kitchen, a soul food restaurant in Northeast. The wall next to it cooled her cheek as it kept her somewhat upright.

"Are you dealing with insomnia again?" Trixie Nguyen fussed

as she slid next to her. Her wavy black hair was pulled into a messy bun. "Sorry I didn't make it home last night. My workshop ran late and it was easier to stay at Andre's. I was too tired to drive."

Lately Trixie was Zoe's roommate in name only. Now that she'd received her sex education certification, she held weekly workshops at her sex-toy boutique. The co-op space she rented was down the block from Hazel's Kitchen, which was co-owned by Trixie's boyfriend and his sister, Keisha Walker.

"You should just move in with him," Reina suggested.

"Hmmm," Trixie replied noncommittally as she sipped some water.

"You can turn the guest room into a play room." Reina winked. "And not the kind for small children."

"I can hear you," Keisha called out from her hidden high-top in the back. She peeked out from behind a tall potted plant and pointed at the women with her ink pen. "Look, I'm happy for the two of them, but I do not need to know about their sex lives."

"What she said," Trixie added as she rolled her eyes at the redhead.

"Morning. Wow, you look, um, tired." Josie Parks, the mother hen of their group, joined them at the table. After handing over operation of her boudoir photography studio to her sister, Josie now managed a co-op gallery. Her warm brown skin was glowing after her recent trip to sunny New Orleans to visit her long-distance beau.

"Not you, too." Zoe groaned as she forced her eyes open to peek at her best friends. She'd found her Boss Babes when she moved home after graduation. They were as much family to her as her parents and brother.

Josie scooted into the spot across from Zoe at the spacious booth. She'd mastered her bohemian artist look, which included a long scarf tied around her beautiful Afro. Her flowy, light cotton dress emphasized Josie's generous curves.

"I have a major dilemma," Zoe said. She closed her eyes, hoping for a reprieve from the bright sunlight filtering through the windows. Instead, Derek's video replayed itself behind her eyelids. She blinked her eyes back open.

"Is it a man? Or a woman?" Reina stood at the end of the table with her hands on her hips. Today she was wearing a blue floral-print halter and wide-legged navy pants.

"Not everything has to be about dating," chided Josie. "Let Zoe talk."

"How about we give Zoe a chance to wake up before we grill her?" Keisha emerged from the bar area with a large mug. The whipped cream floating on top swayed as she gently set the drink in front of Zoe. "It's your favorite but different."

"Mmmm, mocha," Zoe whispered as the deep chocolate scent reached her nose. "Is it time to play guess the flavor profiles?"

The women were used to impromptu taste tests whenever they stepped into Hazel's Kitchen. It was a perk of holding their mastermind meetings at a friend's restaurant.

"If you want." Keisha clasped her hands together but her red-scarf-covered head bobbed in excitement.

Zoe wrapped her hands around the warm mug. Her best friends' banter faded into the background as she lifted the chocolate elixir to her nose and inhaled deeply before sipping. The sweet liquid warmed her from the inside out. The bitterness of the coffee hot-wired her brain enough to squint at her friends.

"Did you put cayenne in this mocha?" Zoe's eyes widened as the spice hit the back of her throat. "And chocolate liqueur?"

"Chili-infused chicory liqueur." Keisha's dark brown eyes sparkled as she laughed. She tucked an errant black curl back into her head scarf. "It's a new recipe I'm testing out for our weekend brunch service."

"Maybe dial down the spice a little?" Zoe coughed, her mouth still tingling from the chili.

"I told Andre we put too many chilis in the bottle!" Keisha said loudly toward Andre, who was restocking the bar. She shook her head and reached for the mug.

"Wait—" Zoe put out her hand. "Let me taste it again now that I know what's in it."

Closing her eyes, she brought it back for a larger sip. The slightly bitter yet sweet chicory root liqueur infused with chilis exploded in her mouth while sweet cocoa rounded out the bold flavors. She reveled as the balance of flavors danced on her tongue.

Zoe shimmied in her seat and hummed in delight. A number from Derek's musical popped in her head so she sang a line from the chorus.

"I'll have what she's having," declared Reina. She waved toward the bar to catch Andre's attention, then pointed to Zoe's mug. He winked and nodded in understanding.

"Better make that four more, babe," Trixie called out to her boyfriend.

"I'm adding 'one sip will make you sing' to the menu description," said Keisha excitedly. "All it needs is a name."

"What about naming it after whatever song Zoe was singing," Josie suggested and hummed the melody.

"No, no, no, we can't do that," Zoe cried out. She clapped her hand over her mouth in surprise.

All four women gaped at her. She didn't raise her voice often, but when she did they paid attention. Worried expressions covered their faces.

"Sorry, I—" Zoe stopped to compose her thoughts. She wasn't

sure how much she could tell them about the musical. Her Boss Babes were her ride or dies, but Derek had been there for her during college. "I promised someone to keep their secret."

"Oooh, sounds juicy." Reina rubbed her hands together in anticipation and slid into the booth next to Josie.

"Hush." Keisha poked Reina's arm and gestured for her to make room on the seat. "Zoe will tell us what she can."

Andre set four more mugs of the elixir on their table and slipped away quietly. He must've sensed the serious vibes. He also knew better than to hover during their meetings. The last and only time he attempted to join them, the women had tried to revamp his bar menu. He'd learned quickly to allow the Boss Babes their space.

"Promise you won't breathe a word about this," Zoe whispered after Andre returned to the bar. She pointed at Trixie and Josie. "Not even your boyfriends."

"Have some faith," said Josie. "Besides, Spencer is in New Orleans right now."

"Puh-lease. Y'all video chat every day," added Reina.

Trixie and Keisha snort laughed. Josie's eyes narrowed as she shushed them.

Zoe giggled. This was what she imagined it'd be like to have four sisters. Their exchange took the edge off her nerves. She took a deep breath.

"On Saturday, I ran into my college best friend, whom I haven't seen in six years. He's in town to direct a brand-new musical that's probably headed to Broadway, and now he wants me to design the costumes because it's based on the play we created together during school, except I gave up theater halfway through my senior year, then yesterday after dinner I gave him a hug and it felt like more than a hug but we're only supposed to be friends and—"

"Breathe, girlie," Reina cooed softly. Trixie rubbed Zoe's back.

Zoe gasped for air. The last two days were a confusing jumble in her head. She wasn't even sure if what she'd blurted out made sense. Her shoulders slumped in relief now that she'd told the Babes.

"That's a lot of emotions in only two days. It's going to be okay," Trixie consoled her and pulled Zoe in for a side hug. Zoe leaned into her roommate as the other women murmured in agreement.

"Let's start from the beginning," suggested Josie, a problem solver who preferred to tackle challenges methodically.

"I'm a bit lost here, Zoe," Trixie spoke into Zoe's hair. "How come you've never mentioned this college bestie?"

"Does this bestie have a name?" Keisha asked. "And are we supposed to like him?"

"Derek," said Zoe. She sat up. "Derek Bui from Auburn, outside of Syracuse. We met freshman year at CNY College."

"Wait, I've heard of that place. Hordes of crows visit the town every spring. The trees are black because there's so many of them." Reina shuddered and her light skin had gone pale. "Can you imagine the noise and bird poop everywhere?"

"Reina, focus," Josie said gently. Reina had a thing for weird facts and obscure documentaries. She also had an irrational fear of crows, yet couldn't stop herself from watching YouTube videos about them.

"We were the only two Asian American freshmen in the drama program that year. We bonded quickly, especially since he's also Vietnamese. I survived that program because of him." Zoe smiled as she recalled the first time she met Derek.

"You never hooked up?" Reina side-eyed her. "You weren't attracted to him a tiny bit?"

"Of course I noticed that he was cute when we first met. But we never dated because everyone expected us to get together because we were both Asian." Zoe shook her head adamantly. She'd firmly put him in the friend zone based on principle and to subvert their classmates' assumptions.

"Holy microaggression, Batman." Keisha rolled her eyes. "Igno-ramuses."

She knew her friends would understand.

"After graduation, we went our separate ways," Zoe continued. "He went to New York and became a successful director. I came home and apprenticed in Lola's shop before opening Something Cheeky."

She left out the part about how she'd hurt his feelings by moving back to DC. Zoe wasn't ready to rehash that again.

"Now he's back, and he wants you to work with him. Did I get that right?" Trixie asked.

Zoe nodded.

"Do you want us to help you make a list of pros and cons of doing this musical?" Josie pulled out her notebook and favorite capless fountain pen.

"Look, if it's not a hell yes, then it's a no," said Keisha.

"Isn't that Xavier's motto?" Reina narrowed her eyes.

"Yes." Keisha smirked, refusing to take Reina's bait. "Sometimes he drops nuggets of wisdom."

Reina snorted in disbelief. Xavier was Andre's childhood best friend and sometimes helped out in the restaurant. He also had a little flame for Keisha. She was oblivious to his feelings or pretended to be.

"So"—Josie glared at Reina and Keisha to keep them focused— "why should you design costumes for this musical?"

"Here's where the secrecy comes in. He and his friend Thảo are working on Vietnamese Cinderella as a rock musical."

"No way! I loved *Tấm Cám* growing up." Trixie's eyes lit up with excitement.

"Right? In college Derek and I joked about doing our own version of it. A fractured fairy tale sort of like *Into the Woods* but super Viet. But it was a game we played to destress."

"Doesn't sound like a game anymore," Reina scoffed.

"Zoe, you have to do it." Trixie tugged at her sleeve. "Can you see all the little girls who are looking for a Vietnamese empress to look up to?"

"I've never designed professionally. Only in college." Zoe buried her face into her mug. Her last design attempt had been a disaster due to what her professor claimed were creative differences. Right, as if standing up against yellow face was creative.

"You own the most successful custom lingerie boutique in the DMV. You are more than qualified," said Keisha.

"Damn right. And didn't you just do a commission for *Lysistrata* with drag queens and kings?" Reina added.

"I only took the designer's drawings and turned them into clothes."

"Give yourself more credit than that. You can design the costumes and have your team sew them," said Trixie.

"This gig has gotta be enough to help fund your new formal wear collection," Josie pointed out. "You should add it to your contract that your crew do most of the construction. Nothing wrong with double dipping."

Zoe's heart swelled. Her Babes believed in her unconditionally, but seeing Trixie's reaction to the idea of the musical—that gave her butterflies. The representation in this musical would change how Asian drama kids saw themselves. They couldn't be what they could not see.

Until yesterday, she'd been perfectly happy with her life. Her shop was thriving and allowed her to grow creatively. Her Boss Babes were the best friends she could ever have. Contrary to stereotypes, her parents supported her creative work wholeheartedly.

Why did she have to run into Derek? Seeing him—hearing him talk about the musical—opened up the dream she'd long buried. It hurt to bury that dream, but what else could she have done? Her professor had asked her to be complicit in yellow face and she'd refused. That'd been the end of her career before it'd even started.

Now Derek was here in DC, asking her to do the complete opposite of her last design experience. This show celebrated its Asianness in a way she'd never expected to see onstage.

How could she pass on such an opportunity? Especially after reading the most empowering interpretation of *Tấm Cám* she'd ever seen. And the songs. She'd watched that video at least twenty times and had already learned the choruses.

"What if I do this and the musical fails? I could ruin his career." Zoe's chest tightened just thinking about hurting his chances at Broadway.

"If it flops, it's more than the costumes," Reina pointed out. "When my guys choreograph new shows, there's a gazillion factors on whether the audience likes it or not."

"I'm putting too much pressure on myself," Zoe admitted. "I wanted to be a costume designer so badly back then."

"Here's your chance," Josie encouraged.

Zoe bit her lip and sighed. This was her chance to revisit her first true passion.

"Now about that hug that could be more than a hug," said Reina. "Would you date him now? Without the pressure from your classmates?"

Zoe opened her mouth but had no idea if she would. She closed her mouth.

"You're hesitating, so it's not a hell no," Keisha pointed out. "You haven't dated anyone seriously in a while. Perhaps it's worth testing the waters?"

"Or you could just bang him and get it out of both your systems," Reina suggested.

"Reina!" Josie cried. "That's not helpful."

Reina shrugged. "All that sexual tension can mess with your head. So why not get it out of the way before you spend all that time working together?"

"I've never allowed myself to see him as more than a friend." Until one hug made her all tingling and she flung him out of her arms like he was hot iron.

"Never?" Josie raised an eyebrow. "I just googled him, and he is fine."

Keisha grabbed the phone from Josie. "Damn, girl, he's hot—in a nerdy way. Not my type but totally yours."

"Babes, give Zoe some space to figure out what she wants," Trixie said. "It's been only two days since she ran into him."

Zoe whispered a thank-you to her roommate.

"I wish you could hear the songs, but he made me promise not to share them with anyone." Zoe hummed what she could remember. If she didn't sing the lyrics, she technically wasn't breaking her promise. "That song was so haunting and beautiful. I had to sketch out some costume ideas after listening to it on repeat."

"Zoe, you have to do this. For me. For us." Trixie squeezed her arm in excitement.

Her friend was right. This was an extraordinary chance to make a difference. What better way to test out the theater again than a show that she'd been dreaming about since college? She owed it to herself to give it a try.

"I'm going to do it." Zoe took a deep breath and smiled. "But when tech week is looming and I'm pulling all-nighters to finish the costumes, I'm blaming all of you."

"Promise me you'll introduce me to some hot actors?"

"Reina!" the other women cried and everyone broke out in laughter.

CHAPTER 12

W hy hasn't Zoe called or texted?" Derek paced the rehearsal room at Prestige Rep. "I don't have a backup plan for our costumes."

"Chill, Derek." Thảo grabbed him by the arms and guided him into a chair. "It's a big ask. Give her time."

"What if she hated the songs? Or I remembered our version incorrectly and fucked it up?" Derek took off his glasses and rubbed his eyes. "Then she'll never want to go out with me."

"That escalated quickly." Thảo laughed.

"I'm pathetic." Derek dropped into the metal folding chair in front of their makeshift worktable. The sticky notes on his laptop screen fluttered.

"You're not. You're in love," she reassured him. "I'd be flattered if a woman felt that way about me."

"Would you date her if she were your best friend?"

"Maybe. Depends how hot she is." Thảo grinned unabashedly.

"Not helping." Derek tossed her a pained expression.

"Kidding. Bros before—"

"Don't you even," he cut her off sternly as her chest shook with silent laughter. Thảo may not be his sister by birth, but she'd acted like one ever since they met working at the diner. He was shit at waiting tables, but thanks to her, he got better at it. Not great, but passable enough to get decent tips.

"I would never, but seriously, Derek, you have to tell her how you feel." Thảo gave him one of her sisterly looks of concern that he was all too familiar with. "You can barely focus on our work now. The more time you spend together and the longer you go without—"

"I know. Let me figure it out," he snapped. Then immediately regretted it. "I didn't mean to yell at you. I thought it'd be easier."

"What makes it so hard to tell her how you feel?"

"I finally have her back in my life. Sunday night felt like we'd barely spent a week apart. What if I tell her and she pushes me away for good?" Derek closed his eyes. His chest hurt at the idea of losing her again. "I'd rather have her in my life as a friend than not at all."

"I don't have any good advice for you except don't wait ten years to tell her how you feel."

"Way to make me sound like a pining fool."

"We're all fools when we're in love," Thảo consoled.

Derek sighed. Normally he thrived under pressure, but this was the first time that he'd written and directed a production. Add in Zoe and Greg's expectations. He was trying to do too much at one time.

"Since you can't control what she decides, let's focus on the script. The entire reason we're here." Thảo tapped her notes.

"You're right."

"I'm always right," Thảo gloated. "The first scene still isn't working."

"You know the opening number is supposed to be the hardest to write," Derek said with more confidence than he actually had. "We should save it for last."

Thảo huffed. They'd known each other long enough that she saw through his fake-it-till-you-make-it energy.

"The cast arrives in two weeks. I want to have a finished script for them." She groaned in frustration.

Her foot shook with nervous energy. The tapping against the keyboard stand echoed in the Prestige Rep's large rehearsal room. The room wouldn't feel so big when the cast and creative team came together for the first time. The idea was both exhilarating and terrifying.

"You can't rush the creative process," he reminded her. And himself. The two of them had been working on the show on and off for several years. Thanks to Prestige's sponsorship, they'd been able to dedicate time to it the past year.

"Everyone will be at the first read through," added Thảo. "Which means Greg, the board, donors, and producers will be judging us."

"Add the entire world while you're at it," he muttered. All he could think about was disappointing everyone. Especially Zoe.

"I heard that! As if I don't know that we have to be twice as good to prove ourselves."

The legs of Thảo's chair scraped the floor as she abruptly pushed away from the keyboard. She paced back and forth in front of him as she mumbled to herself. This freak-out was all part of her process.

Derek hadn't told her everything about his dinner with Greg on Saturday. Thảo was stressed enough that he didn't need to pile on more. He was the one who'd wanted to produce this musical in the first place, so he'd deal with Greg's expectations on his own.

"Story of our lives." He stopped her as she made another pass. "We're going to finish in time. Promise."

Thảo tilted her head and bit her lip. Derek smiled as her eyes began to soften. Though they'd worked on projects together before, his process was more laid back than hers. Derek preferred to allow the feeling of the piece to move him while she hammered away until the music and words came out.

"Fine," she said finally. "We'll save the opening number for last. What about the scene where Tấm and Cám are reunited at the palace?"

"The first or second time?" Derek flipped through his notes. Portraying the sisters as best friends changed the entire dynamic of the Cinderella story. Their retelling of the folktale focused on friendship and love instead of jealousy and hate.

"First," she replied as she settled back down in front of the keyboard.

"Whose brilliant idea was it to sing the entire musical?"

"You and that big brain of yours." She tapped his head.

He groaned. "And you let me?"

Thảo laughed, then played the opening notes to the scene. Derek waved for her to continue. He hummed along as he closed his eyes to imagine how the scene would play out on a stage.

"This scene should be hopeful and exciting until the end, when Tấm reveals her concerns about the emperor's feelings for her," suggested Thảo.

"I agree." Derek sat up and snapped his fingers. "Let's amp up the pop vibes—give it girl-band energy—until the final verse where it starts to fall apart and become discordant."

"Melancholy, too." Thảo nodded.

"Then we jump right into Cám's number where she vows to repay Tấm's kindness. For protecting her from the evil stepmother."

"Hmm. Maybe." Thảo rubbed the shaven side of her head the way she did whenever she was deep in thought. "But the audience needs to see what Tấm means about the emperor. After all, they're supposed to have their happily ever after."

"To prove that she's not imagining the way he takes her for granted."

"Maybe the emperor needs a name," said Thảo.

"You know I'm terrible with names and titles." Derek shook his head. "So many micro decisions. Should it be a Vietnamese name, and do we want to base it off a real emperor or—"

"Keep him as 'Emperor.' To keep with the fairy-tale vibe," spoke a feminine voice from the doorway. "And the story is focused on the sisters' relationship with each other. Not him."

Zoe! Derek spun around. How much had she heard? It was best to pretend that she'd been there for only a minute or two. He swallowed and smiled brightly.

How could she look even more beautiful than the last time he'd seen her? She was wearing what had to be one of her designs. At first glance, it looked like the Vietnamese traditional dress áo dài, but the light blue fabric from the waist down was sheer, giving it a cropped look. Instead of the typical flowy, wide-legged pants underneath, she wore white capris.

"Hey!" He ran over to Zoe and pulled her to the cluttered table, where he and Thảo had been working. "Thảo, this is Zoe, my best friend from undergrad. Zoe, meet my cowriter and composer."

"The famous Zoe!" Thảo pulled Zoe in for a bear hug. She winked at Derek and mouthed *Wow.* "You're the one who helped Derek survive college."

"Nice to meet you," Zoe said as she shot him a surprised look. "*Someone* has barely mentioned you."

Thảo clicked her tongue with the same disappointing tone that his mother made when he forgot to take his shoes off at the door.

"If you'd responded to my texts, I would've mentioned Thảo," Derek shot back.

"So this is the room where the magic happens." Zoe ignored him as she ran her fingers over the side of Thảo's keyboard.

"You play?" asked Thảo.

"If you count scales as playing." Zoe chuckled. "My parents quickly realized that Eddie and I weren't music prodigies."

"I can teach you a few bars of something fun if you want. It makes for a good party trick."

Zoe shook her head. "I'll stick to my riveting topics of stretch lace and corset construction."

"You're in the right place for it," said Thảo. "Speaking of places, what did you think about the video and script Derek sent over?"

Derek shot Thảo a *don't rush her* look, but she shrugged it off.

"That's why she's here, right? To give us an answer."

"I meant to text you, but . . . " Zoe started.

"It's okay. We don't have to talk about it right now. Want to grab lunch?" He looked at his phone. It was only eleven o'clock. "Or brunch?"

It was Thảo's turn to give him a *what the fuck?* look. If Zoe planned to reject him, he'd rather it be one-on-one and not in front of Thảo. She'd be empathetic, but she'd want to over-analyze everything as soon as Zoe walked out the door. He was very capable of overthinking every one of Zoe's words and facial expressions on his own.

"No. I mean, I had a late breakfast with my friends this morning." Zoe drummed her fingers on the top of the keyboard before arching them over the keys. Her hands shook, but soon the familiar warm-up notes filled the rehearsal room.

Maybe he'd put too much pressure on her yesterday. He should've asked her if she even wanted to return to theater. He hadn't realized how the incident from senior year still affected her.

"Zoe, it's okay if you don't—can't—do the costumes." If he gave her an out, then her rejection wouldn't sting so hard. *Right. Keep lying to yourself.* He'd be gutted, but he didn't have time to wallow. The show had to go on no matter what.

"It's not about can't or won't." Zoe's hands curled into tight fists at her sides.

Derek's chest tightened as he braced himself.

"I *have* to do this. I'll regret it for the rest of my life if I don't," she whispered to the keyboard.

"Really? Are you sure?"

"Good grief, the woman has agreed." Thảo smacked him. "Don't let her change her mind."

"Yes. I'll do the costumes." Zoe finally looked at him with a wide grin. Her eyes were bright.

Derek wanted to jump up and down like a kid, but he kept his cool. Instead he smiled so hard that his cheeks started to hurt. Operation Win Zoe's Heart was going according to plan.

"Thank you!" Derek exhaled loudly in relief before he wrapped his arms around Zoe. "I knew you'd say yes."

Behind them, Thảo snorted.

"I'll walk you to the production office so they can get your contract and the rest of your paperwork." Derek turned to Thảo. "Do you mind working on your own for a while?"

"Go," Thảo said indulgently. "Get out of here, you crazy kids."

When Zoe turned back toward the door, Thảo mouthed *Tell her* at him.

Derek shook his head. He wasn't ready to turn their friendship upside down yet. Not when they'd barely had any time together.

CHAPTER 13

I know you said rock musical, but how do you feel about a *Paris by Night* meets Eurovision aesthetic?" Zoe asked as she flipped through her binder stuffed with ripped magazine pages and print-outs of different outfits.

She'd transformed the largest cutting table in the Something Cheeky workroom into her design center. It was stacked with various books on fashion history and Vietnamese magazines that her cousins had brought back from their travels. Her pencils and markers were strewn in between all the reference materials.

"Eurovision?" Derek cringed. He'd set up camp at her tiny desk in the corner. "That's too much spandex."

"You look great in spandex," she teased. "Remember *Into the Woods*? You wore that spandex bodysuit with a big fluffy tail and a codpiece."

"I prefer to leave a few things to the imagination," he interrupted. "Even if your designs were brilliant."

Zoe scoffed.

"I'm serious. Who else could have taken our professor's vision for a Southern-and-vampire-inspired fractured fairy tale and made them look good?" he reminded her.

"Oh my God. He had some weird ideas, but I had fun working on it during junior year."

The head of their theater program was into unlikely mash-ups because he thought it made him edgy. His challenging combinations forced everyone to dig deep into their creative well. Somehow the productions always worked out.

"We need to keep *Tấm Cám*'s fairy-tale energy no matter what," he said as he tapped away on his laptop. "We loved your suggestion to keep the Emperor nameless. Thảo suggested that everyone else's names should be their job or title. Only the sisters will have actual names."

Zoe nodded, but her brain was stuck on the memory of fitting him for that ridiculous costume. He'd looked hot in that costume. Fairy vibes paired with big dick energy. Zoe's eyes widened. Luckily Derek wasn't looking at her or he'd see the blush creep up her neck to her face.

Why was she even thinking about his—she bit her lip and took a deep breath. Yes, Derek was attractive, but they were friends. Semi-strangers, since they'd been out of touch for so long.

"You're right. No spandex. Maybe just *Paris by Night* with a strong Viet historical influence?"

She picked up another binder, in which there were printouts of her favorite outfits from the California-based entertainment show. Zoe's grandparents always had it playing in the background when she was growing up. The flashy American pop covers paired with body-hugging costumes and choreographed dance numbers had captivated her at an early age.

"I'm getting flashbacks to all the *Paris by Night* videos you forced me to watch."

"Forced? As I recall, you were dancing and singing along." She hummed and mimed his moves.

"Don't remind me how much my Vietnamese sucks. My mom would not approve."

"Drunk Derek singing was entertaining. I have video proof."

"Please never show that to the world," he begged her.

She stuck her tongue out at him. Her fingers stopped moving and his cheeks grew pink as he stared at her. Or was he looking at her tongue? Zoe withdrew it back into her mouth. What was supposed to be a playful moment had turned into something she'd never felt around him before. Her abdomen grew warm and her neck tingled. She cleared her throat.

"Fine, I'll stick with historical Viet clothing, but we'll give it modern-day pop-rock inspo." It was better to stick to what was in front of her than attempt to name whatever that was.

"Zoe, why are you still waffling about your concept?" He pushed his glasses back up his nose with a concerned expression.

"I want it to be perfect," she admitted. This was a big show to debut with, and she had to do it right.

"This entire production is a work in progress. The show will change between now, opening night, and closing." He walked over to her. "There will be rewrites and tweaks down to the last DC performance."

"Really?" Her chest tightened as doubt crept back in.

There was so much Zoe didn't know about professional theater. Sewing costumes for *Lysistrata* was only a small part of the process. She hadn't been involved in the day-to-day creation like with *Tấm Cám*. She hadn't even met with the director for the Greek play. Her main contact was the designer and the costume shop manager.

"Yes. Theater is art. It's breathing and evolving. Especially for a new show. Sometimes we won't know if a song hits until it's performed in front of an audience."

"I didn't know any of this. All the main stage shows in college were ones that have been around for a while."

Her armpits became clammy. She'd looked up the scenic and lighting designers once she'd learned who they were. The creative team had years of experience on major shows. Then there was her, a nobody in the theater world.

"I hate to rush you, but we have a meeting with Greg tomorrow. He wants to see your preliminary sketches and go over our progress."

"Tomorrow? I'm not even close!" Zoe's heart raced and she swallowed the acid coming up her throat.

"They don't have to be pretty. Enough for him to understand the concept of your designs," he said gently.

Zoe nodded as she tried to smooth out her face to hide her panic.

"I can help you however you need," he offered. "We're a team, remember?"

"But you and Thảo still have songs to finish. You two are a team, too."

"She understands that meetings are part of my job. And I'm prepping you for one." He smiled reassuringly. "So we're good, okay?"

"They won't be fully colored. And I have no fabric swatches." She gathered up all her markers and put them in a pile.

"Hey." Derek placed his hand on top of hers. It was warm against her clammy hands. "You won't need those till the first read through. And the costume shop manager can help you shop for fabric."

"When is that?" She was almost afraid to ask.

"Next week."

"I can't do this." Zoe pulled her hand away and started to pace in a circle—or was that a rectangle?—around her worktable. She was glad her staff was in the front helping customers, so they couldn't see their usually unflappable boss have a full-blown panic attack.

"Z, breathe." Derek joined her frenetic pacing. "You're making me dizzy. Can we slow down and talk about this?"

She took deep breaths through her nose and exhaled through her mouth. After a few counts, her heartbeat slowed down closer to normal and so did she. She stopped in front of her sketchbook, where Derek had flipped to the drawings she'd stayed up all night working on.

"Do for the other characters what you did for Tấm's designs. Those were perfect." He tapped the paper.

"But I was only playing around. I have to look at the big picture and make them cohesive. They're supposed to tell a story," she said too quickly. She took another deep breath.

"And they will."

Derek was so confident because he'd always nailed his performances. He'd gotten almost every part he'd auditioned for in college. He graduated with a theater degree. Set out on his own in New York. Unlike her. She'd run home with her tail between her legs. Even if it didn't feel like that at the time, she finally saw her actions for what they were: fear.

"If you say so."

"Come on, Z. You tell stories with the lingerie you design." He pointed at the big corkboard where she hung her newest designs. Her team had worked hard to turn her sketches into patterns and to construct lingerie from them.

"Most people don't ask me what story a bra or a negligee tells."

"But they know when they see your clothes and imagine what they'll do when they wear it."

He picked up a hanger with a neon-and-black-lace bra and placed it against his chest. He posed and gave her an exaggerated smolder. "This bra says *I am a badass who can wear this to the club because who says bras have to be hidden under clothes?*"

Derek pursed his lips in a sexy pout as he pretended to dance in a nightclub. He was trying to cheer her up and was successful at it, too. Zoe bit her lip to keep from laughing. She loved that he was never afraid to look silly. What mattered to him was enjoying the character he embodied at the time. He was a natural onstage.

But this wasn't a stage. He did all this for her and to make her feel better about her lack of experience. Somehow he always knew the right way to boost her confidence, whether it was by being silly or giving her a pep talk when she needed it the most.

"And this—" Derek flung a floor-length red chiffon robe around his shoulders. It was too small for him to slip his arms into the sleeves with red marabou feathers sewn to them. More soft fluffy feathers trimmed the lapels all the way down to the hem of the train.

"This," he continued as he glided around the workroom, "says *I just killed my rich husband and I am pretending to be sad until I get my inheritance.*"

"We call that the murder robe—privately, of course." Zoe laughed as he continued to act out the part of a grieving widow. "It's one of our most requested commissions."

"Aha!" He grinned. "Point made."

"Fine, you're right. Now put that back before you rip it!"

He made one more round with it before hanging it up.

"For each launch, I do tell some kind of story, but it's intuitive. I don't actively create pieces to fit into a story when I start out."

"Then pretend you're designing full body lingerie for all the characters."

She snorted at the image he'd created. "I don't think that's the vibe you want for this musical."

"You have to trust yourself." Derek grabbed her hand and placed it against her chest.

She looked down at his hand on top of hers as her chest rose with each breath. His hand burned her skin. Everything around her fell silent except for the sounds of them breathing. At first each had their own rhythm but slowly, they synchronized. Goose bumps spread across her arm.

Zoe looked up right into his eyes. His pupils were dilated and his lips opened in a content smile. A jumble of emotions she couldn't even name swirled inside her. Naming them was too scary, so she removed their hands from her chest and took a step back.

He remained in place but stuck his hands in his pockets. Was he waiting for her to say something about *that*?

"That's easier said than done," she said, pretending she hadn't noticed his earlier expression. "I've designed lingerie for years."

He ran his hand through his hair as he frowned but smiled quickly to cover it up. As if sensing her discomfort, he backed away closer to his workspace.

"Z, I'll trust you until you can trust in yourself," he said quietly but with plenty of confidence.

"That was so cheesy." But she liked it. She felt better knowing that he'd stand behind her as she figured out what the hell she was doing. He'd always stood by her in school, except for that one time. But it had been hard for both of them. She shouldn't have made him choose.

"I don't care if I'm being cheesy. I just put on a murder robe and pranced around the room. I meant it."

"Okay, will you remind me of that whenever I freak out?"

"I wasn't always here for you before, but I am now, Z." He winked at her. "Best friends, right?"

Zoe nodded. Their friends-only pact protected them from relationship drama and awkwardness. Best friends didn't think about the other's body in a tight spandex suit. Would he still stick with her if he knew she was struggling to see him as only a friend?

CHAPTER 14

Derek cringed inwardly. Why did he have to reiterate their best friends status? He thought they'd shared a moment when he placed their hands on her chest. Only two of his fingers were graced with her soft, silky skin. Maybe one day soon she'd allow him to trace lazy circles all over her body while they snuggled in bed watching old Tony Awards performances.

"You're going to kick ass during our meeting with Greg tomorrow," Derek said for both Zoe's benefit and his.

"I'll do my best," Zoe replied with more confidence than she'd had all afternoon.

He'd put together a talented and visionary team to lay the groundwork for his production, but there were too many factors outside of their control. He had to straddle the thin line between staying true to his story and appealing to producers and audiences.

Zoe's phone buzzed on her table. She unlocked it then looked back at him.

"That was my manager. She's locked up for the day."

"I had no idea it was that late already." He peeked into the front of the shop. It was dark and a purplish sunset shone through a crack in the curtains.

"Time flies when you're dancing around in a murder robe." She picked up her phone. "I should've taken photos."

"You should try it some time."

"Believe me, everyone who works back here has modeled one. Including me." She twirled. "How can you not?"

Derek would give anything to see her with the robe on—and nothing underneath. He'd worship her body until she cried for him to stop. And then do it some more.

"You hungry? We can order takeout from my parents' place," Zoe suggested.

The mention of her parents was the cold shower he needed to return to reality.

"I've been waiting for you to ask. I've missed Cô Hồng's cooking."

"I know my mom's food is good, but you have your choice of Vietnamese restaurants in the city," she said.

"I say the same thing about my mom's food. It has that childhood nostalgia. But your mom's bun thit nuong is the best." He mimed a chef's kiss.

"Kiss up."

"It's not my fault that moms like me." He wasn't even gloating. Even Thảo's mom, who was very prickly, liked him.

"How's your mom doing?" Zoe had met his mother only a few times when she'd gone with him for a weekend visit, but they'd bonded when Zoe spoke fluent Vietnamese to her.

"Still working. I don't think she can't not work," Derek replied.

"Sounds like my parents. Every year they talk about retiring but nothing happens."

"I want to help her retire so she can enjoy life more. It's weird watching her growing older before my eyes." Every time he called home, he noticed she'd have a few more gray hairs or that she'd complain about more body aches.

"Is she coming down for opening night? I bet she'd get along great with my parents."

"I offered to buy her a plane ticket, but she said it was too expensive. I'm trying to be a better son." The more he traveled for jobs, the less he'd been able to make it back home to see her.

"My dad says that about every gift we give him," she commiserated before picking up her drawing pencils.

His pep talk must have worked. She bit her bottom lip as she sketched quickly. Then she'd rotate her sketchbook or hold it at arm's length to study it before adding more lines. It was like watching one of those sped-up art videos but in real time.

Derek had to tell her. Thảo was right. He couldn't drag this out for seven and a half more weeks. It wouldn't be fair to his cowriter and composer if his head wasn't completely in the game.

"Z, there's something I've been meaning to tell you."

"Yeah," she said absentmindedly. Her forehead was furrowed as she fumbled around her piles for a marker.

"We've known each other a long time. And, well . . ." Derek swallowed, his throat suddenly dry. What if she never wanted to talk to him after he told her?

"This marker is dried out." Zoe huffed in frustration and flung it across the room toward a trash can. And missed. The marker clanged loudly against the outside of the metal can.

"Sorry," Zoe said, slightly embarrassed about her outburst. "I hate dead markers."

"I can see that."

"What was it you wanted to say?" she asked as she grabbed a different marker.

He opened his mouth right as his phone buzzed. Mouthing *Sorry*, he pulled it out of his jean pocket to check his messages.

"That was Thảo. She's on her way and wants to go over some lyrics together. Is it cool if we work back here with you? The change in scenery might help."

"Let me make some space for both of you." She began clearing the sewing tools off the table next to hers.

"Thanks. She's waiting outside."

Zoe chuckled. "In that case, why don't you two walk over and pick up dinner? I'll order a little of everything."

"It'll be good to see your mom."

"They're not there. They take Wednesdays off."

"Oh."

He was slightly disappointed and relieved at the same time. Cô Hồng always treated him well when he'd come down to visit. But she'd definitely grill him about everything, including his nonexistent love life.

"I haven't told her you're in town. She'd kill me if I sent you over there by yourself."

"Cool. Maybe next time. You keep working and we'll take care of the rest."

She handed over her shop keys and shooed him away as she called Phở-Ever 75. In rapid-fire Vietnamese, she placed an order for them. He understood enough to make out his favorite dishes. When he finally opened the front door, Thảo was tapping her foot with her keyboard under her arm.

"About damn time. Were you two making out back there?" Thảo smirked.

"Shhh. Not so loud," Derek whispered. "Set your keyboard inside. I almost told her, but I chickened out."

"Wuss," Thảo whispered back.

"Shut up and come with me." He pointed to Zoe's parents' restaurant on the other side of Eden Center. "We're picking up dinner."

CHAPTER 15

Zoe shifted in the chair, trying to keep its arms from skewering her sides like a kabob. Meeting with Greg was already nerve wracking, but now she was also squished in a chair clearly designed for smaller people.

The five minutes of waiting felt like fifteen. When Greg finally walked in, she smiled as if she wasn't being tortured by his furniture.

"Zoe, it's nice to finally meet you," said Greg. He shook her hand before sitting behind his desk.

"We briefly met during the opening night of *Lysistrata* a few weeks ago. My team and I were commissioned to make some of the costumes," Zoe reminded him.

"Oh gosh." He squinted at her. "I'm sorry, but I don't remember. Opening nights are a blur for me. So many important donors to schmooze with."

"I understand. We only talked for a minute." She regretted bringing up their initial meeting. It was silly to think that she'd made an impression on him when there had been more important theater people to talk to.

"Hey, we're talking now." He flashed a toothy smile. "You were first on Derek's list for our creative team, which is a pretty big deal."

She glanced to her left at Derek, who wasn't in any danger of being compressed by his chair. He gave her a thumbs-up. He was either agreeing with Greg or telling her that she was doing great.

"I'm excited about *Tấm Cám*, too," Zoe said tentatively. Greg's bright but flippant manner threw her off-balance.

"Good. You should be. Derek is doing something ground-breaking."

"Thanks, Greg," said Derek. "It's an honor to hold the *Tấm Cám* world premiere at Prestige Rep."

"Anyhoo, sorry for my lateness. One of the board members stopped me after our meeting. He couldn't stop telling me how excited he is about your *Tấm Câm*, Derek."

Zoe's left eye twitched at Greg's pronunciation. Instead of attempting to say it the way she and Derek had, he made the names rhyme like in *Tammy* and *Cammy*. Why didn't Derek correct him?

"I hope he can make it to our meet and greet with everyone next week."

"We invited the entire board." Greg pointed to Zoe then Derek. "Want something to drink?"

"I'm good," Derek replied and shifted in his chair, probably due to nervousness and not because it was trying to kill him. Zoe was envious that he didn't have to worry about things like that but also mad that all the furniture in the room seemed geared for people whose bodies were smaller than hers.

Zoe shook her head. She couldn't drink anything while compressed in this chair. Plus, she was too anxious to consume anything. Her fingers cramped from the death grip she had on her portfolio. This wasn't college and she wasn't being graded. This was a collaborative project.

"Madison, can you get us some water? Coffee for me, please," Greg barked into the handset from the phone on his desk. "Water is on the way."

"Thanks," Derek said quietly.

Zoe could barely recognize the man sitting beside her. Derek was a different person with Greg. Where was the funny, confident man she'd been talking to?

"I want to make something clear before we start," continued the artistic director. "This is Derek's show. I'm only here to make sure this production goes smoothly. To be the liaison between you and the board and producers."

"I appreciate the support," said Derek.

"We're only meeting today because it's my job to keep them updated on the progress, since we're investing so much of our resources into this."

"My designs are going to blow away the audience," Zoe added before subdued Derek could give another generic response.

"The board has nothing to worry about." Derek sat up straighter, as if buoyed by her confidence. "Zoe has nailed my vision. Show him."

He nudged her arm. Zoe set her portfolio on Greg's desk and unzipped it. She'd stayed late at her boutique finishing up her sketches after Derek and Thảo had left to work on the script.

"These are preliminary sketches for the five main characters: Tấm, Cám, their Stepmother, the Emperor, and the God. And here's two examples of how the ensemble will look. They won't all be dressed alike, but they'll have coordinating colors and silhouettes."

"They remind me of backup dancers."

"That's exactly what I'm going for." Zoe clasped her hands in her lap, pleased that he understood her concept.

"Tấm has a lot of costumes." Greg shuffled through several pages.

"She's Cinderella, after all. Audiences will want to see her transformations. We need the wow factor for her." One of her favorite parts of the Vietnamese version was how Tấm changed into a tree, a bird, even a persimmon.

"As long as you're able to stay in budget." Greg tapped her

sketches. "I've already stretched our board members' wallets for this. It'll be hard to ask for more."

"We're meeting with the costume shop manager after this to go over logistics and the budget," Derek said.

"I've done more with less." Zoe looked directly into Greg's annoyingly clear blue eyes. She refused to give him any reasons to think she wasn't qualified for this job. Her imposter syndrome didn't need another person on its cheer squad.

Shockingly, Greg didn't have a response, but he tossed her a look that asked her to elaborate.

"I opened up my lingerie boutique with only credit cards and a small loan from my parents. We were profitable in eighteen months. Believe me when I tell you I can design the best costumes you've ever seen and stay within budget." Zoe wanted to stand up to reiterate her point, but the awkwardness of extricating herself from the chair would have undermined her words.

"Well, Derek, seems like you've got a smart businesswoman here," Greg finally said.

"She's her own person, Greg. She's in high demand and we're lucky to have her on the team," Derek replied in a firm tone. "You know this story wouldn't exist without Zoe."

"Yeah, of course." Greg's head bobbed. "One more thing: These designs feel a little too folksy. I thought you were modernizing the fairy tale, not making it look more exotic."

"Exotic?!" Zoe whipped her head up from her drawings. She tried to keep her tone even and steady. "What exactly do you mean by that?"

She'd heard that term used to describe herself too many times. People who fetishized Asian women used it as a compliment when they hit on her. Others used it as an insult, as if she didn't belong.

"Oh, I mean, it looks too much like a fantasy novel and not a rock musical. We want audiences to be able to relate to our heroine, Tấm."

Greg's mispronunciation grated on Zoe even more the second time.

"And why would wearing this keep them from relating to her?" Zoe picked up the sketch of the dress that Tấm's magical fish had gifted her.

To illustrate Tấm's finally coming out of her shell, Zoe had given her an áo dài with a traditional silhouette that included the hip-high side slits. She'd changed the traditional high-collared neckline to a halter and added puffy sleeves. The plan was to construct it out of a black sequined fabric and pair it with leather leggings and brocaded heels.

"It fits my vision perfectly, Greg," Derek said through gritted teeth. "You told me I had complete creative control."

"You do. I'm trying to anticipate what the board might say. They're old and aren't big on trends," Greg explained.

Zoe opened her mouth but thought better of it. Greg was clueless. He genuinely thought he was helping them.

"If anyone has problems, tell them to come directly to me," Derek pushed back. "I trust Zoe implicitly."

"You got it. Derek's in charge." Greg leaned back in his chair. "Welcome aboard, Zoe."

She pressed her lips together to keep a smirk off her face. Derek wasn't being indifferent earlier. He knew how to handle Greg and when to put his foot down. She, on the other hand, wanted to call Greg out for his little microaggressions, which would only make him more defensive. That would've created a contentious working relationship for all of them.

Zoe breathed a little easier now that she'd successfully defended her costume designs. And she was even more confident that Derek had her back no matter what.

CHAPTER 16

erek, can you stay for a minute?" Greg asked after Zoe excused herself for her meeting with the costume shop manager.

"Sure, what's up?" Derek stopped in the doorway, but Greg pointed at the chair Derek had vacated a minute before.

"I don't know how to say this, but—" Greg stopped and sat on the edge of his desk. He sighed heavily.

"Just say it." Derek braced himself.

"I'm concerned about Zoe," Greg finally said. His forehead furrowed as he pursed his lips.

"I'm not," Derek replied without missing a beat. He sat up straighter. "Her designs are great and you know it."

"Her designs are fine. Nothing to write home about." Greg shrugged. "I'm worried she won't be a team player."

"What are you talking about?"

"It's obvious that she has a hard time taking constructive feedback. On a production like this, you want everyone to be on the same wavelength."

"We are. This is the first time I've worked with an all-Asian design team and the experience has been affirming."

"I get it. Asian pride and all that. But I'm talking about us"— Greg gestured as if to encapsulate the entire building—"and the board. They're going to have a lot of opinions after the meet and greet. And if she fights back at every suggestion—"

Greg stopped.

"What? Then what?"

"It's not a good look for us. For Prestige."

"I see." Derek didn't. He tamped down the anger bubbling up inside him.

"We gotta think about the big picture. They help fund the entire season, not just *Tấm Cám*."

"It's pronounced *thum kham*." Derek corrected him through gritted teeth.

"Can you help her understand how all this works? The unwritten rules." Greg ignored Derek's correction as he walked around behind his desk. He sat down and put his feet up on his desk.

"I have complete faith in Zoe and how she'll handle herself. But if it makes you feel better, I'll work closely with her to make sure she's prepared for the meet and greet next week."

"I'm glad we're on the same page." Greg smiled warmly at what he assumed was Derek's agreement.

"You know what? We should hire an assistant for her," Derek announced.

Why hadn't he thought of this sooner? He and Thảo still had scenes to polish, so he couldn't be with Zoe every day. An assistant would be the next best thing.

"That's a good idea." Greg sat back up. His entire tone had changed from solemn to excited. "We should hire someone who has more costuming experience to work with Zoe. Someone who can keep an eye on her for us."

"Greg, you misunderstood."

"I think I know just the right person for the job," his mentor continued as he riffled through his desk.

"Greg." Derek stared down the man until he stopped.

"Yes?" For once Greg waited for Derek to speak instead of talking over him.

"We'll provide the budget, because it's a costume-heavy show, and she'll need more support. Zoe will choose her own assistant," Derek said in a way that left no room for discussion.

"I see." Greg set down the notebook he'd pulled out of his desk drawer. He pressed his lips together and looked Derek up and down before nodding approvingly. "Someone's learning how to lead properly. Good for you."

Derek said nothing. Greg had to work things out on his own, but both of them knew he'd agree to hire someone for Zoe.

"All right then. If this show fails, you'll have a tough time landing prominent gigs."

"You don't have to keep reminding me." As if the pressure didn't keep him up at night. "That's why I'm doing everything in my power to make sure *Tấm Cám* succeeds."

Greg nodded and waved him away. The meeting was over. Derek's shoulders slumped in relief once he shut the door to Greg's office. He was exhausted and the morning was barely half over.

Derek had to keep pushing to stay true to their vision, but it felt like an uphill battle. If Greg challenged him on every decision, what would it be like when the producers and Prestige's board members came to their first rehearsal next week?

He tried to push his insecurities aside as he walked down the hallway. Thảo was expecting him after lunch. She had a different take on the opening number that she wanted to show him. Maybe it was the breakthrough they needed.

"Hey, is everything okay?" Zoe stood up as he rounded the corner.

She'd waited for him. He closed the distance between them with a bounce in his step.

"Of course." He smiled reassuringly, even though his talk with Greg had left him frazzled. "Why would you think otherwise?"

"You had a worried look on your face."

"Oh, I was thinking about the opening number."

It technically wasn't a lie, but Zoe didn't need to know what Greg had said about her. She was already nervous about her work. He didn't need to mention Greg's so-called issues with her. Derek would do whatever it took to protect Zoe from Greg.

"Still having problems with it? You and Thảo will figure it out," she said confidently as she wrapped her arm around his shoulders.

"Thanks." He leaned into her as her hand slid down and rubbed soothing circles on his back. Derek was surprised by how affectionate Zoe had become, but he didn't mind at all.

His earlier anxiety began to fade. Zoe always had high standards and wasn't one to falsely cheer someone on. When she said things like that, she truly believed in his ability.

"Thanks for sticking up for me in there," Zoe added quietly. "Greg is—"

She stopped herself as if worried she'd offend him. She also stopped mid-circle on his back. Derek's anxiety tiptoed back in at the mention of his mentor.

He looked down the hallway in both directions to ensure they were alone before pulling her closer.

"Greg is a lot," he whispered. "But he's our best bet at getting *Tấm Cám* out into the world."

"I know," she whispered back, her breath warm against his neck.

"Remember, I've always got your back, no matter what."

Derek pulled her tighter into a side hug, but she turned around and used both arms to make it a full one. He closed his eyes and inhaled deeply as he etched this moment into his brain forever. With Zoe by his side, he felt like he could conquer the world.

CHAPTER 17

Zoe quickly glanced at her phone before slipping it under a pile of fabric swatches. She tapped her tablet stylus on the cutting table in Prestige's costume shop. Derek couldn't be late because he'd never promised he'd be here at three o'clock. But she'd gotten used to him visiting every afternoon since she began working on the show.

"Will you stop sighing and pushing fabric around?" TJ asked from across the table. He waved a pile of fabric pieces at her like a pom-pom. "It's very distracting."

"I'm not sighing," Zoe replied. She stared at her digitized sketches without focusing on them.

"Sure." He dug through the fabric piles and sighed heavily. TJ picked up a pencil and tapped it on the table and huffed loudly.

"That's not what I was doing!" She laughed and threw a piece of faux leather at him.

"Maybe not that loudly, but I can feel your broody energy all the way over here."

"Our table is only three feet wide, TJ," she pointed out.

"Whatever you call this"—he waved in a circle in front of her—"it's sucking all my creativity."

"Sorry. I guess I'm a little distracted," Zoe admitted. She checked the time on her tablet. It was now eight minutes past three. Derek had come down to check on her every day by no later than 3:05 P.M.

"He'll be here with our caffeine hit soon," said TJ with more sympathy in his voice this time.

"Who?" She feigned ignorance as she zoomed in on her sketch of the Emperor's headdress. Danny was tall, so maybe she didn't need to make it quite as big.

"Do I have *idiot* tattooed on this pretty face?" TJ shook his head. "We both know you're waiting for Derek, your crush."

"Excuse me. We're friends. I don't crush on people."

"Now you're lying to me *and* yourself." TJ slid off his stool and walked around the table to stare her down.

"Derek and I haven't talked in years. I only want to spend as much time as I can with him before he goes back to his busy, glamorous New York life." Zoe wasn't sure who she was trying to convince.

"In the six months we've known each other, you haven't dated anyone."

"I don't date random people or swipe dating apps. It's because—"

"Yes, you're demisexual." TJ cocked his hip. "You need an emotional connection to be sexually attracted to someone."

"Did you memorize that from Wikipedia?"

"I did my research. That's what friends do."

"I'm touched," she said dryly. "But I don't have a crush on my college best friend."

"Your face lights up like Times Square on New Year's Eve when Derek walks through those doors at exactly three o'clock."

Zoe laughed at TJ's flair for dramatics. "Can't I be happy to see him?"

"My dear, have you stopped to ask yourself why that is?"

"We're just friends," she said firmly. So what if she was excited that he checked in with her every afternoon? That's how their friendship was in college, so why would it be any different now that they'd mended their rift?

"Even if you're not crushing on him—and you are—that boy's got a flame burning for you. Or he's being financially irresponsible by buying us boba every day for the past week." TJ returned to his side of the table.

Zoe's jaw dropped. It was a ridiculous idea that Derek was interested in anything except friendship from her. She waited for a quip from TJ but thankfully he'd returned his attention to the swatches they'd pulled for the sisters.

"Once you finalize your fabric choices, I can color them into your sketches on your tablet," TJ offered.

"That'd be great. Once those are done, we can send them to the copy shop."

The brown craft paper covering the table rustled as she slid the device and stylus across the table. Zoe was disappointed and relieved that TJ had dropped the subject. But now she had more questions than answers.

She'd never even considered that Derek had romantic feelings for her. No. No way. He would've told her. How could he not? They told each other everything during college. Unless this was a new development.

TJ didn't know Derek as well as she did. He was misreading Derek's intentions. Zoe should be the one bringing him coffee after cutting all contact with him when they were supposed to move to New York together. He'd forgiven her, and now they were mending their friendship.

She promised herself that she wouldn't do anything to jeopardize their friendship ever again. They'd survived together as the only two Asian Americans in their theater program for their entire four years of college. She couldn't throw that away.

"Hey, beautiful costume shop! Sorry I'm late." Derek's voice boomed from the double doors.

Zoe looked up from her work. The room grew brighter with his appearance. She couldn't stop the giant, goofy smile breaking out on her face.

"You're here!" She hopped off her stool to meet him at the door.

"Girl," TJ muttered, loud enough for only her to hear.

Zoe's cheeks grew warm. Was this what TJ meant about her crushing on Derek?

"I thought my favorite costume designer could use a pick-me-up." Derek set the cardboard tray of drinks on the costume shop's kitchenette counter before hugging her.

"The afternoon slump was hitting me hard. Until now." She grabbed her Vietnamese coffee boba—extra sweet—as Derek passed along TJ's matcha boba.

"This sexy body needs some sunlight. I'm heading outside for some fresh air. Thanks for the boba, Derek." TJ blew a kiss at the two of them before heading upstairs.

"Wait for me," called Shawn, the costume shop manager, from his office. He grabbed his iced coffee and ran after TJ.

"It's the two of us. Finally," said Derek as he bumped her arm with his.

Wait, did TJ and Shawn leave them alone on purpose?

"What does that mean?" Zoe asked, trying for an even tone as she stabbed a straw through the top plastic.

She stepped around Derek to grab a coaster. Most costume shops didn't allow food or drink because a spill could ruin a costume. But they were still in the preliminary stage, so a coaster would keep the condensation from damaging the paper covering the cutting table.

"It means you've been extremely busy and we haven't had any quality BFF time," he replied as he followed her to the table.

"You've been busy, too. Did you and Thảo figure out the opening number?"

"We got enough of it to rehearse. Once we hear it and see it in action, we can smooth out the rough spots."

"That's great! I'm looking forward to the first read through." Zoe had read the script and new pages as they were written, but she was excited to see the musical come to life once the actors arrived.

"How are things working out with TJ?"

"He can be a lot for some people, but his energy keeps me motivated." She laughed. "Like today he said that you have a crush on me."

Zoe sucked in a breath. She had not meant to blurt that out.

Derek's eyes widened and he pressed his lips together in an uncomfortable smile. He seemed as surprised as she'd been when TJ told her.

"What?!" Derek finally replied in disbelief. He shook his head and laughed.

"That's what I said, too." Her shoulders slumped in relief. "It's funny, isn't it? I mean, we've been best friends since college. If there had been anything, why wait so long to say something?"

"Exactly. I mean, that's absurd." He shook his head and shrugged his shoulders.

"Would you like to see the fabrics I've chosen for the Emperor?" Zoe quickly changed the subject.

"Yes, I would." Derek nodded encouragingly. "But I already know I'll love it."

She pulled up the sketches on her tablet and grabbed the metal ring that held the swatches for the Emperor's robes. Derek's close presence projected the calm she needed to prepare for the designer presentations coming up.

Just friends. And they supported each other the way friends did.

Zoe couldn't wait to tell TJ how wrong he'd been—about both of them. She and Derek were best friends and nothing else. Besides, anything more than that would create a complicated work situation for the two of them.

CHAPTER 18

Derek took Zoe's keys from her hand and unlocked her apartment. Her shoulders held tote bags full of foam board, photocopies, and pieces of fabric. To the untrained eye, it looked like a kid's art project.

"Are you ready for the meet and greet tomorrow?" Zoe asked as he swung the door open for her. She dropped the heavy tote bags on the floor right inside and kicked off her flats.

"I've barely had time to think about it. Thảo and I have been working fifteen-hour days to make sure the music is ready for our first read—sing—through?" Derek had her other bag slung over his shoulder along with his backpack. He shut the door behind him and lined his Chucks next to her other shoes on the mat.

"I'm a little nervous to meet the cast and present my costumes to everyone," Zoe said. Her shoulders were tight and high with anxiety. "And public speaking isn't really my thing. It's yours."

"They're going to love your designs!" He waved at bags stuffed with her presentation materials. "I'm glad you hired TJ to be your assistant."

"Me, too. He's got a great eye for mixing patterns. You should see his drag costumes."

"He makes a mean boba and does drag? A man of many talents. I'm glad Greg found room in the budget for him." When he suggested the idea to Zoe, she'd immediately thought of TJ. Derek gave himself a mental pat on the back for winning that battle with his mentor.

"Honestly, I think he took the job because—and I quote—'theater is full of hot gay men.'"

They chuckled.

"He took Thảo out to Dupont Circle to blow off steam. Maybe he'll find more than steam," Derek added.

"How dare you suggest our friends need to get laid," she joked.

"Thảo's been bitching about how boring DC nightlife is compared to New York. Maybe the two of them can have a little fun before we dive into rehearsals."

The closer they got to the first rehearsal, the more wound up Thảo had gotten. There was one song that wasn't working the way she wanted. Derek wanted to wait until the actors had a chance to make it their own, but Thảo wanted to plug away at it. Derek won in the end, because they ran out of time and energy.

Zoe murmured in agreement. From the few times Derek had stopped into the costume shop, he thought Zoe and TJ made a great team. TJ's big personality wasn't for everyone, but his humor kept her grounded as she finalized her designs. According to Zoe, TJ also knew the best places in the DMV to shop for fabric on a budget.

"Thanks for coming over so I can practice. I want everything to be perfect."

"I'm easily bribed with food." What he wanted to say was that he'd drop everything whenever she needed him.

"Our food is on its way, but I need to take a shower. I'm so gross after driving all over the DMV with TJ to swatch fabric. Today's heat was brutal."

"Go. I'll set the table and wait for the food." Maybe that would keep his mind from imagining her in the shower.

"Can you feed Mr. Bobbins, too?" Zoe asked.

"Mr. Who?" Derek looked around the apartment but found

only an empty pet bed that looked like a giant blue Danish cookie tin, similar to the kind his mom kept her sewing supplies in.

"My cat. He's an orange tabby and has a super fluffy tail."

"I will, but for some reason cats don't like me." Derek bit his bottom lip. "Let's just say the last and only time I cat sat for a friend, the cat won."

"You're saying you're scared of a cute little kitty?"

"No," Derek replied a little too quickly. He straightened his shoulders to prove it. "Where is he?"

"Probably sleeping in my room. But he'll come out when he hears you prepping his food."

"Did you say prep his food? Like a sous chef?" Derek mimed chopping food. "How spoiled is Mr. Bobbins?"

"Hush. He's a pretty boy who deserves lots of love and delicious food. I'm feeding you, aren't I?"

Derek opened his mouth but no witty response came to him. Were they still talking about her cat? He was reading way too much into her words. Zoe must've sensed his awkwardness because her cheeks were pink.

"He's also old and has no teeth so he needs special food," she finally said solemnly.

"Oh, sorry. I didn't mean to—"

"Ha! You should see the look on your face! Mr. Bobbins is in his prime and completely spoiled." Zoe laughed.

"That was not cool." Derek frowned, then stuck his bottom lip out in an exaggerated pout the way he used to in college after she teased him.

Unfazed by his fake sad expression, she lightly punched his arm.

"He needs a little spoiling. I've been gone a lot, so he's been lonely."

He hadn't met Mr. Bobbins yet, but her worried expression told him that she adored her cat.

"So he gets to eat his feelings." Derek nodded. "I can relate."

"Mix a scoop of his kibble with half a can of tuna, please? He's got a mat over there." She pointed to his food prep station at her kitchen counter. "I'll get him."

Zoe walked briskly into her bedroom. She came out with a large, very fluffy cat in her arms. Her face lit up as she cooed and petted the animal. Why was Derek suddenly envious of a ball of fur?

"Meet Mr. Bobbins," she said when she finally turned her attention back to Derek.

"Hello, Mr. Bobbins."

"And this is Derek. He's going to feed you while I shower," she spoke in a soft, sweet tone.

He had nothing to be afraid of. Mr. Bobbins seemed harmless with Zoe's arms wrapped around him.

"Go freshen up and I'll take care of the kitty." Derek shooed her away.

Zoe released the cat and went into her bedroom, leaving the two of them alone. Maybe the other cat was an outlier and Derek would make quick friends with Zoe's pet.

The cat sauntered up to Derek's socked feet, sniffed, and hissed. Derek jumped back. He wanted Mr. Bobbins to be the exception to his bad luck with felines.

"Look, you and me, we have to be friends because I hope to be here a lot."

Derek found the container of cat food on the counter. The tabby glared at him as he scooped some kibble into a purple ceramic bowl. It looked hand-painted, like the kind you find at those paint your own pottery places.

"I think we can agree"—Derek paused to make sure the shower was still running—"that Zoe is a wonderful woman and maybe we can both share her?"

Mr. Bobbins's eyes narrowed and his fluffy orange tail flicked rapidly.

"Or maybe not." He grabbed a can of tuna with olive oil from the cabinet above the cat's food station. "Wow, you have fancy taste. Is this from Italy?"

The cat's tail stilled as he spotted the tuna.

"Ah, this is the way to your heart, isn't it?" Derek popped the tab on the tuna.

Mr. Bobbins ran over and rubbed himself on Derek's leg.

"See, we do have something in common. I can also be bribed with Italian food."

The cat meowed in agreement as Derek spooned half of the tuna onto the dry food and mixed them together. It didn't take long for Mr. Bobbins to chow down his fancy tuna. Maybe the cat was just hungry and didn't hate him. Or they'd come to an understanding.

As the cat licked his plate clean, Derek dug around the kitchen for plates and silverware for the two humans. He might as well make takeout feel like a real dinner. He'd eaten too many meals out of boxes and bags the last couple of weeks. Unlike the one Prestige Rep had given him, Zoe's apartment was homey and cozy. He set the table and found a bottle of white wine in the fridge.

They deserved a little celebration tonight. They'd worked long hours in preparation for the cast's arrival. Tomorrow the next stage of *Tấm Cám* would begin, with even more work and long hours.

And maybe tonight, once they were relaxed, he'd tell her that he wanted them to be more than friends.

Derek almost dropped a wineglass when Zoe stepped out of her room. She was glistening. Droplets of water had escaped her hair and were making the most glorious journey down her chest. She wore an oversize light green T-shirt with an extra wide neck so the creamy skin of her shoulder was exposed—with no visible bra strap. He was pretty sure if she turned around, he'd get a gorgeous view of her ass in those leggings.

"You clean up nice," he tried to say in a way that didn't sound like he'd been checking her out.

"I always do. And it feels so good to put on clean clothes." She looked around the room for Mr. Bobbins, who was curled up in his Danish cookie tin bed. "Did he eat?"

"Oh yeah, he loved the tuna." The bowl had been licked clean. "Our food hasn't arrived yet. How about a glass of wine?"

"Sounds perfect. Might as well get comfy while we wait," she suggested as she waved at her couch.

He poured them each a glass before sitting down. She sat in her love seat next to the couch and tucked her feet under her. Zoe looked as content as Mr. Bobbins did in his bed.

"A toast?" She raised her glass.

"To us," he said as he lifted his.

"To me and you. We make a great team." Zoe's eyes were bright. Her wide smile made her rounded cheeks even more prominent.

The clinking of their glasses was as melodic as the Emperor's duet with Tấm when he finally declared his true love for her.

Zoe was absolutely radiant. He'd never seen her this happy. So content. He couldn't help but feel proud that he'd contributed to her joy by inviting her to design the costumes for *Tấm Cám*.

Derek's heart pounded. This was it. This was the right opportunity he'd been waiting for. He gulped his entire glass of wine.

"Whoa, Derek. Don't forget we have to get up early tomorrow for the meet and greet." She laughed but grabbed the bottle of wine to refill both of their drinks.

"Zoe, there's something I've been meaning to tell you." Derek's throat suddenly dried up. He swallowed. "I've felt a deep connection with you from the first time we met. And it wasn't just because we're both Vietnamese."

He laughed nervously.

She turned her body to face him. Her expression was open and kind, like she always was when he had something important to tell her.

"I think—I want—" He sighed and rubbed his jaw. An actor wasn't supposed to trip over his words. But this wasn't rehearsed nor were they someone else's words for him to recite. He had to trust himself.

"It's okay, take your time." She patted his hand gently.

He nodded and took a deep breath. Reset and start over.

"Zoe, I feel that there's—"

Derek was interrupted by the worst sound he'd ever heard.

"Oh my God, Mr. Bobbins." Zoe set her glass down and jumped out of her love seat. Her head spun as she tried to find her cat. "He's throwing up somewhere."

That's what the horrendous noise was? He'd never heard that from a cat, but vomiting was never a good thing.

"He's by the door," Derek exclaimed.

The cat was dry heaving next to Derek's shoes. A few seconds later, Mr. Bobbins's dinner landed inside his Chucks.

Fucking Mr. Bobbins and his awful timing. Derek was convinced the cat was determined to keep Zoe all to himself.

CHAPTER 19

A re you okay, my baby?" Zoe rushed over to her cat.

The cat mewed pitifully. She scooped him up and hugged her fur baby.

"Derek, your shoes!" Zoe gasped. "I'm so sorry."

"It's Mr. B's fault. He hates me." Derek shot the cat an ugly look.

"How can you say that! He rarely throws up. I feed him a very specific diet." She rubbed the cat's head and cooed softly to soothe him.

"What am I going to do about my shoes?"

"I'll clean them up. Here, hold him." She thrust the tabby into Derek's arms.

"I don't think that's a good idea." Derek held Mr. Bobbins awkwardly at arm's length. The cat mewed sadly as his back feet swung down.

"You can't hold him like that. Support his bottom." Zoe demonstrated with her arms.

Derek begrudgingly complied. As grumpy as Derek was, he and Mr. Bobbins looked cute together.

"He could've tossed his cookies anywhere, but he chose the inside of my shoes?" Derek groaned.

"He didn't do it on purpose. Right, Mr. Bobbins?" She kissed his furry nose.

Zoe dumped the contents of Derek's shoe into the trash and took it to her kitchen sink to grab some antibacterial wipes.

"What were you about to tell me?" she asked over her shoulder as she scrubbed the inside of his shoe.

"Oh, um, it can wait."

"You sure?"

"It's weird to say this after what your cat just did, but I'm starving. I wonder where our food is?"

"It was supposed to arrive half an hour ago. I'll call the restaurant after I finish cleaning your shoes."

Mr. Bobbins wiggled out of Derek's arm and curled up in Zoe's love seat. He seemed unfazed by his previous incident. Maybe it was just a fluke that he threw up. She'd call the vet in the morning to make sure.

"I don't think I can wait that long." His stomach grumbled loudly in agreement.

"You know I'm a terrible cook," she reminded him.

"I can't believe your parents own a restaurant and you can't cook."

"I didn't have to." Zoe shrugged. "And Má always sent me home with leftovers."

"Does your fridge happen to have any of those said leftovers?"

"Nope. I ate the last bit of thịt kho trứng yesterday."

Derek groaned. "That sounds amazing right now."

"I think I have some old rice in the fridge."

"Mind if I dig around your kitchen and whip up something?"

"Are we playing *Iron Chef* Surprise?"

"Don't you mean the 'we're broke college students so let's cobble some random ingredients together' challenge?"

"Your dishes were always better than mine." Zoe hated cooking but could put together something edible when necessary.

"I'll never forget your 'tomato' soup made from old ketchup packets and elbow macaroni."

"Don't forget the bacon bits."

"How could I? Your secret ingredient."

"I learned that recipe from my grandfather. I didn't realize until much later that that was how he stretched his paycheck."

"It did taste almost like real tomato soup," Derek agreed. "And it was filling."

"He still makes it, you know, but with fancy tomato paste from Trader Joe's. I think it's a nostalgia thing."

"I hope it's okay if we bypass the ketchup packets today. How old are these even?"

"Don't you dare toss them! They're my emotional support condiments."

"Okay, hoarder." Derek burst out laughing as he shut the drawer with his hip. He held his hands out and backed away as if she'd hurt him for throwing out her ketchup packets.

"I did my best to scrub out the inside of your shoe but it's still pretty damp." Zoe changed the subject. "I don't think you're supposed to toss Converse sneakers in the dryer."

"Maybe they'll dry by the time you're done. I'm not going home until you feel one hundred percent prepared."

"Are you sure? Maybe you should escape now while you still can."

"Nope. You're stuck with me," Derek said softly.

Zoe's stomach did a tiny flip-flop as the corners of his eyes crinkled with a half-smile. She liked having him back in her life, but she shouldn't get used to it. Once *Tấm Cám* opened, he'd be off to the next thing unless funding came through to take the show to New York.

"I'm going to put the finishing touches on my presentation while you play *Iron Chef* Surprise," she said, changing the subject to distract herself from that flip-flop reaction to the way he looked at her.

Zoe carefully unpacked the tote bags she'd left by the door. She tilted her head to the left then to the right to stretch her tight neck muscles. As worried as she was about tomorrow, she was confident in her designs. Both Derek and Thảo had loved them. Even TJ, who always had constructive criticism about clothing, had been helpful because he asked questions about things that might come up during the meet and greet.

"Where do you keep your frying pan?"

"Bottom cabinet to the left of the stove." Zoe placed the costume renderings for the lead actors on her coffee table. "They look beautiful all in a row like this."

"Now you believe me? I've been saying that for days," Derek reminded her. "Soy sauce or fish sauce?"

"Um, maybe in the fridge?"

"Already looked there." Derek continued chopping.

"Let me think." Zoe walked over to her pantry and pushed aside the bags of shrimp chips and instant ramen her mother always sent home after their big family gatherings.

"If you don't have either of those, I'm taking away your Vietnamese card."

"Don't you dare!" She reached deep into her pantry and shuffled some jars and bottles.

"Kidding. Vietnamese Americans aren't a monolith, so it's okay if you don't own any nước mắm."

"Aha!" She pulled out the two bottles he'd requested. "Don't monolith me. I'm a Vietnamese American lingerie designer. I don't think there's many of us."

"We would've made awful doctors or lawyers."

"I don't want people's lives in my hands." She shuddered.

"Same. Theater can be hard, but it's not life or death."

Maybe not for him. But a part of her had died when she quit theater only months away from graduation. This musical was her second chance and she was doing it her way. Not how someone thought her costumes were supposed to look.

"Are you making fried rice?" Zoe asked as she handed him the bottles.

He'd created a mise en place of different leftovers he'd rescued from her fridge. She spotted the slightly wilted bell peppers she'd bought for a salad and dried shiitake mushrooms rehydrating in a bowl of water. There was also a container of old rice that her mom had given her a few days ago.

"With fancy canned tuna. Thought I'd stick with our attempted Italian theme even though our delivery never showed up."

"I've never had fried rice with tuna before." A client had gifted her Italian canned tuna from her trip to Europe. Zoe had stuck it in the cabinet because it felt too fancy to use for a sandwich, which was the most creative way she knew how to prepare it.

"I figure if it's good enough for Mr. Bobbins, then it's good enough for us." Derek waved toward the living room, where the cat was sitting.

"Wait." Zoe glanced at Mr. Bobbins and back to Derek. She ran to the trash can and dug out an empty tin. "Did you give my cat tuna with olive oil?"

"Yes, because that's what you told me to do." He pointed to the counter where she'd set up Mr. Bobbins's prep station.

"No, I said this tuna right here." She opened up the cabinet next to the one he'd pointed at. She pulled out a small stack of store-brand tuna. "Olive oil makes cats throw up. I only feed him tuna in water."

"Oh, shit." Derek's playful tone completely disappeared. His forehead wrinkled with worry and he covered his mouth with his hand. "I thought you pointed to the other cabinet. Is he going to be okay?"

"I don't think it's super serious. I'll call the vet tom—" She turned back to the living room to find Mr. Bobbins sitting on top of her sketches. He looked her right in the eyes before vomiting tuna and olive oil all over them.

"No, Mr. Bobbins! No!" Zoe waved her arms as she ran back into her living room. It wasn't as if she could stop him from throwing up. The tabby jumped off the coffee table and ran into her room. Now she'd scared the poor cat when he was feeling ill.

"Zoe, I'm so sorry. It's my fault."

"They're ruined! And it's too late to get more copies made and buy more foam board." Zoe's voice cracked.

All the work she'd put into making the presentation perfect was undone. The past two weeks of stress and long hours had finally caught up with her. Her eyes burned as tears threatened to spill, but she hated crying in front of others, so she forced herself to blink rapidly to keep them at bay.

Derek turned off the stove and quickly ran over to her. He gently eased her onto the couch and sat down next to her. She leaned into him as he rubbed her back.

"We'll get up early and replace them. Or maybe there's a twenty-four-hour copy center nearby."

"Why did I think I could pull this off?" Zoe muttered. The tightness in her chest made it hard to breathe. "I should let TJ do all the talking tomorrow. He's great in front of people."

"TJ is a wonderful, vibrant person, but these costumes are your creations. You have to be the person to present them tomorrow."

"I'm better at talking to people one-on-one. Like the woman I helped find a strapless bra."

"Well, then I'll sit next to you. You can pretend I'm your customer," Derek offered.

An image of him in a frilly nightgown popped into her head. She giggled. Her shoulders relaxed slightly as her panic subsided.

"Come on, I'd look great wearing a negligee from Something Cheeky. As long as it was all black, obviously."

"We do carry a lot of black negligees. You don't strike me as a lace type person."

"Maybe not, but I'd look fetching in a murder robe." He tossed his imaginary waist length hair. "Can you make me one?"

Zoe barked out a laugh. Derek was a pro at cheering her up. He was good at bringing the best out of people, period. Which was probably why he'd found so much success as a director.

"You look better already." He squeezed her hands. "Now take a few deep breaths with me."

Zoe nodded as she followed his lead. She held on to his hands as if her life depended on it and closed her eyes. She inhaled through her nose and then exhaled through her mouth. He guided her through several more breaths until she relaxed her grip on his hands. But she wasn't ready to let go.

"Good girl." He nodded encouragingly. "Now look at me."

She opened her eyes slowly and found Derek's kind and patient dark brown eyes. This man had seen her at her worst during college. When she'd lost everything that she'd worked for because she dared to stand up to their professor. Even her Boss Babes had never seen her in such a dark place.

He'd done everything in his power to help her then. And now he was back to help her find her way back into theater. A way back to the person she'd wanted to be all those years ago.

"I'm scared, too. As beautiful as your sketches are, they're not why we're doing this." He licked his lips and swallowed hard. "We're going to make this show so fucking Asian that people will either love it or hate it. No in-between."

"No in-between," she whispered.

"Theater is supposed to make people feel something, but we can't tell them how to feel about it. We can only control what we put into it." He squeezed her right hand and placed it on her chest over her heart.

Her stomach did another flip when his fingertips grazed her bare skin. She leaned into his touch. Without breaking eye contact with him, she reached up with her free hand and pushed the hair that had fallen behind his glasses out of his eyes. Derek stiffened at first but relaxed as she ran her fingers down his cheek and then his jawline.

Had he always been so beautiful? She traced the five-o'clock shadow below his bottom lip, the one he bit when he was learning new choreography or when he was nervous. His expression didn't change as she ran her thumb over it.

Zoe leaned in and kissed him. His lips were soft and inviting. Like she'd found her way home where she belonged. He kissed her back gently, as if she might break. Tiny shocks flicked through her body and her chest grew warm. She shivered as Derek ran his hand over her bare shoulders.

She deepened the kiss. He groaned and invited her to explore his mouth, causing a deep moan to escape her throat. A hunger like she'd never felt before possessed her body the same way she tried to possess his mouth. She pulled herself into his lap and wrapped her arms around his neck.

He broke free of her mouth to drop kisses on her neck down to her upper chest. Zoe tossed her head back as each one seared her skin. She reflexively rolled her hips into him and gasped as his hardness pressed into her mound. They'd never been this physically close to each other. Not in this way.

Her body was responding to his touch in ways that it shouldn't respond to your best friend. Derek was her best friend. What was she even doing kissing him? Zoe pulled back abruptly.

"I'm sorry, I shouldn't have done that." She stood up and walked to the other side of her living room.

"Zoe, it's okay." Derek's face was red. He seemed as flustered as she was.

"I-I think you should go home." Zoe's face was hot, but this time it was from embarrassment, not because his kiss had woken up these new feelings inside her.

"We should talk about this."

"Let's talk tomorrow. I'll be up all night fixing this." She waved at the mess on the coffee table. Zoe didn't—couldn't—talk to him because she didn't know what was going on or why she felt compelled to kiss him right then.

Derek stood up and tried to grab her hand, but she backed away. She couldn't trust herself to touch him. What if she couldn't control the desire welling up inside her?

"Here, you can borrow my flip-flops and I'll put your shoes in a bag."

He nodded in resignation as she handed his things over. He was silent as she walked him to the door.

"You can always text me," he said as she shut the door behind him.

Zoe leaned on the door as the kiss replayed in her mind. She touched her lips. With one kiss, she'd ruined years of friendship. But that moment had felt so . . . natural. So right. Her life was stressful enough. She'd complicated it even more by crossing the line with her best friend, who was also her director. This should never have happened.

So why did she want to run down the hallway and pull him back into her arms?

CHAPTER 20

"Exit, pursued by a bear," Derek quoted Shakespeare's infamous stage direction. "My friendship with Zoe is over."

"You actors are so dramatic." Thảo rolled her eyes. "Awkward, yes. Over? Probably not."

He plopped on the plush black leather couch like some television patient in their therapist's office. Thảo, who sat in the love seat opposite him, was scarfing down one of the burrito bowls she'd brought for them.

"You didn't have to cut your night short for me. I should've waited. It's your first night out since you got here."

He'd texted a 911 to Thảo after walking out of Zoe's building. Thảo was waiting in front of his apartment, food in hand, by the time he'd made it back.

"I needed an excuse to bail. TJ's boundless energy was wearing me down."

"You didn't tell him, did you?" Derek sat up too quickly. The room spun.

"Have you eaten today?"

He shook his head.

"Eat," she scolded like a big sister. "I told TJ that a friend was having a bad day and needed to talk. I didn't say who it was."

"Thanks." He pulled the foil lid off his food. His stomach

grumbled angrily. He appeased it by shoving a forkful of rice and beans into his mouth.

"So she kissed you after her cat puked in your shoe and then puked on her sketches?" Thảo shuddered in horror. "Cats are evil."

"It was the best first kiss I've ever shared with someone. I thought she felt the same way, but she couldn't push me out of her apartment fast enough." Her rejection hurt more than all the times he'd lost out on a role combined.

"Can you think about it from her side for a minute?" Thảo asked gently. "It's a lot for her to figure out. She friend-zoned you from the very beginning."

"I'm thinking about her expression after she jumped away from my touch. It was regret. With a side of terror."

"From what you told me, she was in a vulnerable state."

"I'm under a lot of pressure, too." He knew he was whining, but he didn't care. His pride needed time to repair itself.

"Yeah, but have you told her that?"

"I didn't want to add to her anxiety. She's got enough to worry about." Derek felt protective of Zoe. He was the one who'd convinced her to work on this show. If she had a bad experience on her first show since college, she might never come back to theater. Or him.

"For someone who's amazing at communicating with his cast, you suck at personal relationships." Thảo waved her plastic fork at him.

"You suck at relationships," he repeated in a mocking tone. "Tell me something I don't know."

Thảo didn't respond. She scraped the last of her burrito bowl into her mouth and washed it down with some beer.

"Derek, what do you want? Truly, really want?" she finally asked.

"Everything," he replied matter-of-factly. "I want critics to rave about *Tấm Cám*. I want Zoe to feel the same way about me as I feel about her. I want my mom to be happy for me and not worry so much. I want to prove to Greg that shows with an all-Asian cast sell tickets."

"Whoa. That's a lot to put on yourself."

"Theater is one of the few things I'm really good at. I mean *the* Gregory Powers picked me as his mentee. Do you know how many people would kill for that opportunity?"

"Not me." Thảo snorted. "I hate working with old white dudes."

"I know he's not the most culturally aware guy, but I'd still be playing triad gangsters and IT nerds if it weren't for him." He'd be fighting for the same roles against every Asian American actor in New York. Now he was creating the roles he'd kill to play in their musical.

"Derek, we've known each other for, what, five years now? Shared a freaking closet of an apartment together. So don't take this the wrong way." Thảo paused as if she were worried about hurting his feelings, then blurted, "You're a people pleaser."

"I'm what? I wanted you here to talk about Zoe, not insult me."

Thảo gave him a side-eye.

"They are not related." He crossed his arms and leaned back on the couch.

"Sure. Whatever you say." She stuck her empty containers into the bag. "Damn, I should've gotten dessert, too."

"You think I worry too much about what others think?" He cringed. That sounded like he cared.

"You're shortchanging yourself by focusing on everyone's needs before yours."

"I don't do that."

"Example one"—Thảo counted on her fingers—"you ditching me every afternoon to pick up an iced coffee for Zoe."

"I bring you an iced passion tea, too."

"Especially"—Thảo glared at him for interrupting her—"when you know we have songs to finish writing. Número dos: you're putting too much weight on Greg's feedback, even though he knows jack shit about Vietnamese fairy tales."

"He wants us to succeed."

"Dude can't pronounce the title of our show correctly, even though I keep saying it in front of him," she said in exasperation.

"Fine. Maybe I give Greg too much leeway, but he's the artistic director. He's producing the show when other theaters wouldn't or couldn't. Don't forget he has decades of experience over us."

"Number three," she continued, ignoring his objections, "you're so scared of what Zoe will think of you that you've kept your feelings for her a secret for almost ten years. Ten. Years."

"That's not fair. We made a pact freshman year."

"You mean she made it and you agreed because you'd rather be friends with her than nothing at all," Thảo pointed out.

Unwilling to admit that she was right, Derek pressed his lips together. He wasn't the only freshman who had been drawn to her energy, but he was the person she'd chosen to spend time with.

"I know you derive joy from making others happy." Thảo's tone was now calm and gentle instead of tossing tiny daggers into him. "But when was the last time you did something to make yourself happy?"

"Zoe makes me happy, T."

"So tell her."

"Do you know how many times I've tried to tell Zoe that I want us to be more than friends and I couldn't? What if I lose her for good?"

"After tonight, you might lose for good if you aren't proactive." Thảo reached over and patted his knee. "She made the first move and you have to convince her that it was the right one."

"How am I supposed to do that tomorrow during the most important day of our career?" He closed his eyes and groaned.

"You're being dramatic again. Tomorrow will be easy, because everyone who shows up wants to be part of this. The actors, the designers, even good old Greg and Prestige's board."

That buoyed his confidence. Why would anyone working on the show want to sabotage it? He'd gathered people who understood that the musical would open doors for so many Asian Americans.

"You're right."

"Always am," she said smugly. Thảo leaned back and crossed her legs.

"I'll keep things professional tomorrow while we're working. But I'll ask her to meet with me after our first rehearsal. We'll go somewhere and talk it out."

"Promise me you'll tell her? Tomorrow?"

He sighed. The longer he kept his feelings hidden from Zoe, the longer she'd stay in his life. He'd been living in limbo ever since he'd found her again two weeks ago.

"Derek, if you can't tell her, then it's time to let her go. Move on."

He'd kept a spotlight on her for so long but she'd stepped off her mark. He had to adjust his light or turn it off.

Tomorrow he'd pull her aside and tell her everything.

"I promise."

CHAPTER 21

Zoe kept her sunglasses on as she walked through Prestige Rep and down to the costume shop the next morning. The workspace wasn't as well-lit as her boutique's workroom, but it was the room's rainbow of fabrics and boxes that made her smile every time she walked in.

Except today. In between practicing her presentation and taking care of Mr. Bobbins, she'd gotten only a couple of hours of sleep. Then there was the kiss, which she'd tried her best not to think about. Zoe had woken up with bloodshot eyes paired with dark circles under them.

"Zoe, I got the photocopies you asked for," said TJ, without looking up from the table. "I'll make sure everything is ready when the meet and greet starts in an hour."

She'd texted him early this morning when she realized she couldn't leave her cat alone until her neighbor came over. At least that gave her time to put together a confidence-boosting outfit. The puffy sleeves on her deep purple fit-and-flare dress channeled Boss Babe energy. She'd added pockets to the A-line skirt that were deep enough to hold her phone.

"Thanks, TJ," she said quietly as she squeezed in between the table with sewing machines and the big ironing board. It was hard to see everything through her sunglasses.

"Zoe, TJ told me about Mr. Bobbins. You should've called me. I would've come home to help," Trixie piped up next to TJ. She handed him a glue stick as he mounted the new non-vomit-covered copies.

"Trixie, what are you doing here?" she asked in surprise. Zoe could hide her turmoil from TJ, but her roommate could always tell when she was in a mood.

"I'm here to support you. I also offered my services as the show's intimacy consultant and they said yes."

"I'm glad you're finding new ways to share your sex-ed experiences," Zoe replied, thrilled to have one of the Boss Babes working with her on the musical.

"How's your cat?" asked TJ.

"I think he's better. The vet said to give Mr. Bobbins time to work the olive oil out of his system." Zoe hoped her cat wouldn't have anymore "incidents" for both the cat and her neighbor's sakes.

"Why are you wearing your sunglasses inside?" TJ put his hand on his hip and side-eyed her.

"What's wrong?" Trixie asked. "Don't you dare lie to me."

Zoe glanced over to the shop manager's office to make sure his door was closed before pushing her sunglasses onto her head.

TJ gasped and covered his mouth with his hands.

"Have you been crying?" Trixie rushed to Zoe's side. "What happened?"

"No, I wasn't crying but—" Zoe quickly filled them in about kissing Derek the previous night. "I don't know what came over me, but that moment. The way he looked at me like I was the most beautiful person in the world—I kissed him."

"It's about damn time," TJ said as he snapped his fingers. "I saw fireworks between you two that very first day I met him."

"No, it is not," Zoe shot back. "Kissing my best friend wasn't on my bucket list."

"What are you going to do now?" asked Trixie.

"Pretend like it never happened." Zoe shook her head, but a weird feeling in her stomach returned as she replayed their kiss. "Because we have to work closely together for at least four more weeks."

"What if he doesn't want to forget it?" pressed Trixie. "Did he say anything after the kiss?"

"I didn't give him the chance." Zoe felt a little guilty about the way she'd pushed him away. "He also texted a bunch last night after I shoved him out the door but I didn't know what to say."

"What if you just get him out of your system?" TJ asked as he thrust his hips out suggestively. He and Reina would get along very well.

"No!" Zoe cried out. Then she said softly, "People already think I'm only here because we're friends. That would make it worse."

"Since when did you care what people think about you, Zoe? If you had, Something Cheeky wouldn't even exist," Trixie pointed out.

"That's different. No one depended on me when I opened it. I didn't have any employees at the beginning." Zoe pulled out the fabric swatches from her bag so TJ could attach them to the mounted sketches. "As the person with the least theater experience, I'm the weakest link on Derek's team. If the show fails because of me, I'd ruin his chances of taking it to Broadway."

"Your work is fire." TJ snapped his fingers in appreciation. "I say that as a gay Vietnamese man, so it's definitive."

Trixie nodded in agreement. Zoe laughed. They both made her feel a tiny bit less stressed.

"Real talk, Zoe." TJ set down his fabric shears and grabbed her shoulders. "There is something between you and that tasty morsel of a man. Would you regret it if you didn't at least see what that's all about?"

Zoe sat down across from TJ. She double-checked his work even though she knew he'd done everything the way she asked.

"You've already kissed him," Trixie added, "and you can't take it back. Whatever you decide, you should talk about what happened."

Zoe rubbed a strip of silk charmeuse between her fingers as she debated her options. Derek had made an effort to find her even though she'd been such a terrible friend after he moved to New York. Not only that, but he stopped by her boutique or the costume shop every day to check on her and cheer her on. She owed it to him to at least talk about last night.

"Okay, I'll talk to him but I have no idea what I'm going to say."

"Yes!" TJ jumped and clapped his hands.

"You'll figure it out when the time comes." Trixie gave her an encouraging smile.

"But I have to get through the meet and greet first." Zoe turned to TJ. "Did you bring any makeup?"

"I thought you'd never ask." He jumped up to grab his bag. "Let's get rid of those awful circles under your eyes."

CHAPTER 22

Y'all ready to come to the atrium for our meet and greet?" Heather, the theater's resident stage manager, poked her head into the costume shop. "Five minutes till we start."

"Thank you, five," Zoe acknowledged automatically. The four years of college had ingrained the call and response into her.

She and TJ gathered up her presentation boards and headed upstairs along with Trixie and Shawn, the costume shop manager. She still had no idea what to say to Derek about their kiss, so she waited until the last possible minute to join everyone. When they arrived, Greg was escorting Derek from table to table to meet people in suits. They were probably board members and producers. Zoe's shoulders dropped in relief.

The atrium served as a café on show nights so there were plenty of tables and chairs for everyone. A brunch spread of coffee, tea, bagels, fruit, and pastries had been set up on a six-foot table covered with a white tablecloth. Whoever had arranged the food had given a nod to the musical. She spotted a squeeze bottle of sweetened condensed milk. Tropical fruits such as lychees and mangoes were nestled on trays with the usual honeydew, grapes, and watermelon.

Zoe's stomach growled at the sight of baked pork buns, but she was too nervous to eat.

"Breathe," TJ whispered to her before adding in his normal voice, "Heather wants us over here with the rest of the design team."

She followed TJ to a group of tables that had been pushed to one side of the atrium to become the "front" of the room. She'd had video meetings with the other designers but this was their first time meeting in person. Asian faces smiled and waved at her.

Zoe stopped mid-step as she scanned the atrium. Outside of her family and events at Eden Center, Asians weren't in the majority at other group events. Yet right now, the room was at least 75 percent Asian rep. Her eyes welled as she was filled with pride and an intense feeling of belonging. Why had it taken her almost thirty years to be in the room where it happened?

She and TJ began introducing themselves to their fellow designers but were interrupted by Heather. The meet and greet had begun. TJ, always a rebel, snuck away to grab some coffee and fruit as everyone found their seats.

"I don't want to take up too much of your time because this show isn't about me," Greg announced after introducing himself. "However, I want to acknowledge that we're making history today as Prestige Rep's first all-Asian musical production, including the cast and creative team."

The room exploded in cheers.

"We wouldn't be here if I hadn't discovered Derek Bui five years ago playing a bit part in an off-Broadway play," Greg continued. "I invited him to be my assistant director and have taught him everything he knows. I feel as if this production is my grandchild, so to speak."

TJ quietly snorted behind Zoe as he slid paper plates full of food and two cups of coffee onto their table. Zoe hushed him but gave a slight nod in agreement. Greg continued in great detail with how he'd plucked Derek from obscurity to become a sought-after director.

Eventually the stage manager cleared her throat loudly and tapped on her watch. Greg chuckled at her gentle reminder to stay on schedule.

"I've talked enough, so let me introduce you to the man of the hour, Derek Bui." Greg waved at Derek, who was sitting at the foremost table. "Our esteemed director and writer of *Tấm Cám*."

The Vietnamese people in the atrium visibly cringed at Greg's mispronunciation, including TJ, who also rolled his eyes. Still, Derek received an enthusiastic round of applause.

"We can debrief later," she whispered to TJ. "Try to be professional."

He mimed zipping his lips. TJ knew all about her meeting with Greg the previous week when he challenged her designs. She'd also told him how Derek had stepped in to defend her before she said something she'd regret.

"Thank you, Greg," Derek said as he pushed his glasses up his nose. He took Greg's spot in the center of the atrium. Someone she didn't recognize whistled and cheered. Of course Derek had a fan club. He had a way of making everyone feel special without making it trite or cheesy.

Zoe sucked in a breath. He'd transformed from adorable friend to a sexy, well, director. Instead of all black, today he wore a deep blue sateen button-down shirt, which he'd kept untucked from his black jeans. He'd rolled up his shirtsleeves, which accentuated his muscular forearms. Wait, she found forearms sexy now?

He'd also slipped on shiny black leather loafers, which could only mean that his Chucks were still damp from last night's incident with her cat. She didn't even know that he owned any shoes but his Converse sneakers.

Derek's words faded away as images of their kiss flashed in her head. How she'd felt his cock twitch against her body. Her cheeks—and places much lower—heated at the memory. She bit her lip to keep her focus on the meet and greet.

"I'd like to introduce everyone to Thảo Nguyen, my cowriter, the composer, and our musical director," Derek continued. "She's put up with my crazy ideas for the last year and made everything sound good."

Thảo was dressed to kill every day, but she'd injected even more of her chaotic personality into her outfit today. Her typical ripped extra-wide-legged jeans were covered in colored patches. She stood up and waved, making her bangles chime.

"Hope you're ready to sing your heart out," she said warmly. "Because I will push you until you're tired of me."

Several of the actors laughed. Zoe recognized some of them from the headshots that the costume shop manager had pinned next to their corresponding costume sketches on the board downstairs.

"I'm honored that so many of you took a chance to work on a brand-new musical," Derek continued. "The first person to come onboard was Katie Mai Vu as Tấm."

He motioned for one of the leads to stand up. Zoe gasped inaudibly.

"Ho-lee shit," TJ whispered in agreement. "I know we joke that all Asians look alike, but damn."

Zoe and Katie Mai could've been sisters.

The actress playing Tấm was gorgeous and big—in a good way. Zoe had known that, on paper, their measurements were similar. Zoe was excited to costume a plus-size princess. The shock was that their silhouettes were almost identical, except that Katie Mai was taller than Zoe, even without the heels.

While their facial features weren't exactly alike, there was an odd similarity between them. Zoe hadn't noticed this in Katie Mai's headshot, probably because those were usually lit and airbrushed to make the actor look as perfect as possible.

Katie Mai wore a light pink jumpsuit that fit her perfectly, along with chunky heels that screamed summer. She held herself with a confidence that came from years of experience on the stage.

"Girl, I think someone has a type," TJ pointed out under his breath.

"I have no idea what you're talking about," Zoe lied. She thought back to the time she'd spent with Derek since he came into town. She'd missed the signs. His thoughtful glances and how their hugs lasted a little too long. The hungry way he'd returned her kiss last night.

How long had Derek had feelings for her?

The woman who could be Zoe's sister walked over to Derek. She kissed him on the cheek and they hugged for longer than Zoe thought socially acceptable. Were they? No, he wouldn't have kissed her back the way he had if he was in a relationship with Katie Mai. He always told her these things.

At least he used to.

"I can never say no to you, Derek." Katie Mai's laugh was melodic. She probably had a beautiful singing voice, too. Even though they'd pulled apart from their very comfortable hug, her arm lingered around his waist.

Zoe's nostrils flared with—wait, is this what jealousy felt like? She had no claim on Derek. She hadn't even been in his life for the past six years. But it sounded like Katie Mai had been very involved in his life.

"I've played a lot of roles in the past, including a mail-order bride and a prostitute. So many sex workers," the lead actress continued. The Asian women in the group nodded in understanding.

"Never for me," Derek replied as he held his hands out. His eyes shone as he looked at Katie Mai. "You were perfection in every show I cast you in."

"Can you say that again so I can record it?" she teased as she waved her phone in front of him.

There were a few chuckles from the group.

"But," she continued and smiled indulgently at him as if they always bantered this way, "I thought I was too fat to play a princess, much less a Vietnamese one. Thank you for the role of a lifetime."

Katie Mai pulled him in for a side hug before returning to her seat. Everyone applauded. She blushed, which made her more endearing. Zoe wanted to hate her but she couldn't. How could she find fault in a Vietnamese woman who was trying to break down barriers?

The rest of the cast introductions were a blur for Zoe as she analyzed all of her previous interactions with Derek. And she meant all of them, even the ones from freshman year. If she looked hard enough, there were signs of interest. She'd thrown water on that spark before it even had a chance to catch on fire.

Part of her wanted Derek to set her ablaze and see how big the flames could grow. The other part was terrified that she'd lose whatever connection they had as friends if things didn't work out. Now it was too late, because he had Katie Mai.

"Hottie alert." TJ nudged her with his elbow.

Zoe looked up to see a tall muscular man stand up.

"Hi, I'm Danny Kim, proud Korean American. I'll be playing the Emperor." He bowed regally.

"I'd get on my knees anytime for royalty like him," TJ quipped. "Definitely plays on my team."

"He's cute," she agreed. Zoe was grateful to think about something besides Derek and his possible relationship with Katie Mai.

"He's delicious," TJ replied quickly without taking his eyes off Danny.

"He lives in New York so he'll make the perfect fling for you, my little commitment phobe," she teased. "Want me to find out if he's single?"

TJ grunted noncommittally. She snorted.

"Now that you've met our talented cast, let me introduce you to our production team, starting with our costume designer, Zoe Tran," Derek announced and turned to her.

Everyone looked at her as she snort-laughed at TJ. She closed her eyes as her cheeks grew hot. This time it was from embarrassment and not desire. Looking like an idiot wasn't the first impression she wanted to make with people she'd have to work closely with for the next four weeks.

Derek cleared his throat loudly to draw attention back to himself. "Seems as if I didn't read my cues properly."

There was polite laughter. He'd given her a chance to recompose herself.

"Let's try this again." Derek looked at her and she nodded. "I present to you the talented woman who designed costumes for a Southern Gothic–inspired *A Midsummer's Night's Dream*—complete with vampires. Perhaps my best college play ever."

That piqued everyone's curiosity, which was better than seeing her as some jokester who couldn't pay attention.

Zoe took a deep breath and pushed her chair back. TJ grabbed the presentation boards and stood up next to her. Time to prove to Greg and everyone else that she belonged here.

CHAPTER 23

Derek plopped in the seat next to Thảo so everyone could give Zoe their full attention.

"You're doing great," Thảo said as she patted his arm. "Katie Mai is glowing today, don't you think?"

"Hmmm," he replied without taking his eyes off Zoe.

She'd given him a funny look when he attempted to introduce her the first time. He couldn't tell if it was because he'd caught her off guard. Or she was embarrassed about their kiss last night.

He'd caught her entrance into the atrium earlier, but he hadn't been able to break free from Greg's introductions to talk to her. He wasn't entirely confident that she even wanted to talk to him. But she'd cracked the dam he'd built to hide his love for her. They'd talk tonight as friends and not collaborators on a musical.

"Thank you, Derek." Zoe nodded at him as she stood up. TJ followed suit behind her. "This is TJ, my assistant. Both of us are thrilled to work with you all."

TJ curtseyed and made eyes at Danny Kim, who winked in response. Derek was not surprised by the interchange.

"Oh boy, I see trouble," Thảo whispered, "but not the bad kind."

Those two would make a great match. Flings among the cast and crew weren't uncommon but they could cause unnecessary tension or drama that could hinder the chemistry of the production.

Even worse, these relationships could become HR nightmares if there was a whiff of a power imbalance.

"Derek convinced me to come out of retirement by dangling this show in front of me. Like Katie Mai"—Zoe stopped to acknowledge the actress—"and for many of us here, this is an opportunity of a lifetime."

She continued to explain her vision as TJ held up the sketches for the two sisters and the Emperor's costumes. Both Derek and Thảo had agreed with her suggestion to keep the Emperor nameless because the crux of the musical was about the sisters' relationship with each other.

"So while Tấm's dress is fluid and soft, you see hints of her toughness here"—Zoe pointed to the leather cuffs with metal rivets—"and in the traditional headpiece she wears when she marries the Emperor. We're giving it a Lizzo-meets-punk vibe by using lace, leather, and metal spikes."

"Derek, these are fucking gorgeous," Thảo said quietly. "She's making me wish I had a costume."

"I told you she was talented." He grinned.

Even though he'd seen her sketches evolve from the time he almost ruined her sketchbook at the Wharf to the final renderings, he was still mesmerized by her designs. A quick glance proved he wasn't the only one who felt that way. Everyone—the actors, creative team, the board—they were hanging on her every word.

From the very first day he'd met Zoe, she'd exuded some sort of magic around her. Though she didn't speak often or loudly, she had a way of commanding attention whenever she spoke. As if they knew she was destined for greatness.

Their classmates had flocked to her, hoping that some of her glow would rub off on them. Zoe preferred a smaller circle of friends, unlike Derek, who thrived in large groups. Everyone, especially the actors, was on the edge of their seats as she explained her vision behind each character's costumes.

Everyone except for one person. Greg.

Derek sighed. For once, his mentor was in the minority. Even the producers were captivated by Zoe.

"Designing costumes is a collaborative process, so I'm looking forward to meeting with the cast one-on-one to discuss your interpretation of the characters," Zoe said in closing. "Heather will schedule those for us. Thank you, everyone."

Applause echoed throughout the high glass ceiling of the atrium.

Derek fought the impulse to run over and hug Zoe and congratulate her on her presentation. But that wouldn't be professional, not with everyone's eyes on them. He gave her a thumbs-up before introducing the next person on his creative team.

"That was the best meet and greet ever," said Thảo. She lightly punched Derek in the arm. "It's really happening."

"Our musical is coming to life," he agreed. "Even if it still feels surreal."

"Come on, look at all the talented people you've gathered here. We're little orphans you've collected to create your own gang of misfits."

She gestured to the atrium, which was emptying as people shuffled back to their offices or to their cars. The production team was helping the house manager clean up the café area.

"Are you comparing me to Fagin? That must make you Oliver Twist," he teased.

"Please, sir, may I have some more," Thảo said in her best poor British orphan accent.

"Now, that's why you're a composer and not an actor." Derek grimaced, shaking his head at her.

"Alert, Greg is headed our way," Thảo whispered as her eyes

darted to the other side of the atrium. "He looks like his Grape-Nuts got soggy."

"Hush," Derek said but he couldn't help but smirk.

"You're on your own. I'm going back to the rehearsal room to fix the duet between the sisters."

Before he could beg her to stay and be a buffer, Thảo ran off.

"I'll be there in a few minutes," he called after her loudly, so Greg could hear him. Hopefully he could use that as an excuse to cut their conversation short.

"Derek," Greg called out as he walked toward Derek. "Have time for a quick chat?"

"Of course." Did he really have a choice? He might as well get this conversation over with or Greg would hunt him down later.

"We had a great turnout for the meet and greet. I'd say seventy-five percent of the staff and most of the board." Greg clapped Derek on the back in congratulation.

"I'm glad they're excited about this production." Derek breathed a sigh in relief.

"They should be. If we head to New York, we'll make some big bucks and an even bigger name for Prestige."

"I'd like to think they're interested because we're making new and exciting art." Derek envied how comfortable and confident the artistic director was about everything he did, no matter how mediocre.

"That's what I wanted to talk to you about." Greg looked around before pulling Derek to a semi-secluded area.

"What's going on, Greg? Thảo needs me before the actors come back from doing paperwork with HR."

"I know Katie Mai is a good friend of yours, but have you considered switching the two actresses playing the sisters?" Greg's tone was less questioning but more of a firm suggestion.

"What's wrong with Katie Mai?" Derek stepped back to put

some distance between them. "You haven't even heard her in rehearsal yet."

"I'm not sure she's the right look for the lead. Yvonne Le would be more relatable for our audiences."

"What do you mean by that?" He knew exactly what Greg was insinuating, but he wouldn't let him off the hook that easily.

Derek gritted his teeth. He'd cast Yvonne as the younger stepsister, not because she was smaller and thinner than Katie Mai, but because he loved her audition. Yvonne had interpreted Cám as kind yet mischievous. She was the perfect foil for Katie Mai, who portrayed Tám as protective yet optimistic.

"I mean princesses are usually petite and delicate. I think we can both agree that while Katie Mai is tall enough, she doesn't exude delicate."

"She is very—" Derek cut himself off. He didn't have to explain his artistic decisions. "Greg, my casting choices are final and the contracts have been signed. Katie Mai Vu is the best person to play Tám."

Realizing that Derek wouldn't entertain his suggestion, the man pressed his lips together.

"Right. You're the boss," Greg said after a beat.

"You remind me of that all the time, but you don't like any of my decisions." Derek straightened his spine and said firmly, "You said you'd trust me."

"I know you want to make a name for yourself by doing never-done-before things. My suggestions are backed up by thirty years of experience." Greg crossed his arms.

"I appreciate your concern." Derek kept his face expressionless. While he didn't care for the artistic director's advice, he didn't want to alienate him either. Derek couldn't remember his mentor being so pushy. But maybe he'd never noticed because this was the first time Derek was in complete control over a production instead of working as Greg's assistant.

It was time to put more distance between the two of them. Derek needed to make a name for himself without Greg's mentorship. He wasn't sure if their values still aligned.

"I'm only telling you this because it'll be easier to move people around at the beginning," Greg said. "You're like a son to me. I only want you to succeed, Derek."

"I know you do."

"Look, I haven't told anyone, but"—Greg leaned in closer to Derek—"I plan on retiring in five or six years. And I want to recommend you as my successor."

"Seriously?" Derek blinked.

A series of scenes played through his head. A position like this would allow him to commission work by more playwrights of color. He'd have a steady job—with benefits—instead of relying on getting enough freelance work to qualify for health insurance through the union. Not only that, but with the lower cost of living here, he could definitely afford to take care of his mother.

Derek stopped his runaway thoughts. Greg had said five years. A lot could happen between now and then.

"Why do you think they'd hire me to run the biggest theater in DC?" he pressed. Greg had dangled carrots in the past but they often fell through for one reason or another outside his mentor's control. At least that's what the man told him.

"I've taught you everything I know, haven't I? Besides, the board loves me and will hire anyone I tell them to," Greg said with more confidence than Derek had ever heard.

Derek nodded cautiously.

"Don't you want them to love you?"

"I want them to love the show," Derek admitted truthfully. "This musical is bigger than me. It's time for Asian Americans to have something besides *Miss Saigon* to aim for."

"You're excited about this production, but don't forget that no one knows who you are yet. I can help you and your career explode."

Now Greg was repeating himself. Derek needed to extract himself before the man started recalling the "back in my day" stories.

"Look at the time," Derek said as he showed the man his phone. "I need to help Thảo prep for our table read and sing through."

Derek took a step around the man, who had walked him back against a wall. Greg put a hand out to stop him.

"I'm serious, Derek. In five years this could all be yours if you learn how to play the game."

"I'll think about it," Derek said in a tone that indicated their conversation was finished. This time Greg let him leave the alcove.

Whatever relief he'd had at the beginning of that conversation was now replaced with anxious hope. He didn't like who he became around Greg, but the man had gotten him this far. What's another five years if he could finally snag a dream job that would give him everything he wanted? Professionally at least.

Thankfully, Greg had no hand in Derek's relationship with Zoe.

CHAPTER 24

I can't believe I let you drag me out here," Zoe complained to TJ. "I should go home and check on Mr. Bobbins."

The pub was packed for a Wednesday night. Their table was littered with empty and half-full cocktail glasses, some of which were theirs and others were from the other designers who'd left early. Clearly the pub hadn't expected to be this busy on a Wednesday night and were short-staffed.

"Trixie promised she'd take care of your cat," TJ reminded her.

Zoe had wanted to talk to her roommate after the meet and greet, but Trixie had to get back to her shop for the afternoon.

"You can't skip out on our first cast-and-crew happy hour!" TJ protested.

"Everyone's so nice. It feels good to be around people who understand you implicitly," Zoe conceded.

"And not worry someone will accidentally make a racist joke," TJ added. "There's a reason I left rural North Carolina. You don't see too many gaysians there."

Zoe snorted.

"I'd say California is the mecca for gay Asians, but there's plenty in the DMV," Zoe concurred.

"I dragged you here to have fun *and* be my wing woman tonight," reminded TJ.

"Why not Thảo? You two hung out last night?"

"She was such a downer last night," TJ whispered. "Don't tell her I said that."

Zoe glanced over to the half-circle booth a few tables from them. The seating was large enough for them to spread out, but Thảo and Derek had made a Katie Mai sandwich. What secrets were they discussing that made them put their heads so closely together?

"What do you think is going on there?" Zoe asked.

"Are you jealous?"

"No," she replied too quickly.

TJ raised an eyebrow.

"Except for the intro this morning, he hasn't talked to me today."

"Did you really expect him to after last night?" TJ asked.

Zoe sighed. Derek had every right to be upset.

"He could've texted during rehearsal breaks." Zoe hated that she was being childish, but all these new feelings had thrown her off balance.

"*You* could have texted him," TJ pointed out.

"And say what? Sorry I embarrassed myself by kissing you, then kicking you out of my apartment. But maybe I have feelings for you and I think you do for me, too?" Zoe rolled her eyes.

"Honest, if a bit rambly. So you're gonna sit here by yourself and mope while I get Danny's digits?" TJ put a hand on his hip.

"I'll be fine." Zoe didn't sound convincing even to herself.

He gave her a skeptical look but snuck a glance at the actors hanging out by the bar.

"Go," she insisted. "I'll get myself another drink."

"Relax and maybe you'll find a hottie to go home with tonight. Then I won't feel so bad if I leave with the Emperor."

"You know I don't do one-night stands." Zoe shuddered at the idea of hooking up with a complete stranger.

"You demisexuals are so prickly," he teased. "Good thing you have a decent collection of vibrators."

"Keep your voice down! Not everyone needs to hear what's in my bedside drawer." She pushed him out of his chair. "Go flirt and let me be broody."

"You do you, babe." He kissed her on the cheek and practically skipped over to Danny.

She'd nurse one last cocktail to make sure TJ had a ride back to his apartment before heading home to check on Mr. Bobbins. Maybe she'd even cozy up to her well-curated collection of sex toys. It was one of the perks of having a sex educator as her roommate.

If Derek no longer wanted to talk to her after last night, then it was his right. She'd made everything awkward between them. Maybe she needed time to—

"Hey, mind if I sit here?" Katie Mai tucked her hair behind her ear and grinned at Zoe. "I brought you a rum punch. Derek says it's one of your favorites."

The actress set two glasses on the table. Zoe hadn't been able to flag anyone down, so why waste a perfectly good rum punch? Zoe invited her to sit down.

"He's right. What brings you over this way?" Zoe asked. "You three seemed comfortable over there."

"Oh no, they started talking shop. Something about chord progression and repeating a theme? My brain is too tired to follow the conversation." Katie Mai laughed.

"It's been a long day for everyone," Zoe agreed. She herself was running on very little sleep. "I'll probably head out soon."

Katie Mai's face fell, but she quickly covered it up with a nervous grin.

"I'm glad I caught you then." She fiddled with the string of her braided red bracelet.

"Everything okay?" Zoe sat up, her stomach swirling. Maybe Katie Mai wanted advice on dating Derek. It was obvious from this morning's meet and greet that the two had a connection.

"This is going to sound super fangirl, but I've heard so much about your designs and Something Cheeky. When Derek told me you were designing our costumes, I squealed." Katie Mai spoke quickly as if she'd been holding it in all day.

"Oh, thank you." Zoe let out a sigh of relief. She wasn't sure enough about her feelings about Derek that she'd fight another woman for him. Not that he was some prize to be won.

"I wanted to tell you earlier, but Heather rushed us away to get our paperwork finalized. I can't disobey the stage manager on my first day."

"Heather's sweet but a stickler for staying on task, especially during our virtual production meetings." Zoe had dreaded the calls at first, but the stage manager was one of the best people wranglers she'd ever met. She wasn't afraid to cut someone off if they went over their allotted time.

"That's how she was today during our first rehearsal. I'm a little scared of her," Katie Mai stage-whispered and shuddered dramatically while looking at the bar, where the stage manager was sitting.

Zoe smiled for the first time since arriving at the pub. Katie Mai was growing on her. The only reason Zoe had to dislike her was the actress was possibly dating Derek. But it would be too cliché for her to sleep with her director. Katie Mai didn't seem like that kind of person.

No, the actress was genuinely kind. Zoe caught no hint of underlying motives from Katie Mai. Perhaps in a different situation, the two of them would be good friends. She might as well take advantage of the moment to learn if Derek and the actress had a history outside of their professional one.

"You're welcome to stop by the boutique anytime. I'll let my staff know to offer you the friends and family discount," Zoe found herself saying. She could hear Josie's voice in her head about randomly handing out deals, but it was too late to take it back. A smaller profit margin on a few pieces could be worth it, depending on the intel Katie Mai let slip.

"Really? Oh my God, I can't wait!" Katie Mai hugged her. "I'm sorry, I'm a big hugger. I should've asked."

"It's okay. I don't mind." Zoe picked up her drink. "How about a toast?"

"To this show and to new beginnings," the actress said as they clinked their glasses.

The rum punch was cold, strong, and delicious. Not bad for an Irish pub in DC.

"So what's going on between you and Derek?" Katie Mai asked.

Zoe spit out her drink. She grabbed some leftover napkins and wiped the table.

"Sorry, I didn't mean to ambush you."

"Why would you think there's something going on?" Zoe asked cautiously.

"I've known Derek for only a few years, but he's talked about you nonstop."

"All good, I hope."

"He adores you, Zoe." Katie's eyes narrowed as she turned to face Zoe. "I need to know what your intentions are toward Derek."

"Intentions?" Zoe laughed. "Like in a historical romance? Derek is no wallflower."

"Oh God, that sounded super cheesy, didn't it?" Katie chuckled. "Maybe I've had too many drinks."

"I should be asking you that question," Zoe blurted. Screw caution. Her exhaustion combined with the alcohol had quieted her inner editor. "Are you two—"

"Ladies, we brought some snacks," TJ interrupted as he slid a tray of loaded tater tots in front of them. "Danny sweet talked the bartender into a BOGO."

"Voilà!" The actor came up right on cue. He held another tray that was completely covered with deep-fried potatoes. "I had to. The kitchen was closing soon and I'm famished."

TJ had terrible timing, but Zoe's stomach grumbled. Bar food always tasted better after a few drinks. TJ glanced at the actress, then gave Zoe a questioning look. Zoe shrugged. She still had more questions than answers.

"It's as if you read my mind, Danny." Katie Mai dove right into the mounds of melted cheese topped with bacon bits. If she wondered what Zoe's question had been, she didn't mention it.

Zoe would have the actress's undivided attention tomorrow during her fitting. She'd recruit TJ to dig up Katie Mai and Derek's history. TJ would call it procrastinating, but she needed to know before taking the next step with Derek—whatever that was going to be. If the two of them were a thing, Zoe didn't want to get in the way.

CHAPTER 25

"What kind of pub closes at nine?" Thảo grumbled as they walked away from the Wharf.

"When it's a Wednesday night," Derek replied. "We have rehearsal early tomorrow, so I'm going to put on my director hat and send you all home."

"Party pooper," his cowriter mumbled as she tucked her head into Katie Mai's shoulder.

He hadn't seen her get this drunk in a while. Derek had been too wrapped up in his own worries about Zoe and the show that he'd forgotten how much pressure Thảo was under, too. He'd check in with her in the morning.

"I'll walk her back to her apartment. It's next door to mine." Katie Mai looped her arm around Thảo's. "Let's go."

"Are you two good?" Derek touched Katie Mai's arm as he searched her face for the apprehension from their earlier conversation.

"I'll talk to her tomorrow when she's sober." Katie Mai sighed heavily. "Sorry to rope you into this."

"I'm here for you. Both of you."

"And you have some talking to do with you-know-who," Katie Mai added as she nodded her head at Zoe, who was talking to TJ, Danny, and some of the other cast members.

Now it was his turn to sigh heavily. He hadn't meant to avoid Zoe most of the day, but Heather had a schedule they needed to follow. He'd been in rehearsal while she'd been busy in the costume shop.

"Hey, Katie Mai, wait for us," Danny called. "We can all walk back together."

Prestige rented several furnished apartments a couple of blocks away from the theater for their out-of-town actors, which was a majority of this cast. Part of Derek wished that his apartment was in the same building as theirs, but his cast needed space. Even though they were all friends, he was still their director and they'd need to blow off steam the closer they got to opening night.

"Derek!" TJ waved him over. He stood next to Zoe, who was leaning against a large concrete pole that kept cars off the cobblestone pathway.

Derek's body straightened as he went on full alert. He looked at Zoe and back to Katie Mai and Thảo, who now had her arm wrapped around Katie Mai's waist.

"I have everything under control. Go help Zoe," Katie Mai urged.

He ran over to Zoe. Her eyes were glassy as she grinned at him.

"Derek!" Her voice echoed off the dark buildings. "It's about time you talked to me."

"Hey, Z."

"Can you drive Zoe home?" TJ asked quietly.

"Will she be okay?"

"Mostly, but I don't think she ate enough today and Mr. Bobbins kept her up all night. So the rum punches hit her hard." TJ's tone implied it had been more than Mr. Bobbins that contributed to her insomnia.

"Of course," Derek replied.

She wasn't the only one who lost sleep last night. He'd lain in bed, recalling how she explored his mouth and the heat of her soft breasts pressed on his chest. He also couldn't forget the agony on her face as she kicked him out.

"Here are her keys. Don't get lost, okay?" TJ handed him a car fob on a comedy-tragedy keychain. It was the one Derek had given her as a gag gift their sophomore year. He couldn't believe she'd kept it all these years.

"Ha ha," Derek said sarcastically. "That was only one time."

"You know, I'd feel better if you took her back to your place."

"What? I don't think that's a good idea."

"How many drinks did you have?"

"Two? Maybe three?"

"Oh hell no, you're not driving either." TJ tapped his foot as he thought of a better solution.

"How about I bring her back to my place for some coffee?" Derek suggested. "When she's more awake, I'll call her a rideshare."

"Perf. Thanks for taking care of my girl. Now I'm going to take care of me and some royalty." TJ winked and dashed off to join Danny and the rest of the group to walk home.

"Come on, let's get you some coffee," Derek said as he helped her stand up.

"Coffee sounds amazing right now," Zoe muttered as she wrapped her arm around his waist to steady herself.

Once again he found himself close enough to kiss her. Not that he would, considering her state. Zoe leaned into him as he led the way back to his apartment. She smelled of fried food and lavender.

Maybe the caffeine would wake her up enough so they could talk. He'd promised both Thảo and Katie Mai he would. They were right. He'd been living in limbo for too long.

"How the tables have turned," Derek whispered and chuckled.

Zoe had always been the tough one who didn't ask for help. He had to jump in and do things for her so she didn't burn out. For a younger sibling, she had major first child overachiever vibes. Often, she'd been the one who took care of him during college.

"I dragged your drunk ass back to our apartment so many times, I lost count."

"Eventually I got smart and we held the parties at our place."

They'd moved out of the dorm and into CNY's apartments their last year.

"Sorry I don't have any condensed milk."

"Dump a bunch of sugar in it," Zoe muttered with her eyes closed. She was stretched out like a Renaissance painter's muse. Except she wasn't naked. He reminded himself to focus on her and not how great her breasts were in that dress.

"You look better," Derek said. The walk back to his apartment had cleared her head. Her eyes were brighter and her face was less flushed.

"Those drinks snuck up on me." She groaned.

"How much is a bunch?" He held up a bowl stuffed with sugar packets. Thankfully Prestige Rep's company manager had stocked his apartment with all the basics, including coffee and its accompaniments.

She lifted her head high enough to look at him over the edge of the couch. She squinted at him then held up five fingers.

"Five? For this size mug?" He held up the small, white mug with "Keep Calm and Break a Leg" printed on it. Every mug in the cabinet was theater-themed. For himself, he chose one that read "Prop" in bright yellow letters.

"I literally do not have the executive function to make decisions right now. Surprise me."

"Your sweet tooth gets the munchies when you're drunk? That's a new one." He laughed and tore open five packets before sticking the mug under the pod coffeemaker.

"If I hadn't stayed up all night regretting my life choices, it would take more than two cocktails to knock me off my feet," she said before clapping her hand over her mouth.

Derek's hand tightened around the spoon, which was pointed into the air. Right. He couldn't avoid talking about their kiss from the previous night. His chest constricted and he tried to take a deep breath. He had to push past his fear and get this will-she-or-won't-she over with.

There was no such thing as the perfect time. The machine shot its final burst of coffee into the mug. He added a splash of half-and-half. He could feel the spoon scraping the mound of sugar he'd tossed into her mug.

"Are you and Katie dating?" Zoe asked, breaking the awkward silence hanging between them.

He dropped the spoon. It clattered against the side of the mug. The coffee continued to swirl. Whether he was ready or not, Zoe had opened the door.

"No," he replied quickly.

"Sleeping together?" Her voice rose as she pulled herself up to sitting.

"What? Hell, no."

"Have you ever wanted to?" she asked softly, as if she were afraid of his answer.

"Why would you ask that?" He picked up the spoon and stirred with hyper focus so his body language wouldn't reveal his anxiety about her line of questioning.

"You two seem, I don't know, tight," she said as she shrugged.

He wasn't convinced that the sugar could completely dissolve in such a high ratio of sweetener to coffee. Derek gave up stirring and hiding his feelings. He handed Zoe the mug. She wrapped her hands around it. Her face lit up as she inhaled the dark, chocolatey fragrance.

"We're friends, and her heart belongs to someone else."

"Oh." There was genuine surprise on her face. She avoided his eyes by sipping her coffee.

Derek scoffed. That's what Zoe had been worried about? She thought that he and— Katie Mai would have a field day when she found out.

"So you're not even slightly interested? She's beautiful, smart, and funny." Zoe was puzzled, maybe even confused. Was she jealous?

He had no idea where she'd gotten the idea from but Zoe had gotten things all wrong. His heart pounded as he sat down across from her. He set his mug down without drinking from it.

Derek looked into her dark brown eyes. She tilted her head at his serious expression.

Time to blow up four years of friendship. Ten if you added the six years they'd spent estranged.

"Zoe, the only woman I'm interested in is you," he said quickly before he lost his nerve.

Derek exhaled loudly. He'd told her and he didn't die. Relief flooded his body. The room felt brighter. He hadn't realized how holding this in had kept him on edge for so long.

Zoe opened her mouth and closed it. She blinked rapidly.

"The only woman I've ever wanted to be with is you," he repeated with more conviction this time. "Z, I've wanted you since freshman year."

CHAPTER 26

"Freshman year?" Zoe repeated as shock rippled through her. She sat up straight, wide-awake. Whatever effects still lingered from her two drinks had completely disappeared.

He nodded and gave a small, slightly embarrassed smile.

"And you're telling me now while I'm in the middle of the toughest job I've ever had?" She waved her hands in either disbelief or shock—she didn't know which.

"I almost told you so many times, Zoe." He picked up his coffee and sipped it. He leaned back in the armchair and crossed his legs. How was he so relaxed after dropping a major confession on her?

"When? Where? How many?" She replayed their past two weeks together but all she could focus on was last night, when she'd stepped across the boundary of their friendship.

"Since I've been in DC, um, maybe three or four?" He listed all the times they'd been together alone, starting with their impromptu taco picnic.

"I'm a fucking idiot. How did I miss the signs?" She sighed and rubbed her forehead.

"You've been stressed. I didn't want to add to it," he said with his usual kindness.

"And last night when you kissed me back?"

"The best kiss of my life."

She snorted at his hyperbole. He'd traveled all over the country and worked with countless talented, beautiful actors. It wouldn't surprise her if he had a secret fan club somewhere online.

"I mean it." His eyes seemed to pierce into her doubts.

"I have no idea how many people you've kissed," she said, partly to avoid what this conversation meant for their friendship and partly because she still didn't believe him.

"Enough to know."

"Like Katie Mai?" Zoe cringed inwardly as the words flew out.

"Fuck no." He scowled. "Why do you keep bringing her up?"

"She looks just like me." She shrugged, embarrassed that she was jealous of another woman when Zoe had no claim on him.

"What? Please don't tell me you're doing the 'all Asians look alike' thing." He shook his head. "Katie Mai looks nothing like you."

Derek uncrossed his legs and leaned forward to study her. His intense gaze was filled with desire. She shifted in her seat. His eyes crinkled as his lips turned up slightly.

"You're infinitely more beautiful," he said softly. There was no hint of jest or patronization in his voice.

"Are you sure?" Zoe blurted in surprise. "She's gorgeous. And beautiful enough to be an actress."

"You could've been an actress, too."

"My performance at our freshman New Faces showcase was an embarrassment to actors everywhere," Zoe said as she waved off his suggestion. Their theater program required all freshmen to introduce themselves to the rest of the department through a showcase. Everyone had to perform a monologue, song, or scene, even if they weren't acting majors.

"You were nervous. Totally normal. I was, too."

"Your rendition of 'Oh, What a Beautiful Mornin'" was great.

Mine—ugh. I don't know why they make us tech kids act." Zoe was pretty sure that experience had scarred her for life. She hated being onstage for any reason.

"It was probably my only chance to play Curly from *Oklahoma!*" He shrugged. "Your monologue about how much you hated *Miss Saigon* was fantastic."

"Not according to our department head's horrified expression." They laughed.

"Because you tricked them. You rehearsed a completely different piece the night before."

She shrugged. "That 'Fuck *Miss Saigon*' monologue was my way of protesting. Both being forced to act and about the problematic Asian rep on Broadway."

"That was when I knew I wanted you as more than a friend."

"For my potty mouth?" She immediately thought about all the things she could do to him with her mouth.

"No, for standing up for our rights. It was fucking sexy. That's what I've always loved about you, Zoe." Now it was his turn to shift in his chair. "You put your heart in everything you do no matter what others may think."

"That's a nice way of saying I care too much about things others don't." The last part wasn't wrong, but outside of the Boss Babes, he was the only one who made it feel like an asset and not a fault. She'd been accused of caring so much about her projects that she wouldn't compromise. But not everything required give and take.

"You're deflecting," he said quietly. "Z, tell me you feel something between us."

Of course he could tell.

"I feel it," she admitted both to him and to herself. Before she'd learned of the term for it, she'd known long ago that she needed an emotional connection with someone in order to be attracted to them. Maybe she'd felt like this about Derek longer than she'd realized. She'd ignored the signs because she had stuck him so firmly in the friend zone.

"Really? I mean, yes!" He pumped his fist into the air. "I knew last night's kiss meant something to you."

"I don't just kiss anyone." She tried to keep her tone light even though this entire conversation left her feeling unbalanced.

"I'm honored," he replied. She searched his face to make sure he wasn't teasing her but found no signs of it.

"Was that—our—kiss really the best?" Zoe asked quietly. She was annoyed that she needed the validation, but she did want to be his best. In fact, she didn't want him to kiss anyone else ever again.

"Yes. Because it's always been you. Only been you."

Maybe it'd always been Derek for her, too. How much time had they lost because she hadn't allowed herself to see him as more than a best friend? He could've been her partner *and* her lover.

He'd slung a sledgehammer into the wall that she'd put between them. She didn't want to fix it. It was time to tear the whole damned thing down.

"Derek," she whispered, "I've never kissed anyone the way I kissed you last night."

"Well, then kiss me again."

CHAPTER 27

Before she could overthink it, Zoe jumped up and walked around the coffee table to face Derek. Her best friend sat up and smoothed his pants. His eyes shone in anticipation. She took a few steps closer until her right knee touched his.

Her body jolted as if electricity shot through her. His nostrils flared and his breath became shallow. He'd always been Derek, her best friend, but their confessions had peeled back another layer of their relationship.

She paused, suddenly afraid.

In front of her sat a man who knew her better than anyone in her life. One who had seen her at her lowest senior year in college. The man who encouraged her to give her dream a second chance. A dream that was in the process of coming to fruition.

The friend-only filter she'd placed over him had disappeared. This man cared for her more deeply than she'd ever allowed herself to imagine. Until tonight.

And it was fucking hot.

Heat bloomed across her body as she remembered their first kiss. Her desire had been simmering patiently below the surface, waiting for the right moment to make itself known. But now the wait was over and she was shocked by her urge to rip off his clothes and let their bodies become as close as they could possibly be.

She lifted her leg and straddled Derek. He bit his lip as her inner thighs pressed against his outer thighs.

"Are you sure about this?" she whispered. "We can never go back to before."

"How many times do I have to say yes for you to believe me?" He wrapped his arms around her waist and pulled her closer.

Zoe's heart pounded while her breasts rose and fell with her shallow breaths. If she were an inch closer, he'd not only see the movement of her chest, but feel it against his. She ran her fingers through his hair and settled her hand on the back of his neck.

"One more time?" she whispered. Her breath caught in her throat as she waited for him to change his mind.

"It's always yes with you, Z," Derek declared as he closed the gap between their bodies.

Their lips crashed together. This time it didn't matter who initiated. What mattered was that they wanted each other.

Zoe groaned as he parted his lips and invited her to explore his mouth. He was giving himself to her as he'd always done but she hadn't seen—no, she'd ignored the signs until now. After years apart she needed to be closer to him. She reached between their bodies to search for the buttons on his shirt without breaking free from his kisses.

When she grumbled in frustration, he pulled her hands away.

"Let me," he murmured as he kissed her neck.

She shivered, even though his mouth was hot and hungry against her skin. She leaned back in invitation. He complied by leaving a searing trail of kisses down her nape and onto her shoulders.

Zoe reached for his shirt buttons again, but he pushed her hands away to do it himself. She gasped when the back of his hand brushed against her chest. He stopped after the first button and flipped his hands around so that his palms cupped her breasts.

His thumbs circled her nipples through her bra. Zoe arched her back as heat surged through her body and pooled below her belly.

"Derek," she said between gasps, "I need—"

He drowned out her words with a deep kiss that made her toes curl.

Flames licked her body as he stoked the fire within her. She grabbed the hem of her dress and pulled it off her body.

"Fuck, Zoe," Derek exclaimed as he leaned back to trace the lace edge of her bra. "You're so beautiful I can barely take it."

She smiled mischievously and reached for his shirt one more time to finish what he started before her breasts had distracted him.

"Your turn," she said before ripping it open. The buttons popped and scattered onto the floor.

He opened his mouth, but she placed a finger on his lips.

"I'll sew them back later."

He laughed and shrugged off his shirt. His breath caught as she ran her hands across his chest. She bent down and kissed his hot skin before taking his nipple in her mouth.

His body stiffened in shock but quickly relaxed as his head lolled back in pleasure. His reaction empowered her to explore his other nipple by tracing circles around it with her tongue. He grunted as he gripped the chair's arms. She spread her hands over his abdomen, his muscles twitching as her fingers danced lightly across his belly button and teased the button of his jeans.

She straightened up and was met with Derek's hungry eyes.

"Am I moving too fast?" she asked as she traced his skin right above his jeans. She ground her hips against his. There was no mistaking his erection.

"Your speed is the right speed for us," he said as he traced the outline of her dark areolas through her bra.

Zoe's body hummed in pleasure as her nipples peaked under

his touch. Her hips moved instinctually in response and she was rewarded with tiny shocks of pleasure as his hard cock rubbed against the thin cotton of her panties.

"Is that so?" She grinned as she unbuckled his belt and unbuttoned his jeans. She slid off his lap to tug them. He raised his hips for her then kicked them off. There was no mistaking his hard cock under his boxers.

"You're a dream come true," he said softly.

His cheeks were flushed and his lips were puffy from their kisses. He looked at her as if she were a queen and he would do everything in his power to make her happy. His dark eyes were filled with a deep hunger to fulfill her every need.

Desire surged through her body. She needed him as much as he wanted her. Suddenly her bra and panties were too confining. His eyes widened when she released her breasts from her bra and his breathing grew shallow when she dropped her underwear.

"I can't wait any longer," she said as she tugged on the waistband of his boxers.

He licked his lips and reached out for her. She held up a finger to stop him.

"Do you have a condom?"

He nodded and moved to stand up. She pushed him back into the chair.

"I'll get it. Tell me where."

"Bathroom. In my dopp kit." He pointed to a door down the hallway.

When she returned with it, he was grinning ear to ear as if he'd won a Tony Award.

"What? Do I have toilet paper stuck to me or something?"

"I never thought you would walk around my apartment naked. I could watch you all day."

"Maybe later. Right now I'd rather do something else." She reached for his boxers as he lifted his hips for her to pull them down. These too were kicked to the side.

She ran her fingers down the silky smooth skin of his cock before wrapping her hand around it and was rewarded with a groan that made her pussy clench. She swallowed hard. There would be time later for gentleness and exploration. Right now she needed him.

As if reading her mind, he took the condom from her hand and opened it. As soon as he'd rolled it on, she climbed into his lap and nestled his cock between her legs. It slid easily against her wetness. She ground her hips onto him and moaned as his hardness pressed against her clit.

He grabbed her hips to steady her as she rocked into him. She dug her nails into his shoulder as the tiny shocks of pleasure spread across her abdomen. Her skin burned as she rocked her hips faster. It didn't take long for the familiar tightness to spiral through her body.

"You're so beautiful like this," he whispered before leaning into her chest.

She gasped as the heat of his mouth covered her nipple. He wrapped his arms around her waist as her back arched and gave her other breast the same attention. She cried out as her orgasm overtook her.

"I was wrong," he said after she fell onto his chest. "You're a goddess when you come."

"Then worship me," she murmured into his chest before sitting up. "I'm not done with you."

His erection was still pressing against her. She reached down and guided his cock to the entrance of her pussy. Her eyes rolled back as she shifted her body so he could slide deep into her.

"Zoe," he breathed. "You feel incredible."

"Ready?" She didn't wait for his response. She grabbed the arms of the chair for leverage and lifted herself up before sliding deliciously down his hardness.

"Fuck," he cried out.

Pleased with herself, she repeated the movement, except she came down faster and harder.

"I'm not going to last long if you do that," he said through gritted teeth. His cock twitched inside her to reiterate his words.

"Good." She pulled him in for a deep kiss as she lifted her hips until he was barely inside her before slamming herself down and grinding her clit against his hips as his cock was seated deep inside her. He grunted into her mouth as their tongues danced.

Heat bloomed across her body even more quickly this time. She'd already warmed up with her earlier orgasm. It wouldn't take long for her to come again, but she wanted to watch pleasure overtake him first.

Zoe raked her nails over his chest, which caused Derek to buck deeper into her. Each movement, each thrust, brought them closer and closer together. They were breathing the same air as pleasure raked through their bodies. She and Derek had been through so much together.

This was the natural next step. Her thoughts faded as her body took her as he met her with his own thrusts. Everything around her blurred while she focused on Derek and their bodies moving in rhythm.

His fingers dug into her hips as he took over and their rhythm increased. Her skin became taut as her pleasure rose higher and higher.

"I'm gonna . . ." he panted.

"Yes, Derek," she rubbed his bottom lip with her thumb. "Come for me."

He moaned and sucked the pad of her thumb before increasing the pace. All she could do was hold on to the chair and cling to him as he heeded his body's needs.

He tensed as his orgasm began to envelop him. Zoe needed him closer, if that was even possible in this chair. She grabbed the hair on the back of his head and pulled him in to seal her lips over his as he cried out in pleasure. As he came, she closed her eyes and took over, riding him until she exploded into a million pieces.

CHAPTER 28

"Why is the guy always the big spoon?" asked Derek as he re-adjusted the arm that was going numb from their position. Feeling slightly uncomfortable was worth holding naked Zoe in his arms. Well, one arm.

"In heterosexual relationships, maybe. But I'm the big spoon when Mr. Bobbins snuggles with me. Though he usually prefers to sleep on my stomach." She pulled his arm tighter across her abdomen.

"My nemesis doesn't count." He scrunched up his face. His Chucks were still damp thanks to the cat's "present."

The orange fluff ball had ruined his plan, but everything had worked out, albeit on a slightly different timeline. He hadn't pre-dicted that Zoe would make the first move, which made the end result even better: waking up in his bed together after toe curling sex from the previous night.

"Stop. He'll forgive you eventually." She lightly swatted at his hand in a catlike manner.

"Does that mean I'm allowed back into your apartment?" He kissed her neck and was rewarded with a purr.

"Don't tell me you're scared of a fluffy little cat," she teased. Derek could sense her smirk.

"What if I accidentally kill him? You'll never talk to me again no matter how great the sex is."

"You two will have to work things out if we're going to do this."
She placed her hand on his and intertwined their fingers.

"And what does *this* mean to you?" His entire body tensed, worried that she might change her mind. Looking for reassurance, he squeezed her fingers.

Zoe rolled over so they were no longer spooning but were now face-to-face. He closed his eyes as she pushed his hair away from his forehead and readjusted his glasses. She caressed his jaw and kissed him deeply, reassuring him that she cared for him and everything that she'd told him last night was still true. Whatever tension he'd held earlier dissipated.

He wished he could wake up to her kisses every morning.

"Dating. I guess?" she finally said when they pulled away.

"So we're officially dating now?" Excitement coursed through his body. He couldn't wait to tell Thảo the good news.

"But we haven't gone on a date yet." She traced zigzags across his chest.

"That's a technicality we can fix. Dinner on Saturday? No shop talk."

"I'd like that. Our first date." She rubbed a thumb over his nipple until it hardened. His body tingled as he recalled how she'd kissed his chest last night.

"Does this mean I can't tell people we're dating until Saturday?" He was ready for an encore but first he needed to make sure she was truly certain about their new relationship status.

Zoe bit her lip and she looked away from him. Derek held his breath, waiting for her to panic or run out of the room. He knew this was too good to be true. Or he'd waited so long for the two of them to happen that he'd given himself unrealistic expectations. Oh God, he was spiraling while lying naked next to the most beautiful woman in the world.

"Can we keep this between us for now?" she asked tentatively. Worry shadowed her face.

"Z, I've wished for this—for us—since freshman year. Now that we've finally opened up about our feelings for each other, I want to shout it out to the world."

I love you, Zoe, he wanted to add, but he knew that she'd bolt as soon as he said it. Even if he meant it as best friends and now as lovers. Of course they were lovers. What else could they be after last night?

"I'm excited to explore this new part of our relationship, too, but—"

Derek turned onto his back, putting distance between them without completely pulling away. Everything had been too perfect last night. He shouldn't have expected this morning to be all rainbows. That wasn't fair to Zoe. He'd had plenty of time to consider her as more than a friend. She'd had, what, a few days?

He rolled back onto his side to face her and mustered a big grin to hide his disappointment.

"You're embarrassed to tell people that you had the best sex of your life with your best friend?" he half-joked.

"Thank God that chair held up to our rigorous activity." She laughed. "But does that mean sex goes downhill from here?"

He gasped in mock hurt before adding, "Let's find out."

He gave a deep kiss that promised more of what they experienced the previous night. She moaned into his mouth and pressed her bare breasts against his chest. His morning half-erection had become rock hard.

Zoe pulled away, panting.

"As much as I enjoyed that, I want to finish this conversation first," she said.

He tamped down his desire and nodded.

"You and I are working on a really important show. I don't want people to think that I got this job because we're sleeping together."

"But we weren't when I hired—"

"I know that. You know that. But who's going to believe us?" She shook her head. "Can you imagine the tea when people hear I'm sleeping with the director?"

"I don't care what everyone thinks." His words didn't ring true to his ears. He did care a tiny bit. Sometimes.

"I wouldn't either except there are people waiting for me to make a mistake because I'm the least experienced person on your creative team." She pressed her lips together.

"You mean Greg." He frowned. "I have him under control."

"For now. But what happens after the production closes here and goes to New York?"

"You're coming with us," he replied without hesitation. There was no way she'd pass up an opportunity to take the show to Broadway.

"Derek." She sighed. "Even if we do take this musical to the city, the DMV is still my home. I have to come back here to run my shop."

"Your staff can handle things for a while."

"I'm not worried about my staff. It's that DC is a big city with small-town vibes."

"I don't understand."

"Until you dragged me back into theater, I had no idea how much I missed it. I *want* to design more costumes. Maybe not full time, but on the side." She smiled and brushed his cheek with her hand.

"Zoe, I'm so excited for you! People won't know what hit them."

"That's just it. If I fuck this up, Greg will make sure I won't find any more gigs. He knows everyone in the theater scene here. He could easily get me blacklisted."

He couldn't fight her on this. Greg's influence extended beyond DC. His mentor's connections and reputation were how he'd convinced Prestige Rep's board to produce *Tấm Cám*.

"I don't know if I can go through that again," she whispered. Her eyes shone with tears.

"Oh, Zoe," he said quietly and wrapped his arms around her. She laid her head on his chest and sniffed. He hugged her tightly and wished he could protect her from Greg and all the other people like him.

"I let Professor Jerkface push me into quitting theater and I'm not letting anyone, especially Greg, take away my second chance at this career."

Derek couldn't argue with her logic.

"If that's what you really want, then I'll keep quiet until opening night, when your duties as costume designer are complete."

"Everyone will be so surprised. TJ will flip." She giggled.

"But I can't hide it from Thảo. She'll know immediately that something has changed between us," he added.

Thảo would know he'd gotten laid as soon as he walked into the rehearsal room. And she'd pester him until he told her with whom.

"Good point. Trixie will have lots of questions about why I didn't come home last night."

"We'll tell Thảo and Trixie, then?"

"But only them. No one else."

He smiled in agreement, relieved that he could share the great news with at least one person.

"Thanks for being patient with me." She kissed him softly on the lips.

"I know a better way you can thank me."

He rolled her onto her back and kissed her neck. She closed her eyes with a smile and turned her head to give him more access to her silky skin. Once she was relaxed and purring with pleasure, he nudged her legs open with his knees as he nibbled his way down to the soft curves of her stomach.

She tapped the top of his head and he met her hungry gaze.

"Don't you have to be at rehearsal in an hour?"

"Let's see how many times I can make you come in the next hour." He resumed caressing and kissing her abdomen.

"Oh, challenge accepted." She laughed before pushing his head back down between her legs.

CHAPTER 29

Mr. Bobbins meowed loudly as soon as Zoe stuck the keys into her apartment door. He weaved between her legs, almost tripping her as she tried to take off her shoes and set down her bags.

"My poor baby," she cooed as she scooped him up and snuggled him against her chest. "Did you miss me?"

The fluff ball purred loudly and rubbed his head against her chin.

"I'll make it up to you tonight. Promise," she whispered so as not to wake up Trixie. "I had the best time last night, which means you and Derek have to learn to be friends."

He meowed pitifully. She wasn't sure if it was in disagreement or if he could see the bottom of his kibble bowl. Zoe chuckled and set down the tabby in order to feed him.

"Zoe," Trixie said sleepily as she made her way into the living room. "You're home."

"Morning! I picked up some bagels." Zoe knew she was way too perky for nine in the morning, but she couldn't hide it after the numerous orgasms Derek had given her. She'd lost count after the first three.

"Is this a bribe so I don't ask why you didn't come home last night?" Trixie squinted at the overstuffed paper bag on the kitchen counter.

"No. Because I'm going to tell you anyway." Zoe pressed her lips together to keep a giant grin from taking over her face. She should make coffee to help Trixie wake up before dumping everything on her.

"Oooh, chocolate chip ones!" Trixie held up the bagel in a victory pose. "And they're still warm."

"A little something for taking care of Mr. Bobbins yesterday."

Trixie narrowed her eyes at Zoe.

"I slept with Derek," Zoe exclaimed.

Trixie dropped her bagel. It rolled across the kitchen and landed next to Mr. Bobbin's food dish. He hissed and pawed at it before walking over to his bed. Zoe laughed at her cat as she tossed the bagel in the trash can.

"I know! Crazy, right?" Zoe's entire body buzzed with excitement. "Everything happened so fast."

"Nothing wrong with that. I jumped right back into Andre's pants, so I can't judge."

"But?" Zoe sensed there was more.

"It just feels fast for *you*." Trixie's voice was full of concern.

"It is and it isn't." Zoe dug out another chocolate chip bagel and handed it to her roommate.

"I woke up less than ten minutes ago, so explain it to me like I'm a drunk bachelorette at one of my sex-toy demos." Trixie took a bite out of the bagel without slicing it. Happy food sounds emanated from her. "Because the entire time I've been in the DMV, you have rejected all possible dates."

"You know I need some sort of emotional connection with a person before I can be attracted to them."

Trixie nodded as she chewed.

"He's my oldest friend and knows more about me than anyone else. Even the Boss Babes. It never occurred to me that he was potential partner material until I got jealous. I thought he was dating one of the actresses." Zoe laughed. She'd been so upset but now it was silly of her.

"So you finally realized that you had the hots for him and jumped him?" Trixie raised an eyebrow skeptically.

"Basically, yes." Zoe updated her on what had happened at the bar and then at Derek's apartment.

"You're bouncing around the kitchen like one of those karaoke dots over the lyrics, so I assume he's just as talented in the bedroom department?"

"I've never felt so alive." Zoe's cheeks grew warm and she fanned herself with a potholder. "And we did it again this morning."

"I'm proud of you for taking the lead. So what does this mean for the two of you?"

"I've been complaining about how I wanted more excitement," Zoe reminded her. "*This* is what I've been missing. Me and Derek. Me designing costumes for the musical. It's the perfect Venn diagram."

"It's way too early to discuss Venn diagrams," groaned Trixie.

The coffeemaker beeped as if to stall other logic puzzles. Zoe poured two mugs and squeezed in obscene amounts of sweetened condensed milk before sliding one over to Trixie.

"Are you sure this is what you really want—with Derek?"

"You're worried I'm making the wrong decision?" Zoe frowned.

"Make sure you're not rushing into things, okay? You impulsively kissed him two days ago—on our couch." Trixie pointed into the living room. "And now you're suddenly a couple?"

"We're keeping our relationship a secret until opening night, since he's technically my boss on this show."

"Good idea." She didn't seem convinced.

"Even though we're doing this relationship thing out of order, we'll go on a real date soon. Don't you worry about me." Zoe refused to let Trixie's concerns ruin her mood.

"What about your plans to launch your Viet-inspired fashion collection?"

"Everything is going to plan. The costumes for the musical are inspired by my collection. Once the actors are settled, I'll invite the women to model my sample garments at the opening night reception."

"Are you sure you can manage the costumes and sample pieces in time? That's a lot of work." Trixie's brow knotted in worry.

"I don't have a choice. Derek says they're inviting the who's who of Asian celebrities to opening night."

"Like who?" Trixie dipped a piece of her bagel in her coffee and popped it into her mouth.

"I don't know, but we're dreaming big. Can you imagine Kelly Marie Tran or Stephanie Hsu seeing my designs and asking for custom pieces?" Zoe spun around in a circle as if she were a model at the end of the catwalk.

"What if they could get Michelle Yeoh or Priyanka Chopra?" Trixie hopped off the stool and proceeded to catwalk through their living room. "I can model one of your pieces, too."

Zoe laughed and joined her roommate as they strutted around their living room.

The last two days felt surreal, magical, almost like how the gods guided Tấm to her Emperor. It'd been a long time since Zoe felt so exhilarated about what she was doing. And *who* she was doing. Didn't she deserve some excitement in her life?

CHAPTER 30

Derek practically floated on air during his walk from his apartment to Prestige Rep.

Zoe. Zoe Tran. Her name was an earworm that he never wanted to get rid of. He couldn't have dreamed of a better way for them to reveal their feelings for each other. And this morning was the icing on top, because he'd left a very pleased Zoe in his bed. She'd even praised him for his oral skills.

Finally everything he'd ever wanted was coming to fruition. His design team had nailed his vision, especially Zoe with her costumes. The cast had had great chemistry during the table read and that would only grow as they continued to work together.

Nothing could ruin his mood.

"Oh, what a beautiful morning," he sang as he walked into the rehearsal room, only to find that Thảo had beat him there.

"You're forty-five minutes late, Curly." She pointed to the clock that Heather had hung in the room.

"No, I'm early." Derek checked the Google calendar that the stage manager had shared with everyone. "We're not called until ten today."

"Yes, for rehearsal. But you and I were supposed to meet at nine to finish this last song."

He cringed as he vaguely recalled Thảo's text from yesterday.

"Shit, I'm sorry, but I have a good excuse—"

"No more excuses, Derek. We have to finish writing the scene where Tấm and Cám come together to test the Emperor's love. Not to mention fixing their duet by Monday, when Heather has it scheduled for rehearsal."

"I know. I know. It's a pivotal scene that illustrates how we're diverging from the original fairy tale in order to give the sisters more agency." He repeated their previous discussions about the song.

She crossed her arms in front of her.

"Don't be mad," he begged.

She grunted and turned away from him.

"You're mad."

No response. Boy was she was pissed.

"Can I tell you my good news at least?" he tried changing the subject.

She didn't move.

"I finally told Zoe how I felt and she feels the same way!"

Thảo spun around. Her eyes were wide with shock.

"You're making up things to make me react," she accused.

"Zoe spent the night," he said and added, "but we're not telling anyone yet. I told her you're not anyone."

He returned Thảo's look of disbelief with a huge smile so she knew he was telling the truth.

"You finally did it. And you hooked up? Damn." Thảo sat the piano and played the opening measures of "Oklahoma!" as a recall to his singing from earlier.

"I wouldn't have forgotten otherwise. Sorry," he apologized again.

"You're forgiven." Thảo let out a heavy sigh.

His shoulders dropped with relief. They didn't argue often, but he hated when she was upset with him.

"At least one of us is getting some action." She played a sad melody that he recognized as "She Used to Be Mine" from *Waitress*. Thảo played it only when she was really sad.

"What happened with you and Katie Mai last night?"

"Besides getting too drunk? We talked until dawn." She yawned. "She wants to go to LA to take a shot at film and TV. There are way more opportunities in Hollywood for Asian actors now."

"There's good theater on the West Coast, too. Look at East West Players, the oldest Asian American theater in the U.S." It was on his dream list of places to direct a play.

"That's what she said, too." Thảo chewed on her bottom lip.

"What's the problem then?"

"After what happened with my ex, I vowed to never move to a new city for a partner. I have to want to be there, too."

"Thảo, you know Katie Mai is nothing like your ex."

"I wouldn't be dating her if she was."

Thảo's ex-boyfriend had convinced her to move to New York with him even though she didn't have a job lined up. She'd waited tables while she searched for a theater job. Anything to get into the scene. A month in, her ex announced he hated the city and was moving back home to Illinois. He left her with an apartment they'd barely been able to afford on two incomes.

When she'd come into the diner crying, Derek immediately offered to be her roommate. Couch surfing had gotten old. They still shared an apartment, though their current one allowed them to have their own rooms with a door that shut.

"I told her that I'd think about it, but I could tell she was disappointed by my lack of excitement," Thảo said somberly.

Voices echoing outside the room interrupted them. It was almost time for rehearsal to begin. Thảo glanced at the door and back to Derek.

"Don't say anything to Katie Mai, please. People know we're together, but we're keeping things strictly professional during work hours."

"We always keep each other's secrets," Derek reassured Thảo.

He wondered how Zoe would respond if he asked her to move to New York. But he'd never ask her to choose between him and her career.

"Who's ready to learn some blocking?" called out Heather as she entered the room hugging her three-ring binder. She was the most organized stage manager he'd ever worked with.

A chorus of *Me* and *Hell yeahs* came from the cast as they came in behind her. Walking in after them was a face Derek did not want to deal with this morning.

"Greg, are you joining us today?" Derek tried to ask in an even tone. Whatever happy energy he had remaining after Thảo's conversation had completely disappeared.

"I'm only here to observe. Hands off." He gestured to reiterate his point.

"Of course," Derek demurred and nodded at Heather, who quickly pulled out a chair for Greg.

The artistic director had free reign in his theater, but Derek had hoped Greg wouldn't observe rehearsals until much later during the process, when the cast was off-book and had a better handle on their characters. Derek hoped to foster an atmosphere of their shared experiences as Asian Americans in order to create multilayered characters. That would be much harder to do with Greg sitting in.

With only three weeks before tech rehearsal, Derek didn't have the luxury to veer off schedule. Greg was part of the equation whether he liked it or not.

"THANK YOU, FOLKS. Take ten and we'll regroup for the next number," Heather announced. "Then you get a lunch break!"

The cast cheered with tired enthusiasm. For the past hour and a half, Thảo had pushed them hard to hit their notes and express their emotions while keeping the lyrics as easy to understand as possible.

"You all sound great today," Derek added. "It's hard to believe you've been at this for only two days."

The actors gave him a thumbs-up and murmured thanks. They began shuffling out of the rehearsal studio as Heather reminded them to hydrate.

"Good job, everyone!" Greg called out after them, as if he didn't want to be left out of the conversation.

Thảo rolled her eyes and mouthed Greg's words behind his back. Derek snorted and bit back a laugh.

"Derek, can I have a word?" Greg's eyes darted over to Thảo. "Alone?"

"Sure," Derek agreed reluctantly.

"Be back in a few. Gotta take a bio break," said Thảo, and stuck her tongue out at Derek when Greg was turned away. She fled with the rest of the cast, leaving him alone with his mentor.

"I'm proud of you, Derek."

Greg had said this so often, Derek wasn't sure how much to believe him anymore.

"You were right about keeping Katie Mai as the older sister," Greg continued. "Her voice is stunning. And it makes sense why someone like her would worry about whether the Emperor truly loved her."

Derek gritted his teeth. He thought the issue had been settled yesterday.

"Her body size isn't why I cast her in this role, but I'm glad you can see why she's the best person for it," Derek reminded him in a firm voice.

"Exactly. I have some suggestions if you don't mind." Greg pulled out a small notebook from his shirt pocket.

"Actually I do."

"I wanted to bring it up privately," the artistic director continued, "so I don't undermine you in front of your cast."

"Greg," Derek warned, "I have everything under control."

"Some food for thought." Greg shrugged before flipping to a page and squinting at his notes.

Derek cleared his throat loudly to show his impatience.

"There's a lot of Vietnamese in the show, especially the songs."

"I don't see a problem with that," Derek responded carefully. He and Thảo had worked hard to make sure the Vietnamese dialogue and lyrics could easily be understood through context.

"Have you considered translating it? Add the same lyrics but in English right after so everyone can understand what they're singing?"

Derek's nostrils flared as he attempted to keep his voice under control. "The audience will understand. Didn't you tell me not to underestimate them?"

"I did." Greg beamed. "But people come to the theater to escape, not exercise their brains."

"I disagree. Theater is art and good art encourages the viewer to—"

"When you've been doing this as long as I have, it's all about butts in chairs and ticket sales. People are lazy and don't want to 'figure out' what the actors are saying." Greg used air quotes around *figure out*.

"I'll take that into consideration," Derek lied, hoping Greg would stop there.

He did not.

"Second, why does the Emperor have such a small role? If this is your version of Cinderella, people will want to see him sweep her off her feet." Greg held out his arms to an invisible partner and danced the beginnings of a waltz.

"Because the story isn't about him. *Tấm Cám* is about the love the sisters have for each other."

"Just think about it, okay?" Greg licked his finger and flipped to another page.

Derek's left eye twitched. How many more dumb notes were there?

"I read the script last night and there's two unfinished songs."

"Only one. The other one needs a bit of polish but we're ninety percent there."

"You need to finish both ASAP and send them to me," Greg chided. "We've already sent out the press releases and invited everyone to opening night."

"Thảo and I will work on them this weekend."

Derek didn't point out that writing additional English lyrics for the other songs like Greg suggested would create even more work. That would only make this torturous conversation longer.

"Don't forget you'll make changes to the show as you work with the actors. That's the nature of seeing it onstage versus on paper. You can't—"

"I know," Derek interrupted. "I can't make too many changes or the actors will have a hard time remembering the right lines."

"Good. I've taught you well."

"This isn't the first world premiere production I've directed," Derek said. "I know how new plays can evolve during the rehearsal process."

"Yes, but you're doing double duty as the director and the playwright. The director part of you has to keep a short leash on the playwright."

"Greg, I need you to give me some space if I'm going to do that. You can't show up unannounced to rehearsal."

"Yes, hands off. I remember," said Greg.

But Derek didn't believe him.

"It's better if you wait at least a week before sitting in rehearsal again. Give the cast time to gel and learn the material."

"If that's what you want," the artistic director said sharply, as if Derek had offended him.

"It is," Derek said as he squared his shoulders.

Greg's eyes narrowed as if he debated calling Derek on a bluff.

"I want you to give us a week," he repeated as he crossed his arms over his chest.

"Will do," Greg conceded. "One week."

Greg winked as if there had been no tension between them before leaving Derek alone in the rehearsal studio.

Derek dropped back into the cold, metal folding chair and groaned in frustration. His night—and morning—with Zoe had been one of the best of his life. He assumed everything would fall into place once he'd finally confessed his feelings to her.

So why were the past few hours of his professional life so draining? He'd disappointed Thảo by standing her up this morning. Even though it was an honest mistake, they were on a tight timetable for opening night.

He hated it when Greg was right. Derek grunted, disappointed in himself. Maybe Greg expected Derek to fail so he could have a reason that Prestige Rep shouldn't produce more plays directed by people of color. All so he could have the upper hand and feel good about trying.

Not to mention that Derek would have to work with his best friend turned girlfriend without anyone learning about it. All while mounting the most important show of his life. He took deep breaths to push away the anxiety creeping up his chest.

"It will all work out," Derek said out loud to reassure himself, but the words echoed off the walls, making them sound even more hollow.

CHAPTER 31

Zoe set down her fabric shears and unlocked her phone. But there were no new texts since she'd checked two minutes ago.

"Relax. He hasn't missed a day in the past two weeks," TJ whispered as he brushed past Zoe on his way to the sewing machine. "Don't forget his schedule isn't as flexible since rehearsal started last week."

"What are you talking about?" Zoe feigned ignorance and shoved her phone into the front pocket of her work apron.

"Your lover boy who delivers your afternoon coffee."

"He's not my lov—"

"Then explain why you take private 'meetings' in the fitting room every afternoon at three?" TJ glanced at the clock. "Maybe quarter after, since he's late."

"I'm showing him the costumes in the fitting room. So he can see how they're progressing." She wasn't lying to TJ, only omitting what happened after she updated Derek.

Like yesterday, when Derek had pinned her against the wall as he pleasured her with his hand while his kisses swallowed her cries. Zoe's cheeks weren't the only part of her that blazed with heat.

"You mean those costumes?" TJ pointed to the garments hanging on racks on the far side of the costume shop.

She swallowed hard. She didn't know how much longer she could hide her relationship with Derek from TJ. He was twice as nosy as he was observant.

"Those aren't ready for the actors' fittings yet." Those pieces were only partially constructed because they were working in order of most complicated costume to simplest.

"Liar, liar, pants on fire," TJ accused.

"I'm wearing a skirt," she tossed back. She'd taken to wearing skirts or dresses every day to make her afternoon "meetings" with Derek flow more smoothly.

TJ cocked his head and set his hand on his hip. She returned his stare with a sweet yet mischievous smile.

"I will get the truth out of you." He waved a finger at her.

"The truth about what?" Derek asked as he walked into the shop. He held a cardboard tray with four drinks.

TJ looked at Zoe, then Derek, and back to Zoe. He held two fingers to his eyes before pointing them at Zoe in an *I'm watching you* sign. She laughed nervously. Derek stood in the doorway with a confused expression.

TJ grabbed two coffees from Derek and delivered one to the shop manager, Shawn, who was working in his tiny office with glass windows looking into the costume shop.

"Um, here's your cà phê sữa đá," Derek said tentatively as he passed Zoe her usual order.

"I'm taking my break," TJ announced loudly. "You two better behave."

"What was that about?" Derek asked after TJ left.

"He's just being dramatic." Zoe leaned in closer and whispered, "I think he's on to us."

"How? We've kept our relationship very professional while we're at Prestige."

"I wouldn't call yesterday's two orgasms HR-approved."

"You're right. I think it needs to be a lucky three." He leaned in closer, his voice deepening.

"Well, Mr. Bui, we'll have to test your theory," Zoe replied in an even tone as a shiver ran down her back. She closed her eyes as she recalled the sensations that ran through her body the prior afternoon.

"If you insist," he replied with a gleam in his eyes.

"You didn't text me that you'd be late today." Zoe pouted and hated herself for feeling so dependent on him to brighten her day. She'd been totally fine during the years when they'd grown apart. Or maybe she hadn't been fine but didn't realize it until two weeks ago.

"Sorry." Derek rubbed her back in apology but dropped his hand quickly. "I don't think he saw that."

They both glanced at Shawn, who hadn't budged from his computer. Zoe sighed in relief even though she ached for the warmth of his hand on her back.

"Greg popped into rehearsal after lunch." Derek tucked his hands into his jean pockets as if to keep himself from touching her again.

"Again? How many times has it been this week?"

"Every damned day since rehearsal started two weeks ago."

Zoe grimaced.

"But I didn't come down here to talk about Greg." He pulled his hands out of his pockets and sipped on his coffee. No sugar with a splash of half-and-half if she remembered correctly.

"Oh?" She feigned innocence as she pursed her purple lacquered lips around her straw.

"I'm here for my daily update, obviously," Derek said before lowering his voice to say, "We wouldn't have to make excuses if we went public about our relationship."

"We're having fun aren't we? And the sneaking around with you makes sex even hotter."

He pressed his lips together as if to keep from speaking. They'd been having fun with their afternoon trysts. Until today, he hadn't given any indication that their secrecy bothered him. Then again, they'd barely had time to see each other since he'd confessed his feelings for her. He had a full rehearsal schedule, plus working with Thảo to polish the script and the songs.

"I want to spend time with you outside of this theater. I'm here twelve hours a day and it gets old really fast."

"We agreed on opening night, remember?" she said under her breath. "How about we see who can make the other come first?"

"I'll win. You can never hold out."

"Maybe this time I will."

His eyes darkened with lust.

"Let's make our way to the fitting room so I can share what we've accomplished since yesterday," Zoe said in her normal tone.

"It would be my pleasure." His low growl was an invitation to carnal pleasures.

"Shawn, I'm showing Derek the costumes," Zoe called out.

"If Greg comes looking for me, I'm not here," Derek added.

The shop manager nodded and gave a thumbs-up without looking away from his spreadsheet. Zoe grabbed Derek's hand and dragged him out of the shop and down the hallway.

Once they rounded the corner out of earshot, Derek stopped her and gently pushed her against the cold concrete wall of the basement hallway. He looked deep into her eyes as their breaths mingled. Zoe's body, now primed for his touch every afternoon, had gone hot with arousal.

"I'm sorry I didn't text you that I'd be late," he whispered into the space between their lips.

"All forgiven because you're here now."

Her lips tingled in anticipation of his kiss. She tilted her head back to close the gap between them, but Derek only caressed her collarbone.

Before she could protest, he pulled back her hair and pressed his mouth to the sensitive skin on her chest. She'd never thought of the collarbone as a source of pleasure, but her mouth fell open as he dotted it with kisses, each one making her temperature rise.

"How can I make it up to you?" he asked, nibbling her earlobe as his hands explored the curve of her hips.

Zoe moaned. Even after a week of them sneaking around, she was still amazed by how easily he stoked her desire. She'd long accepted that desire would be elusive since realizing her demisexuality. Yet all it'd taken was her best friend—now lover—to wake up her body with a glance or a whisper.

"You can start with a kiss," she grumbled playfully and turned his chin until he faced her again.

His eyes glinted mischievously in the shadowy hallway. He smiled before paying homage to her neck, teasing her with light bites and kisses. Zoe leaned to the side and arched into his body as she wrapped her leg around his and pulled him even closer to her. She gasped as his stiff cock pressed against her belly.

"That's not what I meant," she explained in between the aftershocks that his lips and teeth created in her body.

"Tell me."

"My lips, you jerk." She laughed as she lightly hit his arm.

Derek grinned with no hint of guilt on his face about teasing her.

"I fucking love your lips," he growled, running his thumb over her bottom lip. "It took all my willpower not to throw you across that table and flip up your skirt."

"The cutting table is too high for you to lift up a woman of my size—"

"I've been working out. Maybe we should test it after-hours when no one's around."

Zoe laughed. No one she'd ever dated had attempted to pick her up, but even the thought of Derek's strong arms lifting her up for *that*, well, her entire body blazed.

"Where was I? Oh yes, your soft lips," said Derek.

"Derek, please, kiss me—now."

"I'll never get tired of hearing you beg."

Finaly his mouth covered hers as he kissed her so deeply that she wanted—no, needed—him even closer. For their bodies to join so they could be connected physically as well as emotionally.

Zoe fisted his shirt but fought the urge to rip his clothes off. With her leg still hooked around his thigh, she wrapped her other arm around his neck and reveled in the feel of his mouth on hers.

"I'm sorry I've been working so much," he apologized hastily in between their gasps for air.

"Your work is going to change the world." She accepted his apology by closing the almost imperceptible gap they needed to speak. She kissed him hard and so deeply that she couldn't remember where his lips ended and hers began.

Zoe needed Derek in her life. Not just because he made her body shudder with pleasure, but because she loved the way he made her laugh. His ambition and the way he saw the best in her always.

She loved him as a friend. A lover. Maybe even as a life partner.

She loved Derek.

Zoe shuddered as the realization struck her. Interpreting her reaction as arousal, he grunted and cupped her ass to pull her impossibly closer to his body.

"Let's move this to the dressing room," he suggested.

"Yes, perhaps you should get a room." A stern male voice broke through their reverie.

Zoe's eyes flew open.

"Greg!"

CHAPTER 32

"Fuck," Derek cursed under his breath.

Of all the people to walk in on them, it had to be Greg. The silver lining was that neither of them had ripped each other's clothes off, which would've been even more embarrassing. Though he might have if they had stayed in the hallway.

His heart pounded as he gently extricated himself from Zoe. She quickly straightened her clothes and Derek was glad he'd worn his shirt untucked today. He'd already looked disheveled before this. Hopefully his shirt and the flickering fluorescent lights hid the bulge in his jeans.

"Good afternoon, Greg," he acknowledged the man with as much calm as he could to down play their in flagrante situation. "Did you need something from me?"

"So this is why you've been so hard to find in the afternoon." Greg ignored his question.

"You're keeping tabs on me now?" Derek clenched his jaw. He wished for just one day without seeing or talking to the man.

"Maybe I should've been." Greg's eyes darted to Zoe, who was standing against the wall.

"I can explain," Derek added hastily, though he wasn't sure how he could.

"No need," Greg replied, still staring at Zoe. "Now I understand why Derek was so adamant about hiring you."

"What are you implying?" Zoe snapped back. Her fists were in tight balls by her side, as if she were ready to knock him out.

"We're all adults here. You know exactly what I mean." Greg took a step forward.

Derek sidestepped and put himself between his mentor and Zoe. He was unsure who he was protecting. If fists were thrown, he was 100 percent sure that Greg would be flat on his back.

Greg stopped and studied both of them, his eyes narrowing. Derek's shallow breaths were loud in his ears as they all stared at one another, waiting for something to happen. This was it. Greg would fire him and take over the show himself.

Finally the blond man's thin lips turned into a creepy smile.

"We all have our weaknesses," he said, looking directly at Derek. "But you need to exercise discretion. I used to be young once. Being the artistic director has its perks, you know." Greg winked as if welcoming Derek into some sleazy boy's club.

Derek's jaw dropped but he quickly clamped it shut. Behind him, Zoe snorted.

"You approve?" Derek asked cautiously as he processed Greg's words. Whatever the fuck this club was, he didn't want any part in it.

"We're not in theater to get rich. You might as well enjoy pursuing your passions wherever you can." Greg looked pointedly at Zoe.

Derek's fingers curled up into a fist. How dare he speak as if Zoe were his plaything?

"Don't talk about me like I'm not here." Zoe's voice shook with anger as she stepped out from behind Derek. "I'm here because of my costume designs, not because you think I slept my way—"

"Zoe, it's no use," Derek said with false calm when what he really wanted to do was punch the man in the face.

Instead he grabbed her hand, but she ripped out of his grasp and backed away from him. Her face was flushed and bore an expression of betrayal. Derek tried to plead with her through his eyes and explain to her that Greg wouldn't listen to reason, but she refused to look at him.

"Oh dear, is this your first lovers' quarrel?" Greg frowned and there was genuine sympathy in his tone.

Derek pressed his lips together, refusing to dignify his question with a response.

"Our discussion can wait until later. Come see me once you're done here." Greg clapped Derek's shoulder approvingly, like a father to a son.

Greg didn't even look at Zoe before turning around and taking the back stairwell, which was rarely used by anyone. Except for his mentor apparently.

"What the fuck was that?" The anger spewed out of Zoe's mouth. "How dare he insinuate that I only got this job because I slept with you!"

"Just when you think you know someone," Derek muttered, still in shock over Greg's approval of what he considered a notch in Derek's bedpost.

"Why didn't you say something? To defend me?"

"There wasn't a point to it." Derek shook his head.

"This is exactly what I was worried about. Warned you about." Zoe paced the hallway. "He thinks you hired me so we can fuck every afternoon. Like I'm only here to service you."

"You are pretty hot. Though I'm sure it was me servicing you yesterday."

She stopped mid-step and spun around to face him.

"Derek," she warned. "This is serious."

"You got this gig because of your talent. Anyone who's seen your designs and your costumes knows that," he reminded her.

"Except Greg."

"We can explain it to him until we're blue in the face, but he'll continue to believe what he wants."

Zoe pursed her lips together. Her eyes shone. Were those tears?

"Z." He rushed over to her. "I'm sorry I didn't push back harder. I was still in shock."

She crossed her arms and blinked quickly.

"Let me make it up to you? I'll come over and bring dinner. Plus some tuna in water for Mr. Bobbins." He reached for her hand again. This time she didn't pull away.

"I thought you were scared of him," she said quietly without looking at him.

"How can a little kitty scare me?" Derek lied as he puffed up his chest and placed his free hand on his hip in a superhero pose.

Derek was still scared of the damned cat. That thing hated him, which was why he'd convinced Zoe to spend the night at his apartment every night for the past ten days. It'd been under the guise of how his apartment was only a few blocks away so why fight traffic to Falls Church when they were both so tired?

Zoe gave a weak laugh. He sighed with relief. Maybe this meant she was no longer mad. He hated seeing her unhappy, especially if he was the reason for it.

"Maybe I'll wear flip-flops tonight," he half-joked.

"But you hate flip-flops."

"I don't wear them in New York, but I'll do it for you." He'd made that mistake only once in his first month in the city and ended up stepping in a questionable liquid when someone's book bag whacked him in the back.

Her eyes narrowed in skepticism.

"Fine. Flip-flops are self-defense so I can keep my Chucks safe from any further vandalism," he admitted.

"He's only a cat, Derek. He didn't do it on purpose." Zoe rubbed her thumb on the inside of his palm as if to comfort him.

"You say that but I know how he looked at me." He shuddered dramatically.

Her laughter was music to his ears. He slipped his arm around her waist and pulled her to him until their foreheads touched. When she finally looked him in the eyes, he smiled.

"Everything will be okay. Do you believe me?" he asked.

His head bobbed with hers as she nodded. For as long as he'd known her, Zoe had exuded strength and confidence, but now there was worry in her eyes.

He kissed her gently, as if she might break. Her breath faltered at first but she returned his kiss. She'd put her faith in him and his vision when she agreed to work on the musical. If she broke down like she had in college, it'd be his fault and not their professor's. He would never let things get that bad. This was their dream production.

"I won't let anything bad happen to you while I'm at Prestige. I promise."

It was a promise to himself as much as it was to her.

CHAPTER 33

"A re you sure you don't want me to wait until Derek gets here?" Trixie asked Zoe for the second time.

Zoe reconsidered her roommate's offer after she recounted how awful Greg had been earlier that afternoon. When she'd gotten home, Zoe had taken a long shower to wash off the disgust that Greg had left on her. She felt much better in her cozy tunic and leggings as she stroked Mr. Bobbins, who was purring contentedly in her lap.

"No, you've done enough by taking care of my little floof ball the past week." Zoe kissed the cat's head. "You and Andre need time together."

"I'm prepared to go mama bear on him for not defending you to Craig." Luckily Trixie hadn't had much interaction with the artistic director in her role as the show's intimacy coordinator.

"Greg. His name is Gregory A. Powers." Zoe laughed.

"Whatever." Trixie rolled her eyes. "Does the 'A' stand for Asshole?"

"Honestly I have no idea what it stands for but it fits." Zoe snorted.

The two women giggled and soon it turned into guffaws. Zoe's chest shook from laughter, which also jostled the cat. Mr. Bobbins, unfazed by their outburst, yawned before curling back into a donut. He'd lived with them long enough to recognize their moods. Currently there wasn't any cause for concern.

"My stomach hurts," Zoe finally said after she caught her breath. "It feels good to let it all out. The last few weeks have been intense."

"Stressful. You're allowed to say it," Trixie pointed out.

"Dealing with Greg has been more challenging than my worst bridal clients," Zoe admitted.

"Should we call him Gregzilla?" Trixie asked.

"What if I accidentally call him that to his face. Better not." Zoe shuddered.

"Don't forget he's technically not your boss. Derek is," Trixie reminded her.

"Greg is technically within his rights to offer feedback. The issue is, he has no idea how problematic some of it is."

"Ugh, that's the worst. I guess I've been lucky that we haven't had much interaction."

"How's the intimacy coordinating going?" Zoe asked. This was the first time she'd spent the night at their apartment since she'd started seeing Derek. They hadn't been able to really talk outside of the Boss Babes' group texts.

"It's been a learning experience, but Katie Mai and Danny have been very involved in the choreography of their love scenes. Unlike the western Cinderella, we get to see what happens after the happily ever after." Trixie laughed.

"Our version is definitely more interesting," Zoe agreed. "It's so romantic how the Emperor continues to love Tấm even though she transforms into a tree, a bird, and a persimmon."

"Your turn," said Trixie. "How are you dealing with all of it? Creating gorgeous costumes and secretly dating your best friend while running Something Cheeky?"

"I'm barely keeping my head above water." Zoe sighed. "Maybe I should've let the past stay in the past."

"You're having regrets about Derek?" Trixie sat down on the couch and rubbed Zoe's shoulder. "People mess up. I know he didn't stand up for you this afternoon, but you said he'd defended you to Gregzilla before."

"He has." Zoe smiled as she recalled their meeting in Greg's office. "By the past, I meant working in theater again."

"We're over halfway done, aren't we? The show goes into tech in ten days."

"There's still so much to do. We've got the base pieces finished, but it's all the decorations and embellishments. Detail work takes forever. Plus the headdresses. I want everything to be perfect to prove Greg wrong."

"Motivation à la spite. I'm familiar with that feeling." Trixie tilted her head as she studied Zoe. "There's more."

"I wanted to launch my formal-wear collection this fall, but I have to push it to next year. I've been too consumed by the musical—and Derek—that I'm not even close to creating a cohesive collection."

"You're worried about something else."

"I've put everything on pause for this musical. What if the audience doesn't get my costumes or, worse, the show flops?" Zoe's heart pounded and the room began to shrink around her.

Mr. Bobbins mewed and licked her hand as if sensing her anxiety. He nudged her hand with his nose as if commanding her to keep petting him. She obliged, taking deep breaths as she focused on his soft fur under her fingertips.

"Zoe, I've never seen you this hyped about lingerie or a custom áo dài. You would've kicked yourself for turning it down."

Zoe bit her lip and nodded. Her best friend was right, yet she couldn't shake the doubts swirling in her head. Was this a second chance at an old dream or was she piggybacking off of Derek's vision? She was no longer the young, naive person in college who thought she could change the theater world.

She'd learned the hard way that she couldn't fight back when the villain was a tenured college professor in a small college town.

So why did she think she could do it when she went to New York to pursue her costume design career?

Instead, she'd come home, where she'd made her own damn chair at her own table by opening Something Cheeky. She'd betrayed her shop and her customers by pushing it aside to do this musical.

"If you need, I'll come into the costume shop and hand-sew things. And you know Josie, Reina, and Keisha will help, too. Hell, Reina can get her burlesque guys. They make a lot of their costumes."

"We'd never get anything done except gossip!" Zoe joked. The image of the Boss Babes hunched over costumes and sewing machines together made her smile. Slowly the room returned back to its normal size.

"Nah, Josie would make sure we got work done."

"She'd have to-do lists broken down by tasks and how long they'd take to get done." Zoe hugged Mr. Bobbins. The mother hen of their group was known for her checklists.

"Thanks for making me feel better, Trixie."

"I mean it about coming in to help," she reassured Zoe.

"According to Shawn, our extremely organized shop manager, we're on track. And he hired two additional stitchers who are precise and fast. I might have to ask if they're looking for extra work when we need backup for our busy season."

"See? You're still planning for the future." Trixie leaned over to give Zoe and Mr. Bobbins a hug.

"I'll see things better once the show opens." Zoe hadn't allowed herself to plan past this show but there was a glimmer of something across the finish line.

"Now, one more time, do you want me to stay till Derek gets here? Because I'll glare at him or give him a stern talking to." Trixie put one hand on her hip and shook a finger dramatically.

Before Zoe could respond, a loud knock landed on their front door. Mr. Bobbins's ears perked up and his body tensed at the sound. Zoe made comforting sounds as she rubbed his chin until his tail stopped twitching.

"Can you let Derek in on your way out?" Zoe wasn't ready to kick the cat off her lap. They'd missed each other terribly and she wanted as many cuddles as he was willing to allow.

Trixie slung her overnight bag on her shoulder before making her way to the door.

"And be nice," Zoe whispered. "I've got everything under control."

"One text and I'll drop everything. Andre will understand."

"I've kept you away from him for too many nights now. You need a break from cat sitting." Zoe motioned for her to go. "You two enjoy yourselves."

"I've got some new toys to test out." She grinned and patted her bag before swinging the door open to reveal Derek, who was holding at least six plastic bags presumably filled with take out.

"Hi, Derek!" Trixie said a little too brightly. "Need a hand with those bags?"

"I'm good. I've Tetris'd the hell out of them because I wanted to make only one trip. One bad move and the crispy lechón skin will tumble out of its tinfoil sleeping bag." He nodded to indicate one of the bags in his left hand.

Trixie dramatically stepped back and waved at their kitchen counter.

Derek nodded at her roommate and stepped inside, kicking off his flip-flops.

"Where did you even get flip-flops?" Zoe asked in surprise.

"Thảo lent me hers, in case you can't tell by the floral print on them." He briefly pointed at them with his left foot before setting the bags of food on the counter.

"Please tell me you're buying her a new pair after stretching them out with your big feet," said Zoe.

"I'll buy her as many as she wants," he replied before turning to Trixie. "Are you staying for dinner? There's plenty to share."

"As delicious as that sounds, I have a hot date with my boyfriend, who's a professional chef."

"That sounds fun," Derek said, his fingers still tangled in the bag handles.

Trixie walked over to help him since Zoe was still trapped under Mr. Bobbins.

"These things are like those stupid Chinese finger cuffs," Derek grumbled. "Why are they even called that? Gotta have racist origins."

"Look, theater boy," Trixie said, glaring at Derek. "If you hurt Zoe in any way, you had it coming."

Derek laughed but his face paled when Trixie didn't join him.

"Uh, I don't plan on running into your knife," he joked nervously.

"Ten times," Trixie deadpanned.

"Trixie, stop it. You're not a murderess and this isn't 'Cell Block Tango,'" Zoe said, trying to keep a straight face.

"What kind of best friend would I be if I didn't threaten him at least once?" Trixie shrugged and smirked.

Derek laughed nervously as he squeezed past Trixie to set the bags down in the kitchen.

"Don't wait up for me," Trixie sang as she shut the door behind her. They heard her laughter through the door as it echoed down the hallway.

"I had no idea Trixie could be so intense. Will your other friends threaten to stab or poison me, too?"

"I can't say," Zoe replied honestly. "We Boss Babes are very protective of one another."

"They sound like wonderful friends. I hope to meet the rest of them soon."

"You will on opening night."

"Perfect. I can hide behind you all when the board comes looking for me. I hate schmoozing."

"They'll love you. Whenever you talk to people, you make them feel as if they're the only ones in the room," Zoe said quietly. "You make them feel important."

"Are we still talking about the board?"

Embarrassed, she shook her head. After Greg had caught them making out like teenagers, she thought it'd been a mistake to take her friendship with Derek to the next level. But when they were alone together, he made her feel safe and loved.

Derek set everything down and sat down next to her to hold her hand. The corners of his eyes crinkled as he smiled. Those deep brown irises never strayed from her.

"You're the most important person in my life. Except for my mom," he added.

"Is she coming to opening night?" Zoe asked, relieved to move the conversation away from herself. She wouldn't have to deal with her conflicting feelings about their relationship.

"I bought her a nonrefundable ticket hoping her frugality guilts her into coming."

"Ooh, you know how our moms hate wasting money."

"Fingers crossed. She'll be more excited to learn that we're dating than seeing my bastardization of *Tấm Cám*."

"Retelling," she corrected him. She hadn't realized how stressed he'd been about his mom. "Even if she doesn't like it, she'll be proud that you're telling our stories."

"I hope so." He placed a hand out for Mr. Bobbins to sniff. "I almost forgot, I brought tuna for Mr. B."

"Mr. B?"

"A cool cat needs a cool name. Right, Mr. B?" He scratched the cat's chin.

The orange tabby meowed as if in agreement. Zoe gasped in joyful surprise.

"Now how about that tuna, Mr. B?"

Mr. Bobbins's ears perked up at the magic word. He stood up and arched his back into a big stretch before hopping off Zoe's lap. He nudged Derek's leg and trotted to the kitchen.

"He approves." Derek grinned and rubbed his hands together gleefully. "Let's get you some tuna with *water*."

Finally, her two men were getting along. If Mr. Bobbins could let go of the past, so could she. Dealing with Greg was already hard enough but to be surprised the way they'd been? Derek had done his best to handle the situation.

It was best to focus on the present. Zoe told herself not to worry about their future until after opening night.

CHAPTER 34

I can't believe I ate so much." Derek patted his stomach and groaned. "This is the second-best meal I've had since in DC. Your mom's is the best."

"Maybe we'll get a Filipino restaurant at Eden Center one day," Zoe said wistfully. "There's still a couple of vacant storefronts."

"When was the last time you were at your boutique?" he asked suddenly.

Derek had been so engrossed in rehearsals that he hadn't checked in with her about her business. They spent most of their off hours discussing the musical or naked in bed. Sometimes both at the same time.

Zoe squinted as her lips silently counted the days. "Last Sunday night so I could finalize payroll for my staff."

"You miss it?"

"A little. I have a great manager who's taking care of everything while I'm at Prestige."

"Of course you have everything under control. You basically ran our college costume shop whenever you were working on a production."

"That was different. We were running on naivete and cold pizza," she reminded him.

"Don't forget the late-night energy drinks."

"How did we ever drink that syrupy stuff?" Zoe shuddered as her face scrunched up in disgust.

"Says the lady who dumps a cup of sugar into her coffee."

She giggled. How he loved that sound. If his only job in the world was to make her laugh every day, he'd die a happy man.

"Something Cheeky is different because there's more balls to juggle. There's staffing, inventory management, marketing—and I have to work on next season's designs in advance so my sewists can make them."

"And I gave you one more," he said with a twinge of guilt in his voice. "I had no clue it took so much to run a boutique. I'm glad you agreed."

Zoe frowned instead of agreeing with him. Did she regret accepting the gig? Maybe that was why she'd been quiet most of the evening. He'd chalked it up to general tiredness after their long days.

"Did you talk to Greg after he found us together?" she blurted. The slight relief in her expression meant that she'd held in the question all night.

Derek nodded. His light mood vanished. He'd avoided the topic because Zoe wouldn't be happy about it.

"What did Gregzilla say?"

"Did you say Gregzilla?" Derek cocked his head but he couldn't help but smile. His mentor had many similarities to a self-obsessed, micromanaging bride-to-be.

"All the credit goes to Trixie." Zoe smirked.

He chuckled. Trixie was a firecracker. But he supposed she had to be in order to be a sex educator and the show's intimacy coordinator. There was no way he'd be able to stand in front of people and talk about vibrators and lube.

Zoe poked his arm and waved her hand for him to continue.

"I went to his office after rehearsal. It was the strangest conversation I've ever had with him." He'd replayed it several times on the drive to Zoe's, trying to figure out if he could've steered the conversation differently.

"Did he imply again that I'd gotten this job by sleeping with the director?"

"No. Yes. I mean." Derek clamped his mouth shut. He was doing this all wrong, but Greg's reaction had confused him.

"Tell me."

"He invited me into his office and poured me a glass of fifteen-year-old Macallan," he said quietly.

That glass of whisky in a crystal highball was etched in his brain cells. Greg had planned the entire disgusting conversation before Derek set foot into that office.

"Are you kidding me?" Zoe sat up straight. Her nostrils flared. "So now you're part of Greg's little old boys' club."

"It doesn't matter what he says, okay?" he snapped. "Sorry."

Derek reached for her hand. She didn't pull away from his touch like she had this afternoon. Her eyes were fiery with rage. Her lips were pressed together as if she were holding back a string of curses.

"Fuck Greg and what he thinks about us," he blurted.

Zoe raised an eyebrow at the anger in his words but she waited for him to continue.

"He's part of an older generation who can't see that theater needs to evolve to stay alive," Derek said, more as a reminder to himself than to Zoe.

"I'm having déjà vu." She crossed her arms.

"This is not like what happened to you in college."

"You said the same thing about Professor Richards when he asked me to do yellow face for his fundraiser."

"Look, men like him and Greg know they're becoming irrelevant and finally retiring."

"Greg's retiring?"

"In a few years, he told me." Derek didn't tell her how his mentor had dangled the artistic director position as—what—a bribe, motivation? He wasn't sure. "But until then, we need to get ahead of him."

"How?"

"We go public. About us." He smiled hopefully.

"No," she said flatly and crossed her arms.

"You didn't even think about it." Derek's lips turned down into a frown.

"If we do this because of him, he'll have won."

"He wouldn't be winning. It's about what's best for us and the production." Derek didn't point out that the reason she'd wanted to keep things secret was *because* of his mentor.

"He's going to use our relationship as a leveraging point to get what he wants on this show." Derek's head started to ache at the "feedback" Greg would offer for the next few weeks.

"You waited until I was in a Filipino food coma before dropping this on me so I wouldn't be as mad," she accused.

"It didn't work." Derek shrugged. "Besides, my mom would smack me if I let this food go to waste."

Her lips quirked, but she didn't respond to the frugal practicality that his mother had ingrained in him. She had every right to be upset about how Derek had handled the situation earlier. But they needed to revisit their decision to wait until opening night to tell everyone about their relationship—before Greg did something even more idiotic.

He nudged her arms until her shoulders relaxed. He uncrossed her arms, taking her hands in his.

"Men like him thrive on power—or perceived power." He intertwined his fingers through hers. "If we tell people, he'll no longer have that power over me. Over us."

Zoe bit her lip as she considered his suggestion. Her eyes were dark and slightly unfocused, as if she were recalling how she'd stood up to their professor. And how he couldn't—didn't—stand up with her.

Derek's stomach twisted. That was his second biggest regret from college. The first had been waiting ten years to tell her how he felt about her.

"Can I think about it?" she finally asked.

"I've waited this long for you, so take the time that you need." Derek's easy smile hid his guilt about college. This time would be different. He'd support her 100 percent however she needed.

"Thanks for understanding," she said quietly.

"Is there something I can do to convince you?" He closed the distance between them. She smelled of coffee and lechón. Absolutely fucking delectable.

"What did you have in mind?" she said with feigned innocence, but her eyes lit up.

He brushed her hair aside and caressed the soft curve of her neck. She inhaled sharply. He still couldn't get over the fact that a simple touch from him lit a spark in her.

"Maybe we can finish christening your couch."

Zoe's cheeks reddened. "Oh God, that was so embarrassing. I can't believe I freaked out like that."

"How about we make some new memories here then?"

"Like watching a movie?" Zoe teased as she reached for the television remote.

"Nope." He kicked the remote out of her reach.

Zoe gasped. "Did you just kick—"

She squealed as he pushed her onto her back. Zoe tried to sit back up but he grabbed her forearms and pressed them against the couch. Her fists were still clenched but her body relaxed into his hold. Her eyes were wide and willing.

"The best part about a fight is the make-up sex," he said in a low voice.

Zoe's eyes fluttered.

"I like this part," she whispered as her fists uncurled.

He kissed the swell of her breasts as they rose and fell with the rhythm of her breath that he'd learned to associate with her arousal. A flush grew on her neck and spread to her face as he pressed his lips on every bare inch of her chest and neck.

"Derek, kiss me," she begged. She made a half-hearted attempt to pull her arm out of his grasp but he held firm. "Please."

Her wide eyes implored him. Her lips parted as her pink tongue darted out.

"You're fucking beautiful," he exclaimed before he claimed her lips.

Her head rose up to meet him. Her lips were hot and hungry and—everything he needed. During rehearsal, he was the person everyone came to for decisions. They asked so much of him that he'd barely found time to think.

Tonight he was the one who needed—what? To feel in control of his life when everything else was spinning faster and faster around him.

"Zoe, I need you," he growled.

She parted her lips in invitation for him to deepen their kiss. Her mouth was hot and soft and tasted of sweetness and coffee.

"I'm all yours," she said between their kisses.

Zoe had spent every night since the meet and greet in his apartment, where they spent half the night naked and intertwined. In his bed, he'd been happy to let her lead their lovemaking. But tonight, something had changed.

He groaned against her mouth as heat flooded his body. His cock grew hard and insistent for her body. Not yet. He needed to feel her, skin to skin.

Derek released her arms so he could pull off her tunic. She

didn't have on a bra. Her light brown nipples peaked, as if commanding him to—

"Glorious," he breathed before taking one of them in his mouth.

He was rewarded with a moan as Zoe's body arched to meet his lips. Derek rolled her other nipple between his fingers, feeling her body shudder as he increased the pressure on both. One with his mouth and the other with his fingers.

She reached down and slipped her hand under the waistband of her leggings to pull them off, but he stopped her.

"You're impatient tonight," he teased as he pulled her hands away in order to peel off the damned leggings himself. She lifted her hips to help him.

"So what?" she retorted as she reached for the hem of his T-shirt. "A woman can't want to feel her man's cock inside her?"

Suddenly his jeans were too tight. He wanted to rip off the leggings and sink his dick deep into her wet, tight—he closed his eyes and bit his lip. He took deep breaths until his head—the one up top—was in control.

No, not yet. Tonight he wanted to be a little selfish and in control. He wanted to kiss and caress every inch of her body and make her beg to come. That was what he wanted. What he needed.

"How about a game?" he suggested before taking the other breast in his mouth. He swirled his tongue in tight then wide circles around her nipple.

"Right now?" she squeaked. Another moan escaped her lips as she held his head against her chest.

He pulled away to take in her flushed cheeks and half-lidded eyes. Her lips were swollen and slightly parted. For a moment he imagined those lips wrapped around his—wait. He wanted to focus on her pleasure first.

"Do you still remember how you tried to teach me Vietnamese using bad pick-up lines?" He grinned.

"Are you freaking serious right now?" This time her groan was one of frustration.

"For each line you complete, I'll give you what you want."

"That's easy enough," she said confidently. Her competitive streak was so hot.

"Don't be so sure." He nudged her knees open and slid down. The scent of her arousal almost drove him mad, but he'd challenged her and Zoe never backed down from a challenge. He licked the seam of her outer lips.

"Oh, fuck," she growled.

"I'm pretty sure that's not a pick-up line."

"Jerk." Her tone was playful not angry.

"Let's start easy. Is your last name Nguyen?"

"Because the two of us . . ."

He dragged his tongue up and dove into her until he found her clit.

"Would be a Nguyen Nguyen," Zoe cried out.

"Good girl." He drew the letters of his praise words around her clit until she was gasping to catch her breath.

Derek pulled away slightly to ask, "Do you like phở?"

"Cause I think about you twenty-phở seven." She rolled her eyes. "I'd forgotten how cheesy—"

Keeping his eyes on her face, he pressed the flat of his tongue against her. Now she had a better reason for her eyes to roll back.

"You're so good at this." He rubbed circles around her clit as he tried to remember another one. "It's always bò kho and thịt kho but . . ."

Zoe's eyes were half-closed as she became lost in his touch. He pulled away to encourage her to finish the line.

"But," she said breathlessly, "but when are you gonna kho me yours?"

"Fuck, you're making me so hungry," he growled as he covered her clit with his mouth and sucked.

Zoe moaned and writhed under him. Seeing her fall apart under him was so fucking sexy.

"Derek," she gasped. "I'm going to come."

"One more and you get an A-plus. Are you bún bò huế?" He slipped two fingers inside her. Fuck. She was so wet, so soft. He wasn't sure how much longer he could wait—

"Cause I'm about to come your way," Zoe screamed. Her muscles clenched around his fingers as her orgasm began.

"Yes, baby. Come for me." He took her clit back in his mouth and stroked it with his tongue.

Zoe bucked against him. She wrapped her legs around his head, riding his hand and his mouth. Her moans grew deeper and deeper until they were guttural. Animalistic.

Yes. This was what he needed. To taste her and feel her pleasure as she gasped for air. Her entire body tensed, pulling him deeper into her. His tongue continued against her hard clit.

"Fuck." The way she drew out the word meant she was almost there.

He couldn't see her face but he felt every muscle in her body release as her orgasm overtook her. Gently he straightened her legs and stood up long enough to strip off his clothes. He grabbed a condom from his wallet and slipped it on.

"Don't stop, Z. You're so beautiful," he said as he kneeled between her legs.

She mumbled incoherently but lifted her hips for him. She was so wet from her orgasm that it took no effort to bury himself deep inside her. He groaned as he stilled her to keep things from ending too soon.

"Is this what you want?"

"Yes," she repeated in between breaths. "Yes. Fuck me, please."

She ground her hips, pushing him even deeper.

All the willpower he'd had vanished. He grabbed her hips and did as she requested. This wasn't just what he wanted or needed. It was what the woman he loved wanted. It didn't matter that she wasn't ready to go public about their relationship.

What mattered was that she wanted him. She *needed* him.

"Again," she panted. "Make me come again."

And dammit, he'd give her everything in the world was his last thought as they both exploded in pleasure.

CHAPTER 35

"Derek," Zoe whispered as she tapped his chest softly.

His eyelids fluttered but his eyes moved as if he were dreaming. A leg twitch jostled Mr. Bobbins, who was in bed with them. He mewed in protest.

Derek had helped her off the couch last night so they could cuddle more comfortably in her queen-size bed. Which felt a little too small with two adults and an orange tabby. A sliver of sunlight slipped through the curtains of her bedroom window and bathed his bare chest.

"It's morning," she said instead of kissing him where his skin glowed golden with the sun.

She should let him sleep. Stillness was rare for Derek even while asleep. This was the most relaxed he'd been since coming to DC. She'd peeked in on rehearsal, where he'd been on his feet the entire time as he observed the cast from different vantage points. He was dedicated to his craft and his audience's experiences the same way she was passionate about her customer's fit and confidence.

He needed the rest. Even when they were alone together, he jumped up to do anything and everything for her. Grab a fabric swatch, bring her coffee, and fuck her silly on her couch. He'd put her first almost always.

She'd sensed a deep longing in him yesterday. Maybe she'd been unfair in her wish to keep their relationship a secret. He'd supported her even though he disagreed. Derek had spent more time than necessary helping her present her designs.

It was her turn to support him. He'd asked for only two things since he came to the DMV: for her to design the costumes and to share with the world how happy she made him. How could she deny him that?

"Let's get some breakfast. I'm hungry." She danced her fingers on his chest before stroking his cheek.

He murmured incomprehensibly and turned into her touch. His lips curved into a smile but his eyes remained closed.

Derek was right. Who cared what Greg thought? He was a sad man who was afraid of being left behind. Which would happen once people saw this production. Trixie and Thảo already knew about their relationship and TJ had pretty much figured them out.

She was ready to tell everyone how much she loved this man. Her best friend. Her lover.

If only he'd wake up so she could say all these things to him.

"Derek," she said at her normal volume. "Open your eyes. I have something to tell you."

She kissed his shoulder and ran her thumb over his lips. Slowly, he blinked his eyes open.

"Hi, beautiful," he said with a wide, sleepy smile. "What time is it?"

"Eight in the morning, but don't move."

"Huh?" His arm stopped in midair as he reached for her.

"Mr. Bobbins is sleeping between your legs."

"That's why I can't move them."

"There's more."

He squinted and lifted his head to look at his legs.

"His head is on my balls!"

Zoe bit her lip to keep from laughing.

"Is he going to attack me if I move him? What if he attacks my—"

"Shhh, it's okay." She giggled. "You're the first guy to spend the night, but I think he likes you."

"So he holds my junk hostage?" Derek dropped his head back to the pillow. "Dammit, Mr. B, stop purring!"

"You're being dramatic," she teased. "He'll get up once I open a can of tuna."

Derek closed his eyes and scrunched his face as if he were in pain. His neck and face were beet red.

"Are you hurt?" She looked under the sheet. "Please tell me that's morning wood and not because of the cat."

"Go open the tuna," he said through gritted teeth. "Please."

Zoe pressed her lips together to hold back her laughter but her shoulders still shook.

"I cannot believe my girlfriend will not move her cat off my dick. Which is one of your favorite parts of my body." He enunciated each word firmly.

"You know the rule. If a cat sits on you, you can't move until he does."

"Zoe," he half-whined. "I have to go to the bathroom and you're laughing at my pain."

"Sorry," she squeaked before breaking into peals of laughter.

Mr. Bobbins glared at her for waking him up. She mouthed an apology to the furball. Tired of their antics, the cat hopped off the bed and left the room. Derek threw off the covers and made a dash to the bathroom. He also gave her a very lovely view of his bare ass.

Maybe they should stay in bed and make it a lazy Saturday. Neither of them had taken a full day off in over two weeks. She wouldn't mind curling up in bed with him and watching a costume drama.

"Hurry up! The bed is getting cold," she called out to Derek.

She heard a muffled ring tone coming from the living room. It was her mother! She threw on a plush chenille robe—her design of course—and followed the sound of her phone. By the time she'd located it under the couch, the call had gone to voicemail.

"Six missed calls?" she read aloud. "From the restaurant. Má is never there so early on Saturdays."

Zoe hit the button for Phở-Ever 75, but it rang and rang. Something was wrong. She fumbled through her favorites list and called her mother's cell phone.

"Zoe." Her mom stretched out the end of her name in a worried tone. "Come to Eden Center right away."

"Do I hear sirens?" She couldn't hide the panic from her voice. "Má, are you okay? Are you hurt? Is it Ba?"

"Someone spray-painted terrible things all over Eden Center. They are so bad." Her mom started crying.

Her mother only cried during romance movies.

"I'm coming. I'll be there as fast as I can."

"Okay, con, be careful." Her mother hung up.

Zoe had never heard her strong mother so upset. So scared. She texted her brother.

> **Zoe:** What's going on? Má called but she's freaked out.

She stared at the moving dots until he responded.

> **Eddie:** Fuckers spray-painted slurs all over Eden Center. The restaurant. Your shop. Parking lot. Everywhere.

He sent photos. Zoe's stomach twisted. Her heart pounded in her chest. No wonder her mother was scared.

Zoe: Anyone hurt?

Eddie: No. Thank God. Police are investigating it as a hate crime.

Zoe: I'll pick up cleaning supplies on the way over.

Her brother replied with a thumbs-up.

"Z, what's wrong? Why are you staring at your phone like that?" Derek had pulled on his jeans but was still holding his shirt.

Her lips trembled so hard she couldn't get the words out. She held out her phone so he could read her brother's messages.

"Fuckers," Derek spat. "Come on, let's get you dressed and I'll drive you there."

She nodded and let him guide her back to her bedroom.

CHAPTER 36

Zoe had never seen the Eden Center parking lot so empty on a Saturday morning. She wasn't sure what was eerier, the quiet or all the flashing blue and red lights from the police cars that were parked at odd angles scattered across the shopping center. She had gotten them past the barricade after flashing her ID and a Something Cheeky business card.

"Park in front of my parents' restaurant." She pointed it out as if he weren't familiar with it from his numerous visits during college breaks.

Derek nodded patiently even though she'd snapped at him for missing several turns on the way here. He navigated his rental car around multiple tarps that were held down with cement blocks, rocks, and various tools found in a car trunk.

Someone had covered all the racial slurs painted on the parking lot. Based on what had been painted on the windows and walls, Zoe didn't need to know what was under the tarps.

As soon as he put the gear into park, she bolted out and ran to the front of the restaurant, where a crowd had congregated.

"Má!" she called out as she searched for her mother's familiar rounded cheeks and shoulder-length hair.

Several women who were also mothers turned around in response. When they realized it was Zoe, they made a path for her.

She rushed through and embraced her mom, who was standing next to her brother.

"Má, are you okay?" she asked in Vietnamese. "Where is Ba?"

She'd read stories of vandalism and attacks in other cities but thought they were safe in the DMV. Broken glass could be replaced and paint scrubbed away. Her parents could not be replaced.

"Slow down, con." Her mother stroked Zoe's back. "Everyone is safe. Your dad is over there, organizing cleanup."

Zoe's entire body relaxed in relief. Her father was a man of actions not words. He was sweeping up the glass and directing people to various tasks.

"Hey, you made it." Her brother gave her a tight smile. "I'm sorry about your shop."

"When—how did this happen?" Zoe asked both of them. "Did the security cameras get their faces?"

"Z, breathe." Derek had caught up with her. He rubbed her back.

"Derek!"

"Cô Hồng," he greeted her mom with a kind smile. "Sorry I haven't stopped by yet."

"It's okay. Zoe said you were busy." Her mom stepped back. "Let me look at you."

"Má, you can do that later," Zoe protested.

Derek winked at Zoe to signal that he didn't mind. He stood still with his hands clasped behind his back for her mom's scrutiny.

"You are too skinny," her mom declared. "Come into the restaurant after we open and I'll make sure you eat."

"Yes, Cô Hồng," he replied obediently.

"Now tell me everything," she demanded of her brother.

"I don't know much except Bác Lê arrived early to open his tofu shop and saw, well, all that." Eddie waved helplessly at the damage and horrible, horrible words covering the walls.

"I'll stay until everything has been cleaned," offered Derek. He didn't seem to care that today was his first day off in two weeks.

"Are you sure?" Zoe asked. "You barely know the people here."

"How could I walk away when our community needs help?"

She hugged him, grateful to have him with her. She wasn't sure if she'd have the strength to deal with the damage at Something Cheeky on her own.

"The elders should check on their shops and make sure nothing was taken," Zoe instructed her brother. "They don't need to be out here scrubbing paint and dealing with sharp glass."

"Yeah, we can do all the heavy lifting," TJ said from behind her.

Zoe spun around and gasped. Next to TJ was the entire cast of *Tấm Cám and* the Boss Babes. They were dressed to scrub and clean. Zoe's fears and anger melted into relief. Her eyes were wide as she turned to Derek.

"I might've called the calvary." He answered the question she didn't have to vocalize.

"It's your day off," she repeated, this time to the actors, stage managers, and the rest of the Prestige staff.

"Which means we'll be here as long as you need us," Heather said in a voice that discouraged any argument. Everyone agreed emphatically.

"Andre sends his apologies," Trixie said.

"He's really upset he can't be here, but I told him that we couldn't leave Hazel's Kitchen even more shorthanded for Saturday brunch," Keisha explained.

"I already checked on your boutique," Josie said. "It's mostly superficial damage, but it'll take some elbow grease to clean."

"This is bullshit." Thảo shook her head at the hateful spray-painted words. "Time to rock the boat."

"I'll reach out to my social media connections and make sure this story is covered in the news," Reina said. "I'm not letting anyone sweep this under the rug."

Of all the Boss Babes, Reina had the most experience with publicity. She'd grown her network of influencers and journalists in order to make her burlesque club a success. Trixie, Josie, and Keisha murmured in agreement.

The rest of their friends followed up with "Hell, no!" and "We're not staying quiet."

Zoe blinked away the tears forming in her eyes. She knew her Boss Babes always stood by her no matter what, but the actors and people at Prestige barely knew her. They were all gathered here because of Derek. He'd reached out to their community and they'd dropped everything to help.

"I can't believe you did all this without me knowing."

Derek shrugged as if it were no big deal. But it was. She tossed her arms around his neck and pulled him in for a deep kiss.

After his initial shock, he relaxed into her very public display of affection. She didn't get a chance to tell him this morning that she'd changed her mind about keeping their relationship a secret. Telling him this way was much more fun.

Their friends were cheering at their intimate embrace. She'd almost forgotten how loud theater people were. She laughed against his lips and pulled away from Derek.

"Are you sure about this?" he whispered.

"No more hiding."

"Yes!" He picked her up from the waist and spun around like people did in the movies.

Somewhere in the distance she heard clapping and more cheering. When he finally set her down, she smiled shyly at her friends, new and old.

"I knew it!" TJ yelled indignantly. "You lied to me."

Everyone laughed. Danny hushed him. TJ pouted but gave Zoe a nod of approval when they made eye contact.

"Finally, my daughter comes to her senses," her mother announced to her friends. "Derek is a good man."

Zoe cringed. She'd made out with Derek in front of her mom and all her aunties and uncles. At least they'd gotten her mother's approval.

"Okay, everyone, kissing time is over. Let's get to work," her brother announced as he clapped his hands. He turned to Zoe. "For the love of God, I don't need to see you suck face with anyone ever again."

"Get used to it, Eddie." She laughed as he led people away to assign them various jobs. Now that everyone's attention was diverted, she should have an actual conversation with Derek. Using words.

"You're magical," she said.

"No, they're here because they respect you. Like you."

"I get it now."

"Get what?" Derek's head tilted in confusion.

"Why you wanted to tell our friends. They don't care that we're working on the show together."

"I'll refrain from an *I told you so*," Derek teased.

She smacked his arm. Not too hard.

"Ow!" he exclaimed dramatically.

"That didn't even hurt. Don't make me regret dating an actor." She pointed a finger playfully at him. "But what are we going to do about Greg?"

Derek worried his lip as he considered her question. When he didn't respond, Zoe frowned in worry. Maybe she'd been too rash in her decision. They should've talked it over—what, for the third time? No more overthinking. Their friends knew about them and she couldn't take it back.

"I'll figure something out," Derek reassured her. "Right now we have to take care of our own."

She nodded and tilted her face up for a kiss. Derek quickly complied.

"Cut it out," her brother cried.

Zoe ignored her brother. Now that everyone knew about them, she could kiss Derek whenever and wherever she wanted. They'd deal with Greg and the aftermath on Monday when she was back at Prestige.

CHAPTER 37

O h good, I caught you during a break," announced Greg as he entered the empty rehearsal room.

"I'm tweaking the lyrics for a song," said Derek flatly, hoping to discourage any conversation.

He'd actively avoided Greg the past few days since his mentor had welcomed Derek into what Zoe called the "little old boys' club." Sidestepping Greg wasn't what he meant when he told her he'd take care of things with the artistic director.

Avoidance should count for something, considering the man had made it a habit to drop in every day to observe and then offer a litany of suggestions once the cast was out of earshot. Greg's feedback had gone from a trickle to a firehose since rehearsals began. Derek pretended to take notes and ignored all of them.

Greg had been a no-show on Monday and Tuesday, which had been a huge relief. Derek had been able to pull so much vulnerability and intensity from his actors that he'd gotten chills.

Derek knew it was too good to last.

"I was thinking we should extend the run," Greg suggested.

"What do you mean?" Derek asked cautiously. The man had a motive behind everything.

"We're skipping previews and invited dress rehearsal," Greg clarified. "Let's start the run earlier."

"That means moving up opening night by almost two weeks!" Derek exclaimed.

"Exactly! It'll coincide with the start of DC's Asian Pacific Islander Heritage Month Festival. The festival organizer thought it was a great idea—which I put into her head." He squared his shoulders proudly like a child waiting for a compliment from his parents.

Derek silently counted to five so he wouldn't scream.

"Greg, we can't possibly be ready for the public after two and a half weeks of rehearsal." Derek spoke slowly to hide his growing panic.

"You'll still have tech."

Derek fought the urge to roll his eyes. The only thing predictable about tech rehearsals was that nothing ever went according to plan.

"Derek, isn't this what you wanted?" Greg's face fell in real disappointment.

Derek clenched his fist.

"Yes, but not like—"

"Now that the show is one of the headliners for the festival, you'll get more publicity. Word of mouth will spread across the DMV." Greg spread his arms out to demonstrate.

"If we keep our current schedule, people will see a more polished production," Derek attempted to reason.

"Two extra weeks of shows means more ticket sales and will prove to the board and producers that there's an audience for *your* musical."

Greg's emphasis implied that the success of the show rested on Derek's shoulders. Of course it did. As the director, he'd made all the casting and creative choices. It was his vision and he couldn't let his team down. Or all the Asian people who needed to see themselves represented onstage.

"I also want to give us a fighting chance. Which means giving the cast and the designers the time they need," Derek said in a firm voice.

He'd allowed Greg too much leeway and now the man was trying to steer the production. Derek needed to regain control of the ship.

"You said it yourself that they're talented. Even the inexperienced designer, Zoe. Your team will figure it out."

The man had tossed his words back at him. Derek opened his mouth but nothing came out. At least nothing that wouldn't get him fired.

"You're in shock now, but this is a good thing. Besides, we can't change our mind because marketing has already sent everything out to the printers."

"What?" Derek's chest tightened as he forced himself to breathe slowly through his nose. He'd have no chance to change Greg's mind because the decision had already been made before the man walked through the door.

"I believe in you, Derek. I know you won't let me down." Greg clapped him on the shoulder. "Don't forget the better this show does, the bigger your chances of getting my job when I retire."

"But what if I don't want—"

"I'll give you the chance to personally share the good news with the cast," Greg continued, ignoring Derek's protests.

Greg flashed his perfectly white teeth in a smile, but all Derek could see was red. Greg gave Derek a thumbs-up before leaving the rehearsal room.

"Fuck!" Derek screamed silently. Everyone would be back from lunch soon and he needed to regain his composure. He walked along the tape that the stage manager had used to mark out the stage as if it were a meditation circle but rectangular instead.

"What the fuck was that?" Thảo exclaimed. She'd come back early with two iced coffees in her hands.

"You heard?" He rubbed his forehead.

"I'm not even sorry for eavesdropping. I was headed up here when I saw Greg practically skip toward the rehearsal room." She set the drinks down.

He increased his pace, this time making tight military turns at the corners, something he'd learned during private school assemblies. Heather had done a great job with the tape because it didn't budge with the pressure he put on it.

"Derek, stop." Thảo grabbed his arm. "We can't open the show in two weeks."

"We can make it work," he said with false cheer. He had to set an example for everyone and keep their spirits up.

"Don't you fucking Tim Gunn me. This isn't a game. It's real life. If we fail, you know this show won't get another chance. We're not Andrew Lloyd Webber. People aren't lining up to throw money at us."

"I know that!" Derek snapped. He immediately regretted it.

Thảo's lips quivered. She turned away from him and picked up her coffee. He followed her.

"Sorry," he whispered. "I need time to process the news."

"Well, process faster because we only have ten minutes before everyone comes back." She thrust his coffee at him with a wry smile.

He stabbed the straw into the lid and took a deep breath before sucking down half of it. The ice cold elixir calmed the panic threatening to take over his body.

"Thanks. I needed that."

"Yeah, you did." Thảo lightly punched his arm. "Now what?"

"The good thing is that I get to break the news to the team instead of Greg."

"Silver lining." Thảo's voice dripped with sarcasm. "Does Heather know?"

"I don't think so. Greg's only told the marketing department."

"She's gonna shit a brick."

They both grimaced. Their superbly organized stage manager had scheduled their entire production, including rehearsals, tech week, and preview performances, down to the half hour. Greg's news would throw her fine-tuned machine—and her—completely out of whack.

"I'll tell her when she gets back. She's always back before the actors." Derek drank the rest of his coffee in one long sip, as if it could inject energy into him for the long afternoon ahead.

"I'm so glad you're the boss because that is a job I don't envy." Now it was Thảo's turn to walk the tape on the floor.

She'd been a little distracted this morning during vocal warm-ups but he'd chalked it up to her having an off day. Something else was bothering her because she was pacing way too fast. Greg's news had exacerbated whatever it was.

Derek sighed. He hadn't been a very attentive friend to Thảo since rehearsals began. He'd been too wrapped up in his own problems and completely missed how miserable she'd been since Katie Mai arrived in DC.

"You cool?" he asked quietly.

"No. I'm not." She sped up, making dizzying turns at the corners. "Katie Mai wants me to give her an answer by opening night. And now I have two less weeks to avoid making the biggest decision of my life."

"Come on, you must know deep down," he prodded gently.

"I'm too chicken shit to drop everything and move to LA," she blurted. "My life is in New York."

"Even though you love her?"

Thảo stopped and turned to face him.

"It's *because* I love her. I don't want to hold her back."

"How would you do that?" Derek asked.

"She's so smart and talented, but Hollywood is hard for people like us. Asian and queer. That's two things against her. Us."

"Katie Mai knows that already. It's no different than theater."

"But if she's worried about me finding work in LA, it'll be even more difficult for her." Thảo rubbed the shaved side of her head the way she did when she was worried.

"That's not the only reason you don't want to go," Derek said.

She bit her lip and blinked rapidly.

"I'm in a good place here—I mean New York," she admitted. "Our musical is my best work yet. Even if we don't take it to Broadway, I've already received queries about commissioned work."

"That's great news!" Derek's spirits lifted. This musical was already opening doors for Thảo. Soon the designers and actors would get more opportunities.

"If I move across the country, I won't be able to network with New York theater folks. I don't want to compose for movies. I want to write musicals!" She opened her arms out and danced as if she were in *A Chorus Line*.

"You would definitely get cut dancing like that," Derek teased. "It's okay if you don't want your career to take a back seat. You've worked so hard to get where you are."

Part of him wondered if he was pushing Zoe too far out of her comfort zone the way Katie Mai was with Thảo. Zoe had established herself in DC as the premiere plus-size lingerie designer and she ran a successful boutique. If they took the show to New York, would he be asking her to sacrifice doing what she loved?

No, he couldn't be. Zoe practically glowed whenever he saw her working in the costume shop. She'd told him how much she loved being back. Yet he'd had to beg her to join the production. Now Zoe would be under more pressure to complete her ambitious costumes with their shortened timeline.

How much strain would the new timeline put on their relationship? He couldn't lose her now, yet he'd put too much work into the musical. Derek would have to work even harder to make sure the production was everyone's best work while making sure Zoe had everything she needed to finish the costumes on time. Even if it meant twenty-hour days.

"Hey, folks, are you ready . . ." Heather's voice trailed off as she walked into the room to their somber faces. "Did someone die?"

She laughed nervously. Derek took a deep breath and pointed to her work station.

"No, but you better sit down first."

CHAPTER 38

"M s. Tran."

Zoe jumped in surprise. She'd been so focused on beading the headdress that she hadn't heard Greg enter the costume shop. TJ and the rest of the staff had gone for a coffee run. She didn't want to lose her flow so she'd asked them to bring her a double shot extra-sugar latte.

"Hi, Greg," Zoe said with too much fake cheer. "If you're looking for Derek, he's not here."

They'd agreed to stop their afternoon trysts and his coffee runs for now. Zoe hated not seeing Derek every afternoon. But keeping things more professional at Prestige meant less fodder for Greg to do whatever the hell Greg did to make their lives harder.

"That's not who I'm looking for. As artistic director, it's my duty to make sure everything is running smoothly."

"Of course." She set down her beading needles and slipped her snips into their leather cover less she be tempted to stab the man with them. Lucky for him that blood stains were a bitch to clean off fabric.

"Since you were preoccupied on Friday"—he cleared his throat loudly—"I'm here for my tour today."

Zoe's heart raced and her mouth felt like she'd swallowed cotton balls. *This isn't college. I already have this job. I don't have anything to prove to him*, she reminded herself silently.

"Please, over here." She walked briskly to the other side of the room, where the mostly finished pieces hung.

He followed so closely behind her that a breeze accompanied his strides. She took a deep breath to calm her nerves. Huge mistake. His heavy cologne assaulted her nostrils.

"Why don't we start with our leads?"

Zoe reached for Katie Mai's costumes, which were a little farther down. She was grateful for a little distance between them.

"Katie Mai has the most costume changes, since she's reincarnated into various things but those are mostly accessories," Zoe explained. "She wears a simple midi-length áo dài that's sheer from the waist down and pencil pants."

"Hmmm" was all Greg said, but he waved for her to continue.

"My favorite is what she wears to the festival, since it's her transformation moment. The first one at least."

Zoe pulled the costume off the rack and laid it on the worktable closest to them. She'd designed a gown that Tấm could slip over her plainer outfit. The formal dress was bright red, the color of luck to foreshadow her marriage to the Emperor. Katie Mai loved the long, billowy sleeves, which worked well with the choreography for the festival dance number.

"We can't forget the shoes, which are the catalyst for her relationship with the Emperor." Zoe unclipped a Polaroid photo from the hanger to show Greg.

He took the picture from her, frowning as he studied it.

"They're at the cobbler right now so he can add rubber soles to them. We can't have Katie Mai slipping during the dance numbers," she quickly added.

Zoe knew she was talking too fast, but Greg's silence increased her anxiety. This man had an opinion about everything. Was he holding back because he didn't want to give her bad feedback? Would he make Derek fire her instead of being the bad guy?

The more costumes she showed the artistic director, the more her thoughts spun. She fumbled over her words and basically sounded the opposite of confident. Instead of reassuring him of her ability, she made things worse.

The torture was over after she'd shown him the final costume. Or so she thought.

"Well, Ms. Tran, the story your designs tell will read very well onstage."

"Oh, thank you." It was the second time this afternoon that Greg had surprised her.

"But I'm concerned that you still have so many unfinished pieces."

He leaned in so close that she started to choke on his cologne. He pulled back so she didn't cough in his face.

"Has Shawn not spoken to you about your time management? You're not even close to finishing the rest of the costumes. You'll need to scale back. Make compromises."

He pressed his lips together like a disapproving school teacher. Or maybe even like her college professor, who'd told her that she had no choice but to do as he asked or he'd flunk her from the theater program and tell everyone who asked that she was too difficult to work with.

She plastered on a smile, hoping that she didn't look like a deer in headlights.

"I-I-it's all under control," she stammered, taking a step back, but she was stopped by the worktable.

He'd trapped her. She breathed through her mouth and shot a glance at the door. TJ and Shawn had to come back from their break soon. They'd been gone for at least thirty minutes.

"Derek's not coming to rescue you today. He's got problems of his own." The man's blue eyes crinkled with glee. He was enjoying his power over her.

"What did you do?" she demanded.

"You'll find out soon enough."

"You're trying to sabotage the production," she accused.

"Why would I do that to a theater that I run? To my mentee of all people?" he replied innocently. But she knew better.

"You can't stand the fact that he's going to be even more successful, more famous, than you'll ever be."

Greg's face blanched. He stepped back at her boldness. Zoe edged herself out from between him and the table. She inhaled air that hadn't been poisoned by his fragrance.

"Derek will never be more successful than me unless I allow it," Greg sneered in condescension. "He hasn't earned his dues yet. Neither have you."

"I don't need to earn anything. I'm here because I want to be." Zoe straightened her spine as her confidence returned. "I already have a successful business."

"Lingerie, how classy."

"I don't need you or your approval, Greg."

"Keep telling yourself that."

They both turned to the door as voices echoed in the hallway. Finally she wouldn't be alone with the awful excuse for a human.

"If you change your mind, come up to my office. I have a few suggestions on how you can pay your dues." Greg's smile left no question as to what he meant.

Zoe swallowed and kept her face neutral. She refused to give him the joy of watching her squirm.

"Thank you for your feedback," she said coldly. "I'd appreciate it if you scheduled any further meetings through Shawn or Heather."

Greg huffed and stomped out of the room, almost running into the staff coming into the shop. TJ's head swiveled as he tried to figure out what had happened.

"Excuse me," TJ yelled down the hallway, but Greg had long disappeared. "What happened here?"

"Greg wanted an update. And he got more than he bargained for." Zoe laughed uneasily. She fought the urge to run home and take a long hot shower.

She needed to warn Derek. They had to stick together and stand up to Greg.

CHAPTER 39

"Great job today," Derek said at the end of rehearsal. "Before you head out for the night, I have some news."

From behind the cast, Heather and Thảo nodded encouragingly. The three of them had agreed to wait until the end of the day to announce Greg's news. As the director, he shouldered the responsibility.

"We've been presented with a great opportunity to be one of the headlining shows for DC's API Heritage Month Festival," he said with false excitement.

The actors cheered.

Thảo rolled her eyes, obviously annoyed that he hadn't blamed Greg for the "opportunity." Derek couldn't change the timeline, so there wasn't a point to inciting drama or hard feelings against the artistic director. He needed this team to focus.

"Which means, we have to move up opening night." He swallowed before dropping the bad news. "By two weeks. Which means we're skipping previews."

Their cheers turned into groans.

"We're not even close to ready!" cried Katie Mai.

"I'll make sure you're ready," he reassured them. "Memorize your lines and nail those songs."

"I'll be here if you want to schedule one-on-one time," Thảo offered. "Talk to Heather and we'll make it work."

"What about Equity rules?" Danny asked. "We're already working our max hours."

"I can't—won't—ask you to break Equity rules." Derek bit his lip as he searched for a solution. Tech meant twelve-hour days and he wanted them to be as well rested as possible before then.

"Thảo and I will work with Heather to redo our rehearsal schedule," he said while looking at the two women.

They flashed him four thumbs-up in agreement.

"I know we're under a lot of pressure now that opening night has been moved up, but I've worked with all of you before. You have talent and drive. You're going to do this show justice no matter what."

They responded with "Hell, yeah!" and "You got that right!"

"Now go home and get some rest. I'll see you all tomorrow morning." Derek's smile was real this time.

He slumped into a chair once the actors left. Heather waved good-bye before heading to her office.

"You should've thrown Greg under the bus," Thảo said.

"There was no point. What's done is done."

"Yeah, but every story needs a white dude as the villain," she half-joked. "You give him too much leeway."

"Don't you start. I still have to tell Zoe." He sighed.

She'd sent him a *We need to talk* text over an hour ago. All he'd managed to tell her was *After rehearsal*.

"You're going to see her now? What about us?"

"What do you mean?" Derek's forehead furrowed in confusion.

"You forgot again." Thảo's exasperation was all over her face. "We have to finish the fucking song. Something's not right and I need your ears."

"Thảo, I'm wiped. I'd be no good to you."

"If you were my boyfriend, I would've dumped you already with all your excuses."

"Ha ha. Can it wait until I talk to Zoe?" He pleaded.

"I'm so tired of you putting Zoe ahead of our work. I know that the two of you came up with the concept, but I'm the one writing the music and all the Vietnamese lyrics."

"I'm sorry. I thought I had more time, but she needed my help." The excuse sounded pathetic in his ears.

"I'm starting to think this entire production was just an excuse for you to confess your love to her," she accused.

"That's not fair. You know there are bigger reasons! We need more than *Miss Saigon* on Broadway."

"Yeah, yeah, blah, blah. You keep saying that but your actions tell me the opposite." She frowned and crossed her arms.

"We can work on the lyrics tomorrow. I promise."

"Sure. Whatever." She waved dismissively. "I'll finish the song myself and you can't argue with it because you are too busy for it."

"Thảo, I'm sorry. It's going to take everything I have left to break the news to the creative team. They're professionals and will roll with it. But Zoe—this is her first pro gig. She needs extra help."

"Thanks for letting me know where I am on your list of priorities." Thảo tossed her bag over her shoulder and stormed out.

Derek rubbed his temples. He didn't know how much longer he could keep all his plates spinning. He only had to make it to opening night.

As soon as the costume shop shut down for the day, Zoe ran upstairs to find Derek. He hadn't responded to the cryptic and slightly panicked text she'd sent him after her incident with Greg.

She stopped in the doorway of the rehearsal room. All the lights were off except for a small lamp on the stage manager's station. Derek was lying on the floor under the six-foot folding table that Heather sat at during rehearsals.

"Derek?"

He didn't respond. She'd never seen him like this except when he slept.

Keeping her footsteps soft so she wouldn't wake him in case he was taking a nap, she crept into the room for a closer look.

Derek was flat on his back, wide-eyed and staring at the underside of the table.

"Hey, you. You ready to go home?" Zoe tried unsuccessfully to keep the worry out of her voice. She tried to crouch down but the day had caught up with her. She sat her ass on the cold floor.

"Zoe." Derek blinked quickly, as if waiting for her to come into focus. "What time is it?"

"Eight P.M.," she said without checking her phone. The exact time didn't matter right now. "What are you doing under there?"

"Thinking. When I was a kid, I was home by myself after school. I didn't like the emptiness of the house without my mom, so I'd sit under the dinner table."

"That's really cute and kind of sad. What's on your mind?"

The silence stretched as she waited for his response. He'd tell her when he was ready. After a few minutes, he crossed his arms over his chest and rolled out from beneath the table. He pulled himself up to sit next to her, their shoulders touching.

"I knew putting on this show would be challenging, but the obstacles are not the ones I planned on." He sighed.

"Let me guess. Gregzilla," she said dryly.

Derek covered his face with his hands and groaned.

"Greg moved up opening night by almost two weeks."

"He what?!" Zoe exclaimed. Her voice echoed off the walls. This was what Greg had alluded to this afternoon.

"Thảo and I got into an argument. She stormed out," he added.

"Oh." Zoe frowned.

"I'm going to make it work." He combed his fingers through his hair. "As soon as I figure out how."

"Once you get some sleep, you'll come up with something." She gave him a side hug.

"I will. I will," he repeated as if to convince himself.

The man who could never stop moving needed rest. He'd spent all Saturday and Sunday cleaning up Eden Center then dove back into rehearsals on Monday. Even the strongest person had to take a break.

Her altercation with Greg could wait. She refused to add to his stress. Derek needed her strength right now and that's what she'd give him.

"Let's go back to your place." She helped him up. "How about I order some Indian food? Want some goat curry?"

He finally smiled and nodded.

Seeing Derek like this only increased her anger at Greg. The artistic director was fucking with people's livelihood like they were his puppets. She'd dealt with a man like him before. While that didn't end the way she'd wanted, this time would be different. She had her Boss Babes to help her figure out how to solve this.

She'd prove to Greg that she wouldn't crumble under his machinations. These costumes were going to be the best work she'd ever done.

CHAPTER 40

"Have you noticed that every time one of you starts dating someone seriously, we have an emergency Boss Babes meeting?" Reina asked.

Zoe rolled her eyes at the redhead, even though she had a point. She'd put Derek to bed and sent an SOS text to her friends. They were waiting with wine when she got back to her apartment. Their teasing was as cozy and comforting as Mr. Bobbins sleeping in her lap.

"Why are you excluding yourself?" asked Trixie. "Wait until you fall in love."

"I'm never falling in love," Reina declared as she topped off everyone's wine.

"I can't wait to rub this in your face." Josie laughed.

"It's too messy. Y'all are exhibit A, B, and C." She waved at Trixie, Josie, and now Zoe.

"Girl, stop," said Keisha. "You're going to fall the hardest of us all."

Trixie and Zoe exchanged glances. Keisha had no idea that Andre's best friend had a thing for her. Keisha would figure it out when she was ready.

"Wanna bet?" challenged Reina.

"Now, now, let's focus on the task at hand," Josie reminded the women. "What are we going to do about Gregzilla?"

Zoe had already filled them in on everything from the costume shop visit to how he'd pulled a dirty one on Derek by forcing them to open the show sooner than planned.

"I can't believe the name stuck." Trixie snorted.

"I haven't met the guy, but I want to kick him in the nuts." Keisha's curls bounced as she demonstrated.

"I don't want anyone to get arrested." Zoe bit back a laugh. "But I have a plan. I don't know if it's too bananas."

"Let's hear it." Josie grabbed her notebook and flipped to a blank page.

"Greg is doing everything he can to sabotage us but he pretends that it's for our benefit. That way if the musical is a success, he'll still get credit for it."

"Not if, when," Keisha corrected her.

"*When* it succeeds," Zoe repeated. "I don't have control over the actors or rehearsal, but I can make sure the costumes are done in time."

"Please don't tell me you're pulling all-nighters for the next ten days." Trixie shook her head. "You were a terror to live with the last time."

"It was one time for a high-profile bridal client." Zoe pushed back. "Besides, she referred several less high-maintenance clients, so worth it."

"Does the plan involve my dancers coming to help sew?" Reina offered.

"No offense, sewing G-strings are a bit different from sewing the costumes I designed."

"G-strings might sell more tickets," Reina joked.

"I'm going to close Something Cheeky for two weeks and pay my staff to come to Prestige and finish the costumes."

Her friends began to protest but Zoe held up her hand.

"I told you it's bananas, but it's the best solution. I trust my team and they can do detailed work quickly at the quality I demand."

Her friends were speechless. Even Reina, who had a snappy response to everything. The women all turned to Josie as if imploring her to talk sense into Zoe.

"Is it really a good idea to close your boutique for two weeks at the beginning of wedding season?" Josie appealed with her no-nonsense practicality. "Especially if you're spending your own money to bring your team in?"

"I don't see any other way." Zoe swallowed down the doubts her friend raised. Even Mr. Bobbins flicked his tail in concern.

"How about just one or two people go to Prestige so you can keep Something Cheeky open on the weekends?" suggested Keisha, who managed all the finances for Hazel's Kitchen. "We don't want you to lose your main source of revenue."

"We can help run the register," Josie offered. "The other artists at the co-op can take my shifts for the next couple of weeks."

"Those are all great ideas, but I need all hands on deck. That way Derek doesn't worry about me. He needs all his energy to get the actors ready." Zoe's voice cracked.

He'd done so much to help her ease back into costuming. Now it was her turn to stand on her own. She blinked away tears.

"Oh, sweetie," Keisha hugged her. "You know we're here for you one hundred percent."

"Tell us what you need from us," Josie said, picking up her pen.

"We're not going to let Gregzilla win," declared Trixie.

"Hell no!" Reina raised her glass for a toast. "To kicking Greg in the proverbial balls!"

CHAPTER 41

Derek arrived at Prestige at eight in the morning. He still had a spring in his step from the love note Zoe had left in his apartment. He missed waking up with Zoe in his bed, but it was the first night in weeks that he'd slept for more than a handful of hours.

The situation didn't feel as catastrophic once the sun rose. It turned out getting eight full hours of sleep was good for him. He probably didn't need the coffee he'd bought for himself and Thảo. He still hadn't figured out how make the new opening night date work, but at least he now had energy to work it out.

Music echoed into the hallway leading to the rehearsal room. Of course Thảo was already at the keyboard working her ass off to finish the rest of the songs while he'd fallen into bed with Zoe. He knocked on the door so as not to surprise her.

"Well, look who decided to show up." Thảo played the opening bars to "Good for You" from *Dear Evan Hansen* to match her sarcasm.

"I bring a peace offering." He held up the cardboard tray with his coffee and a macchiato, her favorite. A takeout bag with breakfast burritos were snuggled in between the drinks.

"You're bribing me with breakfast?"

"Is it working?" He waved the food under her nose. The smell of the cheese and sausage made his stomach grumble hungrily.

"Maybe," she said sternly, but a corner of her mouth quirked into a tiny grin. She grabbed her coffee and waved for him to join her at the stage manager's table.

"I'm sorry I've been a jerk," he said sincerely.

He'd spread himself too thin trying to make sure Zoe and his creative team felt supported. Everyone except for Thảo. They were too close to getting what they wanted to ruin it because he couldn't admit that he'd let her down.

Thảo unwrapped the burrito and inhaled deeply.

"Oh my God. Is this from the taco place by the Wharf?" She closed her eyes and took another deep breath before taking a huge bite.

He nodded.

"You're right. I've been hovering around Zoe too much. I need to trust her to do her job," he admitted.

Deep down he was still worried that she'd break down the same way she had in college. But she'd handled everything with finesse, even Greg.

"I'm sorry. Can you repeat that? I was chewing too loudly."

"I need to trust her to do her job," he repeated.

"No, the first part."

He laughed. "You were right, Thảo."

"Music to my ears." She danced in her chair. "You should eat before your food gets cold."

She pushed out the folding metal chair with her shoe and patted the seat next to her. Derek breathed out in relief. Thảo had forgiven him.

The two of them ate in a comfortable silence that was only broken by murmurs of joy about their food.

"So, you've been coming here every morning at eight?" he asked after they finished eating.

She nodded.

"You hate mornings." For as long as he'd known her, she'd had to set multiple alarms just to wake up at ten o'clock. Arriving here that early meant her waking up well before eight.

"We have to make sacrifices for things we love," she said quietly.

He'd heard the *and friends* she omitted from her declaration. Hopefully she and Katie Mai could work things out soon.

"I've been a shit friend. It's time for me to sacrifice some sleep and time with Zoe so we can make this the best musical ever."

"Yes, please. I'm so tired of Gregzilla and his fucking tiny notebook." Thảo groaned. "If he mispronounces *Tấm Cám* one more time . . ."

"I might have PTSD from that notebook." Derek mimed the blond man thumbing through it.

They belly laughed. Finally they were vibing with each other again.

"So what's the game plan, boss?" Thảo asked.

"Actually, I was thinking we should change the title of the show to *The Brocaded Slipper*."

"You better not be doing that because of Greg." Thảo's eyes narrowed.

"Let me explain." He held out his hands to stay her anger. "I know this play is for us, but we need it to appeal to a wide audience. *The Brocaded Slipper* will help people compare it to Cinderella, and you know people can't resist a rebooted fairy tale."

"True. I mean, people love *Into the Woods* and that's all the fairy tales tossed into a wok."

"We're cooking the baker and his wife now?" he joked.

"You know, I like it. *The Brocaded Slipper* is how *Tấm Cám* has been titled in some English translations, so it works."

"I'm so glad you agree." He hugged her. "Now let's finish this Vietnamese duet between the sisters before Greg gets here so I can inform him of the change. Maybe he lied about things going to the printers already."

"You mean *I* write the Vietnamese lyrics and you give feedback," Thảo half-joked. "The marketing department is gonna hate you, but it'll be easier for them to advertise it."

Derek took a deep breath. His gut told him that this was the right decision, but standing up to Greg took fortitude. He knew Thảo, the cast, and the creative team would support him. They trusted him enough to work on this show. It was up to him to ensure it was a success.

DEREK TOOK THE stairs two at a time from the upper floor where Greg's office was down to the costume shop. The elevator was quicker, but his nervous energy needed an outlet after his meeting with his mentor.

Greg's gleeful acceptance of the name change stung, even though it was his and Thảo's decision. At least there was enough time to redo the program cover and artwork for the API Heritage Month festival.

The hardest part was done. Now he had to tell Zoe. She had been oddly quiet since leaving him alone at his apartment last night. Maybe she'd been waiting on him, but he'd thrown himself into working on the songs with Thảo until the cast showed up for rehearsal.

There was chatter combined with the whir of sewing machines emanating from the costume shop's open double doors. It was louder than it had been the past week, which made sense due to their shortened timeline.

"Hey, Z," he called out at the door so he wouldn't surprise anyone.

Zoe smiled and waved him in quickly before returning to her work. She was hand-sewing trim or some other embellishment on a costume. The bright red fabric contrasted against her pale green top.

"You look beautiful today—and every day," he added.

"Thank you." She smiled as she attached a tiny bead to the costume. "Feeling better today?"

"Can we talk? In private?" He glanced around the room. Was he imagining things or were there more people in here than usual?

"I thought we weren't doing that anymore." Zoe's spine stiffened, but she didn't look at him.

What an idiot. It was almost three o'clock. The time when they usually—he should've known better than to be so cryptic. After Greg walked in on them, they'd decided to avoid personal displays of affection while inside the theater. So why was she acting so strangely?

"Sorry, I—it's not *that*." He shifted his weight and tried to ignore the heat on his face. "It's an important update about the show."

"In that case, sure." Zoe set down her work and turned around to the worktable behind her. "Shawn, can we use your office for a quick meeting?"

"All yours," the shop manager replied with a smile. He was also hand-sewing embellishments.

"Are you okay?" Derek asked as soon as Zoe shut the door. He stopped himself from grabbing her hand. The blinds to the office windows looking into the shop were open.

"I'm fine." She sat behind Shawn's desk and crossed her legs, which were covered in a pair of deliciously snug dark green jeans. "I should be asking *you* that. You weren't so hot when I left last night."

"You didn't need to see me like that." He was supposed to be the one who kept her motivated. Not the other way around. "Sorry I was such a mess yesterday."

"Who helped cheer you up after you got drunk because some white kid got cast as the lead instead of you?" she reminded him. "You're allowed to have unhappy feelings."

"I'm no longer unhappy. I got a ton of sleep, the sun came out, and I'm a new man," he declared. If he said it enough, maybe all the tension in his shoulders would dissipate.

"Oh God, please don't start singing. You're too old to play Orphan Annie," she teased.

"I'm more of a Daddy Warbucks." Derek sat in the chair opposite her and crossed his arms like an overconfident billionaire.

"Stop it!" She laughed but then turned serious. "What's going on, Derek? You've been on a roller coaster of emotions and I don't want you to hit bottom like last night."

"Thảo and I worked everything out this morning. We even finished the sisters' duet."

"That's wonderful!"

"We also made a big decision about the show." Derek's stomach twisted. He didn't want her to think that he was giving in to Greg.

Worry shadowed her face.

"No, it's nothing bad," he said quickly. "Thảo and I have changed the title of the musical to *The Brocaded Slipper.*"

"Oh." Her expression was unreadable.

Fuck. She was trying to hide her disappointment.

"Is it because your Vietnamese sucks?" she finally asked.

Derek's mouth dropped. Was she serious? Of all the reasons for the new title, this hadn't been on his radar. Wait, there was a gleam in Zoe's eyes. She was teasing.

"I had you going!" Zoe giggled. She was adorable when she giggled. He especially enjoyed the way her chest gently shook with joy. "Thank God you changed it, because if I had to hear Greg mispronounce *Tấm Cám* one more time, I'd be arrested for assault."

Derek snorted. "You and Thảo both."

"All those lessons I gave you in college—did you remember any of it?"

"I thought I did pretty well the other night." He winked.

"Besides the pick-up lines." She rolled her eyes at him, but a blush crept up on her cheeks.

"That's not fair. I didn't grow up around a bunch of loud, nosy Vietnamese aunties and uncles so my Vietnamese is limited." He stuck out his bottom lip in an exaggerated pout.

"You're so cute when you're offended." Zoe's breath hitched. "I miss our three-o'clock quickies."

"Aha! You miss them, too," he accused.

Derek met her eyes. They were dark and dilated. Her mouth was slightly open and her cheeks were turning pinker by the second. Even though they weren't pressed against each other in the fitting room, their bodies remembered. Suddenly the air grew hot in the tiny office.

They both looked away. Zoe cleared her throat.

"Rain check later tonight?" she whispered hoarsely. "We still have a lot of work to do out there."

"Wait—" Derek stared out the office's window. Every sewing machine was occupied. "Did you hire more sewists? We don't have that in the budget."

He'd stretched their budget more than the producing director had originally allowed. There was no way he could sweet talk Greg into more over-hires.

"You don't have to worry about it. Those are my staff from Something Cheeky." She swelled with pride. "They're the best."

"I'm confused. If they're here, what's going on at . . ." He trailed off as his stomach dropped. What had she done? No, no, no. It couldn't be.

"I've closed down Something Cheeky until opening night and redirected my team here to work on *Tấm*—I mean *The Brocaded Slipper*."

"Zoe, that's too much. How will you pay them if you close

down the boutique for two weeks?" Derek rubbed his forehead. Everything was going wrong again.

"We're not flush with cash, but I can cover payroll for a few weeks." She brushed some invisible lint off her jeans.

"I didn't ask you to come on board to put you on the hook financially. Why don't we scale back the costumes? Until we get some more investors on board and hire out the costume construction," he suggested. He hated how frantic his voice sounded.

"No. I've invested too much time, energy, and now money to scale back. This is my chance to design the costumes my way without some white dude telling me how Asian things are supposed to look." Zoe white-knuckled the arms on her chair.

"We're not in college anymore, Zoe. You don't have to prove anything to anyone."

"That's not true. We're proving ourselves every time we walk into Prestige. I don't care if *you* want to make this show easier and more palatable for people like Greg." Zoe stood up. Her face was red and her hands were balled into fists. "I refuse to hide my voice and my aesthetic."

Dammit, he wished he could touch her, hold her hand, or even better hug her. But he couldn't. Their raised voices had caught the staff's attention. They quickly looked away when he turned to look out.

"Zoe, I love every single one of your designs. They tell the story as much as the music does."

She bit her lip but didn't speak.

"But I won't have you risk your livelihood for these costumes. You've invested years of your life to create a place that helps women feel beautiful. One musical isn't worth closing Something Cheeky."

"That's not your decision to make, Derek. It's not one musical but *the* musical. This is my chance at a do-over and I'm not going to fuck things up again."

Derek opened his mouth but she shushed him.

"You're under a lot of stress right now, and I refuse to let my costumes be part of that. Now, if there's nothing else about the show you'd like to discuss, I need to get back out there and sew."

He shook his head, worried that if he pushed back anymore, she might quit. That's what had happened in college when their professor gave her an ultimatum about putting the actors in what amounted to yellow face.

Zoe gave him a wide berth as she walked out of the office. There was shuffling as the staff returned to their work, pretending they hadn't heard their raised voices.

His phone vibrated. It was a text from Heather. The actors were back from their afternoon break. Derek was late but Thảo was working on some songs with them until he got back. Once again Thảo was covering for him.

Now he'd pissed off Zoe. One thing at a time. He'd talk to Zoe after rehearsal was done for the day. Maybe he could ask the producing director for a little more money so they could hire a few of Zoe's staff in as over-hires while the rest kept her boutique open.

This day was supposed to be better than yesterday. How the hell did Annie stay so optimistic when her life was so shitty?

CHAPTER 42

Derek hid a yawn behind his notepad as Thảo led the actors through vocal warm-ups. Next she'd walk the cast through the song they'd finished writing last night.

He gulped the fresh coffee Heather had made for rehearsal and texted Zoe.

> See you at the designer run aka our first stumble through. We start after lunch at one.

It wasn't the first time he and Thảo pulled an all-nighter, and it wouldn't be the last. They'd drunk obscene amounts of coffee as they finished writing two songs, including the pivotal duet between the sisters. Besides the opening number, this one had been the most difficult to write because his Vietnamese wasn't good enough to help Thảo refine the lyrics. But he trusted her judgment on them.

It was also the sisters' most emotional moment of the show. The duet began with Tấm's impassioned plea to her stepsister to break free from their stepmother's abusive hold. Cám is paralyzed by the fear that her mother's anger instilled into her as a child. Eventually Tấm wins her over and they hatch a plan to bring Cám to the safety of the palace.

Today's designer run would be rough with the two new songs, but with only twelve days until opening night, they had to stay on schedule. Rehearsing the entire show from beginning to end with as few stops was a tall order right now, but it wasn't called a stumble through for nothing. At the very least, their design team would have a better idea about the show's staging and emotional beats in order to finalize the lighting, sets, sound, and costumes.

Derek tapped his phone. Nothing from Zoe.

The last time he'd checked in at the costume shop, she and TJ had also stayed late to work, but then actually went home before the sun rose, unlike him and Thảo. Zoe should be awake by now because the costume shop started work an hour before rehearsals began. But the app gave no indication that she'd read his message, nor were there bouncing dots to indicate she was forming a reply.

> Missed you last night.

His thumb hovered over the on-screen keyboard after he hit send. *Screw it.* They were dating. He could send her multiple texts without coming off as needy.

> I sleep better when you're in my arms

One—no, two—nights without spooning Zoe and he was already heartsick. He hoped she felt the same way, but the last conversation between them had been awkward at best. What if she was still mad at him? He hadn't meant to imply that she wouldn't be able to handle the pressure.

Thảo handed out the new sheet music, which was still warm from the copier. He didn't have any more time to fret about texts from Zoe. He had only an hour or so to block the new songs then give the actors a chance to rehearse them one more time before lunch.

Zoe was an adult and would show up on time. She was too professional to show up late or, worse, not at all. He had to trust her the way she trusted him to get this musical in shape for opening night.

"Okay, folks," he said after Thảo was finished running through the songs. "Let's block these numbers and make the audience fall in love with Câm."

"CALLING IT A train wreck is too kind," Derek muttered so only Heather, who sat next to him, could hear. "That was the worse stumble through of my life."

Her expression didn't change except for a slight cheek twitch. Damn, that woman was a pro. She cleared her throat.

"Do you want to give notes now or after the break?" she asked.

Twenty minutes wasn't long enough to fix all the problems that had walked across the rehearsal room.

"Give them an extra-long break. An hour, okay?"

Heather nodded and penciled a note into her binder.

"Let's take an hour break so I can chat with our design team. Thank you for your hard work!" He clapped his hands. "Be prepared for notes when you return."

The tired and sweaty actors weren't happy with their performance either. They quickly shuffled out of the room with their shoulders slumped. Hopefully the break would help.

Derek turned behind him, where Greg and the designers had observed the full run through of the show. Zoe waved at him and pointed to her phone to indicate she'd texted him.

He pulled his phone out of his pocket. She'd sent him three.

Need to get back to costume shop. Come down later?

I missed you, too.

Wanna stay at my place tonight?

Like magic, her words soothed the disappointment of the designer run. He couldn't think of a better way to destress than to spend the night in her bed. He could even put up with Mr. Bobbins's glare to hold her in his arms.

He smiled at Zoe and mouthed *Yes* twice in response to her text. Her red lips curled into a bright smile. She waved and left the room with TJ.

Derek invited the other designers to sit at the stage management table. Thankfully, Greg didn't come down with them, but Thảo joined them.

"That was fantastic," exclaimed Eugene Wang, his lighting designer. "I knew your retelling would be different but to see it come to life—wow!"

"It's going to be amazing," agreed set designer Amy Lê. "I'm a little emotional. I can't believe even more people will learn the story of Tấm Cám."

The sound designer, a man of few words, nodded in agreement.

"Um, thanks, it was a team effort." Derek flipped through his notes to hide his surprise. Maybe the rehearsal hadn't been as terrible as he thought.

Eugene and Amy asked very thoughtful questions. Amy was almost ready for them to come onto the stage and rehearse on the set. She offered some ideas on how to use the wider space they'd have for dance numbers. Heather took copious notes during their meeting.

"Wow, that was awful," Thảo groaned after the design team left. "It was as if we hadn't rehearsed for eight hours a day, six days a week for two and a half weeks."

"I know." Derek sighed. "Maybe having an audience combined with all the changes confused them."

"Are you sure we'll be ready in time?" Thảo whispered as she glanced back at Greg, who hadn't moved from his chair.

Derek bent his head closer to Thảo. "We don't have a choice."

"After you give the actors their notes, I'll pull the sisters aside to work on their music while you focus on the other scenes," she suggested.

"Derek," boomed Greg, who had somehow snuck up on the three of them. "Can we talk? Alone?"

Greg looked pointedly at Thảo, who looked as if she might bolt. Derek placed a hand on her arm to steady her. Heather kept her head down as she scribbled something in her big binder.

"I'm meeting with my composer. We can meet at the end of the day," Derek said firmly. He met his mentor's eyes and dared him to push back. "We have a lot to do before opening night."

Greg huffed, then laughed. "Finally, you're becoming a real leader. I'll come back to watch the end of rehearsal. We'll talk then."

"Thank you." Derek hoped his tone didn't betray his shock that Greg had actually listened to him.

"Look at you!" Thảo exclaimed after Greg was a safe distance from the rehearsal room. "Finally growing a pair."

"Hey!" Derek feigned hurt. "After that stumble through the last thing I needed to hear was Greg's criticisms."

"Well, we're proud of him, aren't we, Heather?"

"Uh, I need a bio break." But a smile slipped out onto Heather's usual poker face. She winked at Derek.

If Derek had known it'd be that simple to get rid of Greg, he would've stood firm sooner. Unless Greg was biding his time to give Derek worse news. He wouldn't worry about that right now because after rehearsal, he was heading straight to the costume shop to kiss Zoe and take her home.

As long as things were good with him and Zoe, then everything else would fall into place.

CHAPTER 43

TJ had run ahead of her down to the costume shop, so Zoe stopped at the bottom of the stairwell to reread Derek's texts to her. She was grinning like a fool and she didn't care.

As miffed as she'd been with him after their conversation yesterday about scaling down the costumes, she'd had a tough time falling asleep without him next to her. Mr. Bobbins would only put up with her snuggles for so long before leaving for his cushiony cat bed.

The costume shop was thrumming with the same exciting energy as when she'd left to watch the stumble through. The happy sounds of a well-running workroom filled her ears: the whirring sewing machines, the snipping of scissors through fabric, and the whooshing of steam from the irons.

Her staff and Prestige's sewists worked together as if they'd known one another for years. Everyone had gelled almost immediately, which impressed the usually stoic Shawn.

"Oh, wow," Zoe whispered. A craftsperson had left the finished heels on Zoe's workstation. Now that the show had been renamed, they'd upgraded Tấm's brocaded slippers to brocaded power heels.

"Zoe," TJ called as he walked up beside her. "Damn, those heels look like they came brocaded!"

"Right? Jules did a fabulous job on these." Zoe picked them up to get a closer look. If she'd been alone in the shop, she might have tried them on. She and Katie Mai wore the same size.

"Can you take a look at this pattern placement before we cut it?" TJ nudged her elbow.

He guided her toward the back table, where a very expensive piece of matching brocade had been spread out and covered with patterns drafted onto kraft paper. It was a little quieter than the front of the shop, where all the sewing machines were.

Zoe ran her hand over the luxurious golden silk they'd sourced from the Fashion District in New York. Gold was a color reserved for Vietnamese royalty. Tấm and the Emperor would have coordinating costumes after their wedding.

"Shouldn't you have Shawn double check? He's got way more experience in matching patterns." She didn't want to be responsible for screwing up the fabric. They'd stretched the budget too far already.

"There's something you need to hear," TJ whispered. "Join me in the fitting room in two minutes. The main one."

She nodded in acknowledgment, though she was unsure why he was being covert. This wasn't like him.

"Do you still want me to make sure the patterns line up?" she asked.

"Please, but first I need a bio break." He tilted his head toward the fitting room outside the shop and mouthed, *Two minutes.*

For 120 seconds more or less, Zoe surveyed the paper patterns pinned to the silk brocade. TJ wasn't formally trained but his eye was impeccable. The pattern placement looked great, though one wouldn't know for sure until the overcoat was sewn together.

Maybe TJ would come work at Something Cheeky after their gig here was complete. He'd be great in the workroom and on the sales floor. The idea of not working beside him every day made her sad. His snark and slightly chaotic energy had made all their long hours flow with ease.

Two minutes had to be up by now. Zoe was worried about her

staff judging her for leaving the shop so soon after returning, but they were all focused on their work.

Right. The main fitting room was where TJ told her to come. Her breath hitched as she stopped in front of the closed door. The last time she'd been close to this door had been the afternoon that Greg had walked in on her and Derek. She'd moved all subsequent costume fittings to the smaller room, because it was a bit warmer for the actors as they had to change in and out of their costumes. At least that's what she'd told herself.

TJ flung the door open and popped his head out. He looked both ways down the hallway before pulling her inside.

"What is going on?" Zoe exclaimed. She froze.

Danny and Katie Mai were sitting on the vanity where actors sat to put on their makeup. They were lit by the halo of warm yellow lightbulbs around the mirror behind them. Their skin was still pink from the stumble through, and Katie Mai's hairline held a glimmer of sweat from the dance numbers.

"What are you two doing here? Your fittings aren't scheduled till later this week." Zoe tried to remember this week's schedule.

The costumes were running a little behind, but not so much that she'd lost track of the fitting schedule. Shawn would've reminded her. Zoe checked Heather's calendar on her phone.

"That's not why we're here," Danny said somberly. He exchanged worried glances with Katie Mai.

"Something's wrong. You hate your costumes? Oh God, we don't have time to redo them." Zoe paced the tiny room.

Her mind raced through time and fabric calculations. Both of their costumes were 75 percent complete, but if she pulled a couple of all-nighters then maybe, just maybe—

"Zoe, you're overthinking again." TJ placed his hands on her shoulders to stop her. "Sit down."

She complied and rubbed the furrows out of her forehead. She'd told Derek that the costumes would be completed in the time and stay true to her vision. Zoe refused to prove Greg's expectation by failing to finish the costumes in his accelerated timeline.

"We love our costumes," Katie Mai reassured her. "You're the first designer I've worked with who knows how to dress someone my—our—size. You have no idea how affirming our costume fittings have been."

"Oh, thank God." Zoe sighed in relief. Her anxiety had caused her emotions to run amok. She had to reel it back in. "Why are we here then?"

"We're worried about the integrity of the show," said Danny.

"Greg has tried to steamroll it every chance he gets," Katie Mai added. "And Derek has given in to his 'suggestions' way too often." She used air quotes around the word *suggestions*.

"How so?"

The two actors looked at each other again as if debating on how much to tell Zoe. Katie Mai bit her lip while Danny crossed his arms in front of him. Were they worried about ratting out Derek?

"I'll tell her if you can't," TJ jumped in. "Greg claims there's too much Vietnamese spoken and sung in the show."

"Which there is not," Danny defended adamantly as he slid off the counter as if to stand up for the musical. "I don't speak Vietnamese, but I didn't feel lost at the first read. I felt the emotions and figured out what was happening based on context."

"But has he changed anything to English?" Zoe asked. She couldn't believe that Derek would do that. He'd stood up for her when Greg pushed back. He'd do the same for the musical.

"No, but Derek still could." Katie Mai looked down at her shoes.

"Did you tell me that Greg wants Derek to make the Emperor's role bigger?" TJ reminded Danny.

"Greg came to me about it." Danny rolled his eyes. "He said I should demand a bigger part."

"I know Greg is—uh, well-meaning in his own way, but so far Derek has stayed true." Zoe sighed.

"What about changing the musical's name because Greg says it's too hard to pronounce?" Katie Mai asked. "I can't believe Derek caved."

Zoe's back stiffened.

"Don't you dare say Derek caved," Zoe spoke firmly. "He talked to me about it. It was purely a business decision and I stand by him."

All three of them fell silent. They looked chastened.

"Zoe, you've known Derek the longest, so if you trust him, we will, too," Danny finally said.

"But my gut tells me that something is wrong or something is about to go wrong." Katie shuddered. "Could you at least tell him about our concerns?"

"Me? What am I supposed to say?" Zoe shook her head. She already had the costumes to deal with. She certainly didn't want to tell Derek how to handle Greg when she avoided the white man every chance she could.

"How about you tell Derek that the cast is concerned by how much Greg has his hand in the show?" suggested TJ.

"Wouldn't it be better to hear this directly from the cast?" Zoe pointed out.

"It'll sound less threatening coming from you, since you two are dating." Katie Mai smiled sheepishly.

Zoe sighed. She didn't want to tell Derek how to do his job, but everything the two actors had recalled worried her.

"Would it make you feel better if I talk to him about your concerns?"

Katie Mai and Danny nodded enthusiastically.

"Fine, I'll talk to him. But he really does have everything under control." Zoe knew they wouldn't stop unless she promised to speak to Derek.

"Thank you." Kaite Mai hugged Zoe. "We have about ten minutes before our break is over. You can catch him if you go upstairs now."

"Now?"

The three nodded in unison.

"I'll be less rushed if I speak to him at the end of rehearsal. So let's wait," she suggested.

"Yeah, that makes more sense," Danny admitted. "I'll text TJ as soon as I'm out of rehearsal."

Zoe sighed. Whatever the miscommunication was, she was sure Derek would clear the air right away. This show was their baby, and they weren't giving up on it so easily.

CHAPTER 44

Derek was relieved when six o'clock rolled around. The cast had been dismissed. Heather had cleaned up her stage management table and gone home.

"I could sleep for a week," declared Thảo as she stretched her arms over her head. She sat on the floor leaning against a black wooden cube that stood in for a chair or stand or whatever it needed to be until the set was completed.

"You're too much of a workaholic to do that," Derek teased.

She stuck her tongue out at him.

"Go home. Or at least to Katie Mai's for the night."

"Oh, I plan to." Thảo grinned. "As soon as I can make myself stand up."

He offered a hand to help pull her up.

"Am I interrupting a trust exercise?" Greg asked as he entered the room. "Do I get a turn?"

He laughed loudly at his own joke.

Crap. Derek had forgotten about his meeting with his mentor. He could barely stand up straight after their all-nighter. Now he had to deal with Gregzilla. A small delirious laugh escaped before he bit his lip to stave off the rest of it.

Thảo gave him an *Are you okay?* look. He nodded.

"Yes. I mean not a trust exercise." Derek helped Thảo stand up. "We were just wrapping up for the night."

"Perfect time to finish our earlier discussion. Alone." Greg looked pointedly at Thảo.

"That's my cue." She grabbed her bag with newfound energy and stuffed her binder of sheet music into it. "I'll check in with you tomorrow morning, Derek. Have a good night, Greg."

She waved and bolted out the door. Derek couldn't avoid Greg any longer.

"Let's sit." Derek nodded toward Heather's table.

Greg sat across from him and pulled out his annoying, tiny notepad. Instead of flipping it open, he set it down and stared at Derek, who shifted uncomfortably in the folding metal chair. Whatever the man had to tell Derek, he didn't want to hear it.

"The stumble through was abominable, Derek."

Derek's stomach knotted. Greg wasn't sugarcoating anything this time.

"It's my fault. We gave them a song at the last minute and changed up the opening number." He pinched his thigh to force himself to stop rambling.

"I'm going to put everything on the table." Greg crossed his legs and sighed dramatically. "I'm extremely disappointed in you."

Derek's gut twisted. It was one thing for him to think about his failure but another to have it spoken so plainly. He'd spent years working with Greg as a mentee in order to earn an opportunity like writing and directing *The Brocaded Slipper.*

"I'm disappointed in myself, too," he admitted after a beat. In his head, Derek replayed scenes of the actors actually stumbling over their choreography during the stumble through. He rubbed his temple.

"It's obvious that you're in way over your head."

"I'm what? No, we'll get it right before tech starts." Derek shook his head. "I have a plan."

"I'm your mentor. You can admit it to me." The man's smile was almost predator-like.

"I told you. I have a plan." Derek gritted his teeth. He was almost too exhausted to repeat himself so that Gregzilla actually heard his words. But he would if he had to.

"Of course. But if you can't pull this show together by tech, it'll reflect badly on me. I put my reputation on the line for you because I believed in your vision, Derek. What will I tell the board if you fail?" Greg ran his thumb across the bottom edge of his notepad.

"That's not going to happen," Derek said unconvincingly. His sleep deprivation made it challenging to keep his defenses up against his mentor.

"If you can't make this show look good before we start tech, then I'll take over as director."

"You'll do what?" Derek wanted to punch the smirk off Greg's face. "Has this been your plan all along?"

"Why would I do that? I'm offering to save your ass." The man's blue eyes grew hard.

"I've worked too hard for you to take this from me. I'll do whatever it takes." Derek despised the desperation in his voice.

"I'm glad to hear that because I have some ideas." Greg picked up his notepad and flipped it open.

Derek wanted to burn that notepad full of Greg's stupid suggestions. Acting irrationally now would only prove Greg's point.

"I have one major note after the stumble through: too much Vietnamese." The man pronounced it with an extra syllable: vee-et-nam-ese. "Audiences will be confused. How can they fall in love with the musical if they don't understand it?"

Derek's eyes twitched but at least that meant he could keep them open.

"I disagree."

"You need to," he continued as if he hadn't heard Derek, "change all the Vietnamese dialogue *and* all the Vietnamese in the songs to English."

"How am I supposed to find time to do that when you moved up opening night?" Derek threw his hands up in frustration.

"If you'd taken my advice and wrote everything in English the first time, you wouldn't have this problem. We need this show to make money and right now ticket sales are almost nonexistent. And Vietnamese songs won't sell to anyone else but Vietnamese people. Unless you know a millionaire who's Vietnamese and wants to become a producer?"

Unable to come up with a retort, Derek shook his head. Deep down, he'd had doubts about the all Viet numbers but chalked them up to being unable to understand their nuances. Thảo had her heart set on them and he'd been happy to give her creative control for the songs.

"If you want to remain the director of *The Brocaded Slipper*, you'll need to take my advice." Greg grinned. "That's so much easier to say. You took my advice about the title, so now just take it for the rest of the musical."

Derek sighed. If Greg took over the show, he'd absolutely ruin it. Or what if it was a hit? That would be even worse. Greg would take credit for everything. Derek would rather make concessions than have the show taken away from him.

"I'll change the songs. But not the dialogue." He hoped his concession was enough to appease the man.

Greg raised an eyebrow as he considered the counteroffer. Derek's stomach sank as the silence stretched.

"Dialogue, too. For the good of the production." Greg stood up and tucked his notepad into his shirt pocket. He offered a handshake. "Can you have everything rewritten for tomorrow's rehearsal?"

"I'll do my best," Derek said dejectedly as he shook the executive director's hand. Greg had shoved him in a corner and this was the only way out.

"See you tomorrow at ten then." Greg smiled smugly. "I knew you'd see it my way."

The man patted Derek on the back and left.

Derek's skin burned where Greg had touched him. His stomach threatened to empty its contents. That man had never been his mentor. He was a bully who'd only used Derek to make himself feel bigger and more important. Deep down he'd known that but Greg had given him so many opportunities that Derek never thought he would be bullied, too.

"What the fuck, Derek?" Thảo stood in the doorway with her fists clenched by her sides. Betrayal shadowed on her face.

Derek cringed. "How much did you hear?"

"Enough to learn that you're undoing all of my hard work, especially that duet. That song is my favorite." Her voice wavered as if she might cry.

"I had to."

He ran up to her but she held her hands up and backed away from him.

"He threatened to take—" He stopped, unable to repeat Greg's words. He was embarrassed to admit that the situation had gotten to this point.

"I don't care if he threatened to kick you in the balls. How could you agree to that without talking to me first? We're supposed to be cowriters."

Derek blew out a breath in relief. She'd missed the part where Greg basically blackmailed him. Thảo would've told Katie Mai and then news would spread like wildfire. Once that happened, he'd lose control of the show. Worst of all, he'd lose everyone's trust.

"It's too late. I already agreed to put all the lyrics in English."

His voice sounded flat in his ears, as if he were still numb from his conversation with Greg.

"We worked hard on that duet. It's the moment when the sisters' bond is solidified. It's the most pivotal part of the retelling because without it neither of them has agency."

"That's why we need to make it more mainstream. Most of our audience will be English speakers." *Including me,* he almost added.

"That mediocre white man wants you to dumb down the show and you didn't even push back."

"Not true." Derek's spine stiffened. "We're meeting people where they're at."

Thảo shook her head as if she didn't believe him.

"You fucking let him get into your head," she accused.

"Thảo, we originally wrote half of the duet in English. We can rewrite the other half tonight," he pleaded.

"You do it because I'm not pulling another all-nighter. I have a girlfriend who needs me." Thảo ran over to the keyboard they used for rehearsal and dug through a bin. "I forgot my notebook."

"Thảo." Derek took a deep breath before forcing himself to say, "I'm the director, which means I have the final call. The song will be rewritten as soon as possible."

It hurt to put his foot down with Thảo, who was basically a big sister to him. But he didn't see another way of saving the show from Greg.

"You did not just pull rank on—" Thảo huffed. "I'm going to pretend we didn't have this conversation, because neither of us has slept in forty-eight hours."

She found her notebook and shoved it into her messenger bag. Avoiding his eyes, she ran toward the door, only to be stopped by Zoe.

As if the day couldn't get any worse. Derek wished he could hide under the table and wait for everything to fix itself.

"What's going on?" Zoe asked as she looked at him and Thảo.

"Apparently my name on the show doesn't mean shit to him," Thảo exclaimed as her eyes shot daggers at him. She turned back to Zoe. "You're the only person he's ever cared about. Talk some sense into him."

CHAPTER 45

Zoe jumped out of Thảo's path as she stomped out of the rehearsal room. Derek's shoulders sagged. His face was pale and contorted, as if he might cry. The conversation she'd promised Katie Mai and Danny would have to wait.

"I came to see if you were ready to go back to my place. What happened?" She spoke quietly and touched his hand.

Derek pulled her into his arms and hugged her. Hard. His body was hot and his heart was racing. She'd never seen him so upset. But Thảo had very strong opinions about everything, so maybe it wasn't as bad as it looked.

"Talk to me," she whispered into his shoulder.

Zoe breathed him in as they held each other in the empty room. His fragility tugged at her heart. It hit her. She loved him.

She loved Derek.

As if sensing her realization, he squeezed her tighter for a few seconds before releasing her.

"Today has been a terrible, horrible, no good, very bad day," he mumbled and frowned.

"My poor Alexander," she cooed, referring to the musical he'd adapted based off the children's picture book for a college final. "Talk to me. Pretend we're on the roof of our college apartment."

They'd rented a crappy apartment that was a fifteen-minute

walk from their classes. It was all they could afford then but it was their refuge from class.

"We solved a lot of problems on that rooftop," said Derek.

Zoe nodded and smiled at the memories of their late-night conversations. He pushed two black wooden cubes together and laid on top of them. She dragged two more next to him and did the same. In acting class, she loved how a silent agreement between actors and the audience turned these humble wooden blocks into beds, rocks, or, tonight, a rooftop.

"The stars are pretty tonight." Zoe waved at the ceiling. "Is that the big dipper?"

"That was the only constellation we could pick out." He laughed.

"Hey, I majored in theater, not astronomy." She was glad to see color returning to his cheeks.

"Thảo is mad because I made the call to change the songs to all English lyrics, specifically the duet." He looked at the "stars" as he spoke.

"That song brought tears to my eyes. It reminded me of my grandfather's favorite cải lương but with a more modern sound."

"Thảo would love to hear that. She gets all the credit for that song."

"The lyrics are beautiful and the music evocative. Her rhymes were super clever, too."

"That's what all the Viet speaking actors said, too. But I don't know my mother tongue, Z." He ran his fingers through his hair and massaged his head.

She couldn't believe it. All these years and it still bothered him.

"I can translate it for you," she offered.

"Thảo did that already, but it's not the same."

"Oh."

"I—" He swallowed hard. "I can't direct that scene the way it deserves because I can't understand it properly. Besides, it'll alienate the non-Viet audiences."

Zoe's eyes narrowed. What was he hiding from her?

"Yeah, that stumble through was rough but you're good at what you do. You could always provide supertitles like they do at the opera," she suggested.

"That's too distracting. The musical would be more viable if we change all the songs to English." He kept his eyes on the stars instead of looking at her.

"You're scaring me, Derek. You sound like Gregzilla." She hoped the inside joke would bring some levity.

"Greg wants the show to have universal appeal."

"Sisterhood and a love story with magical transformations isn't considered appealing?"

"Maybe not." Derek shrugged.

Zoe huffed. What had happened to the confident man she'd been working with—sleeping with—the past few weeks?

"Wow. I didn't believe them, but Danny and Katie Mai were right."

"What are you talking about?" he asked, finally sitting up.

"They came to me today because they were concerned that you were no longer following your vision for *The Brocaded Slipper*. And that you kept changing things to make Greg happy."

"It's more complicated than that. I have to think big picture. First, we need people in DC to love the show so we can bring it to New York."

"How can you compromise who you are, Derek? You're removing all the Vietna—all of us from the show."

"The story is still Vietnamese. Removing the language won't change that." Hurt filled his eyes. "I'm still Vietnamese, aren't I?"

"I didn't mean to imply that you're less Viet because you don't speak it." Zoe took a deep breath. "Of course you are."

"Z, once we get the go ahead for Broadway, we can rework things. I can bring the original Vietnamese lyrics back. We just have to get there first instead of being DOA."

"What aren't you telling me?" Zoe asked.

"Tickets aren't selling the way they should. If people won't pay to see the show, how will they even learn about our stories?"

"Derek, people already see us. As a community we're more visible than ever—but not in the ways we want. We're still sidekicks in movies and bánh mì is so trendy than random food content creators are creating their own versions."

Zoe was telling him what he already knew. Or maybe he'd forgotten it because he was so focused on the show's commercial success.

"This musical will be another way to show others that we're more than all those things," he reassured her.

"You know what I don't see? Our people telling our stories instead of some French guys writing a tragic white savior musical about our parents' civil war. I want us to be seen. Not the way other folks want to see us but as who we truly are."

"Does that even matter if people don't come to the show?" he asked flatly.

"Derek, if we don't take control of our own narrative, then who will?"

"Zoe, we won't have a narrative if this show flops. I have to do what it takes to get this show to a wider audience. And if that's changing the songs to English, then so be it."

"You're sacrificing what makes this show ours in order to make one white guy happy," she pointed out.

"It's a compromise."

"Is it really okay to compromise our Asianness in order to make white people more comfortable around us? Don't you remember what they spray-painted at Eden Center?"

Zoe didn't care how loud her voice had become. Her body shook at the memory of those hateful words in what was supposed to be her safe place.

"I'll do what it takes to survive so we have a seat at the table," he protested.

"There's no room for us at their table," shouted Zoe. "I knew that in college when I refused to dress people in yellow face for Professor Richards's gala."

"Not all of us have the financial support of our parents to make our own table," Derek blurted.

Stunned, Zoe's jaw dropped open. Her heart twisted. How could the man she loved say that to her?

"That was low. I paid them back every cent plus interest." Her voice shook with anger.

Derek hung his head.

"When you pitched this show to me, it was our vision. Our retelling. That's why I am investing my own savings in order to get the costumes made in time for Greg's accelerated timeline. I closed my shop and I'm paying my staff to help sew them."

"I never asked you to do that."

"But I did it because I believed in this musical. I believed in you." Her voice broke.

"I'm sorry I've let you down." He dropped onto the block as if he'd given up.

"That's it? You're actually going to take out all the Vietnamese from the musical?"

"Only the songs," he muttered.

"I can't believe this is happening again." Zoe walked over to where she'd dropped her bags. The large rehearsal room had shrunk around her. She needed some air.

"Come on, Zoe. This is nothing like what happened in college.

People depend on me to make sure this show does well both artistically and financially."

Zoe scoffed. She'd given up her dream in college instead of going against her values. And here he was, just doing what made Greg happy.

"If I push back too hard, Greg could take it all away. Or he'll never have me back. Then how would I continue to tell our stories?"

"You're smart and resourceful. You'll find a way." How many times would she need to say it, so he'd believe in himself as much as she did? Maybe it was too late.

"So you expect me to give Greg an ultimatum and possibly sabotage the entire production? To sabotage Katie Mai and Danny Kim, and all the other actors' job security, because I think the art is more important?"

"Wouldn't you rather put on a production you're proud of instead of one you've whitewashed?"

"I'd rather have a production happen than not at all. If I push back, he'll just find someone else to take over my job."

"You know, in college you didn't join our protests against Professor Richards because you could have lost your scholarship. But here's your chance to really stand up for something important. To stand up for yourself and our—" Zoe blinked away tears.

"Not everything in life is cut and dry. Please try to understand," Derek pleaded.

He took a step toward her but she shook her head and backed away. If he touched her right now, she didn't know if she'd slap him or try to kiss some sense into him.

"I can't be with someone who can't stand up for our community. Who can't stand up for me." She slung her bag over her shoulder and took a deep breath. Even though she loved him, this was one thing she refused to compromise on. What did she have if she didn't stick to her values?

"After the show opens, I don't want to see you ever again," she said flatly. Zoe walked out with her head held high but the tears fell anyway.

CHAPTER 46

Their final five days in the rehearsal room had been grueling. The actors worked their asses off learning the English lyrics that Derek had rewritten. Thảo had begrudgingly helped so he didn't make a mess of them.

"Thank you, everyone," said Derek as he officially ended rehearsal for the day. "Make sure to rest and drink some tea with honey to soothe your throats."

His weary cast nodded as they gathered their things and headed out.

"Thảo!" Derek called out as she followed the cast out of the room. After a grueling five days, tech rehearsal started tomorrow.

She stopped but didn't turn around until Katie Mai nudged her.

"Want to grab a drink and go over notes for tomorrow?" he asked with an embarrassing amount of hope.

"I'll email you my notes tonight," Thảo replied flatly, but there was still sadness in her eyes.

He nodded and stuck his hands in his pockets. Every day after rehearsal, he'd asked Thảo if she wanted to go over notes and received the same response.

Thảo and the rest of the cast had barely spoken to him outside of rehearsal. They still maintained an expected level of professionalism, which he should be grateful for. Except he didn't want to spend another evening alone in his apartment remembering the disappointment on Zoe's face before she walked out after their argument.

He turned to Heather to seek her company.

"Sorry. I have to meet with the crew," she apologized. "Things will get better, I'm sure."

He shrugged. Thảo was as stubborn as all the other Viet women in his life. He didn't expect her to come around anytime soon, but that wouldn't stop him from trying.

DEREK TOED OFF his sneakers and dropped his backpack on the floor then slammed his apartment door shut. His keys clanged loudly as he tossed them onto the coffee table. He overshot and the keys slid onto the carpet with a jingle.

"Whatever," he muttered. He'd pick them up tomorrow before he left for tech.

The space had felt like home only when Zoe stayed the night. Now it felt more like a hotel room: a place for him to shower and sleep before walking back to Prestige. He'd lost everything and everyone else, but at least he was still the show's director.

Like the past four nights, he ripped open a frozen dinner and stabbed the plastic film before microwaving it. How the food tasted didn't matter as long as it filled his belly so he could do the same thing again tomorrow. He reached into the fridge to grab a beer, pushing aside Zoe's squeeze bottle of sweetened condensed milk.

All he needed to do was make it to opening night. Then he'd return to New York, where the distance would make it easier to forget about Zoe.

No, he wasn't letting her ghost him as easily as she had after college. He needed *The Brocaded Slipper* to succeed so she'd understand what he was sacrificing. He vowed to send her every rave review. Not to gloat but to demonstrate that compromising didn't dilute their people's story.

His phone rang as he settled down on the couch with his dinner.

"Mom," he answered in surprise. She didn't normally call on Thursdays. "Is everything okay?"

"I can't call my son to see if he's still alive?" Her face filled his entire phone screen.

Shit. He'd missed several weeks of Sunday calls. Yet another way he'd let someone close to him down.

"Sorry. *Tấm Cám* has been taking up all my time." *And Zoe,* he added.

"I'm not important enough for you?"

Why were mothers so good at mom guilt? Did they get some kind of handbook?

"Mẹ," he said in exasperation. "You know that's not true."

Her eyes narrowed.

"Are you eating a Lean Cuisine?" She tsked and shook her head. "You are in Washington, DC, and eating bad frozen food."

"I'm too tired to fight, Mẹ."

"You look too skinny. Something is wrong." It wasn't a question but an observation.

"I'm fine," he protested.

"Why are you sad?" The corners of her eyes crinkled in worry.

Had those wrinkles on her forehead always been there? He suddenly wished his mom was sitting next to him. Or that she was in the kitchen cooking a pot of bún riêu, his favorite spicy crab noodle soup.

"I'm not—" He sighed. After five days of not talking to Zoe, barely talking to Thảo, and spending his evenings all alone, the dam burst. "It's been a bad week."

Derek propped his phone on top of the couch cushions. He

filled her in on everything that had happened since they last spoke. Well, not quite. He told her about Zoe but left all the sexy parts out. His cheeks grew hot as he told her about Greg and how his mentor had turned out to be a bully.

"I refuse to give up," he finished. Derek was relieved to talk to someone about the pressure he'd been under since arriving at Prestige Rep.

Surprisingly, his mother was silent the entire time and listened intently to him.

"I'm proud of you, Sang." She only used his Vietnamese name when she was angry with him, but she was smiling tonight.

Derek blinked in disbelief. "You are?"

"And it took you long enough to get together with Zoe!"

"Wait, you knew?" Derek didn't know if he could take any more surprises from his mother.

"I saw the way you two looked at each other when she visited. She's a smart and brave girl."

"She is. I fu—messed things up with her." He rubbed his temples. "She won't return my texts or calls."

"Do you love her?"

"Yes, I love her," Derek replied without hesitation. The feelings he had for Zoe now were real love, unlike his infatuation from their college days. His heart had ached for her these past five days. Food no longer had flavor and sleep was elusive without Zoe in his life.

"Then make things right, because I need grandchildren before I die," she teased, but he could tell she was serious about grandkids. Her phone shook as she set it down on her coffee table.

"Don't talk like that. You're still young. Wait, did you paint the walls blue?" Now it was his turn to peer into the screen. His childhood home was no longer drab and beige.

"I did. And bought a new couch." She stood up and stepped to the side to show off a blue damask sectional.

"Now it's my turn to ask if you're okay."

"I got it on sale. Don't worry." She came back into frame and waved at the wall. "I painted it myself because I quit my job!"

"You what?!" Derek exclaimed.

"Technically I retired and I saved up so much vacation time that they are paying me to redecorate my house."

His mother's face lit up as she belly laughed. He barely recognized her. Never in his life had he seen her so happy.

"Your turn. Tell me what happened."

"I found out my boss has been stealing from the school for the past ten years. He tried to bully me into fixing the books and lying for him. He threatened to report me to immigration." She rolled her eyes.

"But you got your U.S. citizenship when I was in middle school." Derek had drilled his mother until she knew all the test questions and answers perfectly. She'd passed on her first try.

"He's not very smart. I told him that if he paid out my twenty-four weeks of saved vacation time and a bonus, I'd retire. Then he can do whatever he wants."

"Mom! You could get in trouble as an accessory."

"No way. I cashed the check right away. Then I mailed the school's snooty board of directors an anonymous tip plus the flash drive with all the evidence." She smirked.

Derek's mouth dropped.

"So now I'm free of my bully boss."

"How did you know he'd agree?" asked Derek.

"I didn't. But I'm too old to put up with his threats and the disgusting way he looks at me." She shivered. "You're old enough to know that now."

"Mom! Did he ever—" Anger welled up in his chest. He'd jump in his rental car right now and drive the eight hours home.

"No. I would kick him in the balls before I let him touch me," she spat.

Derek barked with laughter and his shoulders dropped in relief.

"This means you'll come down for opening night?" he asked hopefully.

"You already got me a plane ticket. You know I hate wasting money."

"I'll email you the details." He'd buy the ticket as soon as they hung up. "I miss you, Mẹ."

"Sang, I know I taught you not to make trouble, but making trouble is fun." A giggle escaped her lips. "Now, I need to buy some new clothes before I come see your big show."

She looked happier and lighter than she'd ever been. His mother had found the courage to stand up to her boss *and* demand what she wanted.

"I'm proud of you, too," he said. "And I love you, Mẹ."

"I love you, Sang. Make sure you eat something better than a frozen dinner."

Before he could react to what she'd said, his mother hung up. Derek sat with his mouth open in shock. Not only had his mother said she was proud of him but she'd actually told him that she loved him. He'd always known that she loved him, but to hear those words aloud smashed the self-pity he'd wallowed in all week.

He couldn't let his mother down when she flew in for opening night. Before he and Zoe came up with the musical, his mother had told him her version of *The Brocaded Slipper*. He wanted a production worthy of her bedtime story. Derek wanted his mother to hear her native tongue and see herself on that stage when Katie Mai sang.

He'd actually missed the Viet they'd removed in the show. He was more comfortable with English, but the songs had lost their magic without the melodic tones of Vietnamese.

Tomorrow he'd walk into Greg's office and tell Greg that he was putting the Vietnamese back into the show. His mentor would have no choice but to accept it because it would be bad PR to fire a Vietnamese American director and take Derek's place.

Then he'd march downstairs to the costume shop to apologize and tell Zoe he loved her. He should've kept her in the loop about everything instead of worrying that he'd look weak for being unable to protect her. It was too late to change the past but it was time to make things right.

Everything would either work out as planned or blow up in his face, but at least he would try to do the right thing.

CHAPTER 47

Zoe slumped into the wall of their favorite booth inside Hazel's Kitchen. She'd been on her feet most of the day as they finalized the costumes for tomorrow's tech run. Now that she'd eaten Andre's delicious gumbo, all her achy body wanted to do was curl up in bed and sleep for three days straight.

"Want a drink?" Keisha stopped by the booth on the way to the kitchen with dirty dishes she'd bussed from the tables. "He's already closed the bar, but I know he'll be happy to make you something."

"Coffee with lots of sugar, please." Zoe forced herself to sit up straight. "We have a long night ahead of us."

The rest of the Boss Babes exchanged worried looks.

"I saw that." Zoe pointed her finger at them.

"Zoe, it's been five days and you haven't talked about Derek," Reina said gently.

"It's over between us. There's nothing to discuss." Zoe groaned. "Can I at least have my caffeine before you grill me about my failed love life?"

Keisha ran into the kitchen and returned with the entire pot of coffee plus a restaurant-size squeeze bottle of sweetened condensed milk.

Zoe grabbed the bottle and kissed it. Sugar was a sad substitute for her beloved sweetener.

"Okay, now I'm really worried," Josie said as she carefully pried the bottle from Zoe. She flipped the cap open to squeeze the sweetener into Zoe's coffee. "Tell me when."

"Keep going." Zoe waited until the mug threatened to overflow before shouting, "When!"

"Wow," exclaimed Keisha as Zoe tried to stir her coffee without spilling a single drop. "Does that mean you don't want any leftover bread pudding?"

"We never turn down Andre's bread pudding," Trixie answered for the table. "Thanks for letting us hold the meeting here after hours."

"Anything for my babe," Andre called from the kitchen door. He held a large tray of dessert. "I'll set up a spread and y'all can help yourselves."

"Thanks, sweetie." Trixie wrapped her arms around her boyfriend and pulled him in for a deep kiss.

Zoe looked away. It wasn't their fault they were so stinking cute, but their public display of affection only reminded her of Derek. Or rather, how she'd probably never kiss anyone like that ever again.

"I love—*loved* him." Zoe's voice cracked. But none of that mattered now.

"Aha! She finally admits it."

"Reina, you're not helping," Josie chastised the redhead before turning to Zoe. "She's right. You can't bottle your feelings like that."

"He's not the person I thought I loved," Zoe replied before taking a sip. She let the sugary coffee coat her tongue before swallowing.

"I'm sorry." Her roommate hugged her. "You're allowed to be mad and talk about your feelings."

Zoe had said awful things to him and she couldn't take them back. She'd replayed that evening in her head over and over, trying to figure out how she could've handled it better. But the ending was always the same. She couldn't be someone who was afraid to do the right thing. Someone who wasn't strong enough to stand up for their values.

The bell over the door dinged.

"We're here!" TJ announced as he held the front door open for the cast of *The Brocaded Slipper* and Thảo.

"Please, come in and help yourselves." Keisha welcomed them and guided everyone to the huge buffet that Andre had set up.

"Wow, it smells amazing in here." Katie Mai grabbed a plate and filled it with a scoop of everything.

The others agreed and followed suit.

"How DID REHEARSAL go today?" asked Zoe after everyone had filled their bellies. She sat on a barstool so everyone could see her clearly.

"The lyrics are still in English," Danny said dejectedly.

"And the dialogue, too," added Katie Mai.

The two had given Zoe daily updates on all the changes Derek had made to the musical. For four nights, she'd hoped with all her heart that he'd come to his senses, but he'd remained steadfast.

"He pulled rank on me, so my opinion doesn't matter anymore." Thảo was uncharacteristically subdued. "I had to stop asking him to revert the lyrics because I couldn't take the rejection anymore."

"Your original lyrics are beautiful, darling. Maybe you can use them for something else." Katie Mai slipped her hand into Thảo's, and Thảo kissed her in return.

"Yeah, it's way better with them," added Danny. The others murmured in agreement.

"You know what pisses me off?" Thảo grumbled. "If this had been Derek's idea, I would've kept an open mind, but Greg wants to change things for all the wrong reasons."

"We can't let him win," declared TJ. "We can't have white men dictating how we tell our stories."

A chorus of "Hell, no!" filled the restaurant.

"It's clear that Derek won't stand up to Greg. We have to do something about it before it's too late," declared Zoe. If she didn't prioritize standing up for her people, then what was the point of everything she'd fought for since college?

"What are you proposing?" Thảo asked.

"A walkout. Tomorrow." Zoe's voice rang into the restaurant.

Several of the actors' eyes widened. Others had worried expressions.

"We all signed union-approved contracts." Katie Mai stood up and waved at her fellow cast mates. They nodded. "What if we get in trouble with Actors' Equity? Unauthorized strikes have serious consequences."

"I'm asking a lot from you. This can't be a strike because we want the show to open as planned." Zoe bit her lip as she explored options.

"What if we walked out for an hour?" Thảo suggested. "Union rules dictate that we're allowed two hours for a dinner break on tech days."

"Yes!" Danny clapped his hands. "Derek and Greg don't have to know that it's *not* a strike."

"Genius. They'll be terrified for sixty glorious minutes." Katie Mai laughed. "We'll return to rehearsal after an hour and Heather can deduct it from our dinner break."

"So we're in agreement?" Zoe asked.

The rest of the actors nodded *yes* even though a few were still worried.

"If you're only walking out for a short period of time, you need to make a splash," Josie piped up from their booth. "A cannonball-size one."

"We need to alert the media!" cried Reina. "This is a big story: Asian American actors stage a walkout to protest their production's whitewashing."

"How can we get media to show up at Prestige tomorrow morning? That's only thirteen hours from now," Trixie pointed out.

"I have a list of bloggers and content creators who owe me favors." Reina's wicked grin hinted at secrets she'd gleaned at her burlesque club. "Not to mention some mainstream media."

"I can put out an SOS to the food content creators we work with," added Reina. "They have no problem covering social justice issues like this."

"Hot damn, this is really happening." Thảo hugged her girlfriend. "Do you think it'll change anything?"

"I don't know, but I'll regret it if I don't try," Zoe said as her chest swelled with hope.

"Someone needs to make a speech if we convince these people to show up and cover our walkout," said Reina. "And it won't be this white lady."

Everyone laughed but Reina had a point.

"I nominate Zoe!" cried out one of the chorus members.

"No, I like staying behind the scenes. They don't want to hear from me," Zoe protested.

"You've stood up against Greg since you joined this production. We'd be honored for you to lead us." Thảo turned to the actors. "Zoe! Zoe!"

"Zoe! Zoe! Zoe!" they chanted.

"Okay! I'll do it!" Zoe cried out and was met with cheers. She had the least to lose. It was her idea so her responsibility to lead them tomorrow.

They might be able to pull it off, unlike her college protest. Back then no one in Syracuse cared about whitewashing or a tenured professor bullying his students. She'd had no power in that situation.

Tomorrow would be different from college. She had an army behind her.

"Now, let's make a plan for tomorrow so we're all on the same page." Josie pulled out her notebook and fountain pen to make one of her famous lists.

After another round of bread pudding and coffee, they'd agreed on a timeline for tomorrow's walkout along with roles for everyone. They were in good hands. Josie's planning skills rivaled Heather's.

Heather. Their stage manager would not be happy with *this* set of plans. Zoe caught Thảo's attention and waved her to an empty booth.

"What about Heather?" Zoe asked.

Thảo sucked her teeth and cringed. "She's either going to be pissed or she'll join us."

"I don't want her to get in trouble because she works full time at Prestige. The rest of us are contract workers."

Thảo bit her lip as she considered Zoe's words.

"What if I tell her right before we walk out. Like, five minutes. So she can at least be mentally prepared," Thảo suggested.

"You're the best person to tell her. I'll be downstairs in the costume shop." It also meant she didn't have to come upstairs and run into Derek. He'd know immediately that she was hiding something from him.

"Are you sure we shouldn't give him a heads-up, too?" Thảo's forehead wrinkled in worry.

She didn't need to say Derek's name for Zoe to know who she meant.

"No. He's part of Greg's old boys' club now. All he cares about is selling tickets so they can take the show to New York." Zoe crossed her arms. They probably drank scotch together in Greg's office after rehearsals now.

"If you're sure . . . " Thảo trailed off, clearly torn.

Zoe had spent almost a week trying to forget about Derek, which had been slightly easier due to the long hours in the costume shop. But Thảo saw him every day at rehearsal and had to listen to new versions of the songs she'd written. Derek was Thảo's best friend, too.

"You're mad at him, too. He undid all your work!" Zoe reminded her.

"He's trying to hide it, but he misses me. And you."

"I don't miss him at all," lied Zoe.

Thảo raised an eyebrow in disbelief. Zoe focused on folding and smoothing out the napkin in front of her.

"Every night this week he asked if I wanted to have a drink and work together. Tonight was harder to turn him down because the rest of us were going out together—and he wasn't invited." Thảo sighed. "I wish things hadn't come to this."

"He chose Greg over us." Zoe shook her head. "As long as he's on Greg's side, I can't be with him. This isn't some fundraising gala in small-town central New York. Prestige is the biggest theater in the DMV."

"I know you were best friends in college and became more than friends, but I've known him almost his entire adult life. There's something he's not telling us." Thảo traced outlines around the silverware on the table.

"If he can't tell either of his best friends, then we have to do what's right. For all of us." Zoe's eyes softened. "For Derek, too, even if he won't."

Zoe had lost her fight in college and she refused to give in so easily this time. Not when they were going to make even bigger waves about the racism in the DC theater scene. Hopefully their walkout would grab the attention of those in New York, too.

"Thảo, babe, you ready to head home?" Katie Mai called over to their booth. "It's almost midnight and we have an early day tomorrow."

"We're almost done. Can you get a rideshare?" Thảo turned

back to Zoe. "I hope this is the right thing to do. If we fail, we will all have a mark against us as troublemakers."

"I believe in what we stand for and my Boss Babes are here for us," Zoe reassured her.

Thảo hugged Zoe and left with the actors.

Zoe's chest tightened. Is this how Derek felt when he spoke of the cast depending on him? She had her boutique to fall back on but what about the actors and Thảo? If they failed to change anything, Greg would gleefully punish everyone involved, including Derek.

No, she couldn't give up now. Reina was lining up media while Trixie had commandeered a karaoke machine to use for the speech tomorrow. They needed as many people there as possible to rock the boat.

They'd voted for her to be their spokesperson and she would make sure their voices were heard by as many people as possible. Zoe pulled out her phone and texted her brother for backup.

Whatever happened after, she'd have her best friends and family with her. Everyone except for Derek.

CHAPTER 48

erek chugged his third coffee of the morning as he worked to add the Vietnamese back to work with the changes they'd made to the show since removing it. He tried his best to sing the words to himself to make sure the Viet and English flowed well together, but he couldn't remember the correct pronunciation for everything. Hopefully Thảo could help him clean things up later.

Once he'd fixed the script, he headed over to Prestige early to find Greg. Derek wouldn't ask for permission but would inform him that they had reverted the script to his and Thảo's original vision.

He arrived to learn from the artistic director's assistant that Greg would arrive before ten, when tech was scheduled to begin. Derek found himself walking the stage multiple times, both alone and with the set and lighting designers, who were finishing some last-minute things before the actors arrived.

He could hardly believe that everything was coming together. This was his first musical as cowriter and director. As long as he stayed on course, this production would open more doors for not just his actors but for all Asian American actors. Thảo and Zoe would understand after they saw the latest version of the script. *And* after he apologized.

From his seat in the sixth row from the stage, he tried to etch this moment in his memory. His set designer had transported them to a Vietnamese fairy tale with touches of modern elements as a nod to the rock songs. At first glance, it looked simplistic, but it would transform to become the different locations: the sisters' home, the palace, and his favorite, the persimmon tree where the Emperor vowed to never take Tấm for granted again.

The only designer he hadn't spoken with recently was Zoe. She'd done an admirable job of avoiding him, but she'd remained professional by emailing updates to him and the rest of the production team. They weren't working in costumes yet, but Heather had scheduled final fittings for many of the actors.

Rehearsal started in ten minutes. Derek hoped he could pull off a pep talk that would keep everyone motivated. The next five days would consist of ten-to-twelve-hour days. Longer for the crew, who'd been here at nine to prepare for all the behind-the-scenes work.

Thảo, who'd also managed to avoid him all morning, was in deep conversation with Heather. She'd been in a meeting with her assistant musical director and the musicians who would be performing live later during tech after everyone had a better handle on the technical elements.

At ten o'clock sharp, the twelve cast members gathered on the stage for the pre-tech rehearsal meeting. The actors' eyes widened as they *ooh*'d and *ah*'d over the set, as it was their first time seeing it complete. That's exactly how Derek felt this morning, too.

"Welcome to tech," Heather announced. "We have long days ahead of us, so make sure to stay hydrated and eat. I don't need anyone hurting their voices or passing out because you're not eating."

She stepped back to give Derek the floor. Behind him, Greg's voice boomed as he finished a phone call. He hadn't expected the artistic director to come to the first day of tech. Derek groaned inwardly. That man had the worst timing.

Derek took a deep breath and ignored the swirling in his stomach. He'd talk to the actors first and send them to the assistant musical director to warm up.

"Before we start rehearsal, I want to thank you for believing in me and taking a chance on a brand-new musical. You, too, Thảo." He turned around to meet her eye but she was sitting several rows behind him, tapping on her phone.

Derek cleared his throat and continued. "We're about to change how the world sees us with this production. Vietnamese folks—no, all Asian Americans—will be able to see themselves in this story. A fairy tale full of hope, love, and—"

Katie Mai and Danny walked downstage and hopped off into the audience. They walked past him and out of the theater. The rest of the cast followed suit.

"Where are you going? I wasn't finished." Derek looked at Heather, who looked at him blankly.

Thảo stood up and faced him.

"We refuse to be in a production that allows that man"—Thảo pointed at Greg—"to dictate how we tell our story. Until you both agree to revert to the original Vietnamese lyrics, none of us will step foot inside this theater."

Before he could tell her that he'd already changed everything back, she walked out.

"Derek, how could you let this happen?" Greg fumed.

Derek's mouth dropped. Thảo and some of the actors had given him the cold shoulder, but he didn't think they'd walk out over it. If only he'd told Thảo before rehearsal started, he could've stopped this.

"You get your cast back onstage right now. We've invested too much money in this show for this. Wait until I call Actors' Equity for this unsanctioned strike," Greg threatened no one in particular.

"Maybe we should see what they're doing?" Heather suggested.

Derek forced his legs to move. He needed to tell Thảo—and Zoe—that he was ready to stand up to Greg. Heather and Greg followed him into the lobby. A crowd had gathered outside in front of Prestige.

"How dare they protest in front of my theater!" Greg exclaimed. "I'm calling the police to disperse them."

"Police? We can take care of things ourselves," Derek said, trying to calm down the artistic director, but the man stomped off.

"I'll go after him," Heather offered. "You should go out there and talk to Zoe."

She ran after Greg, leaving Derek alone in the lobby. He stared out the large glass windows until his eyes focused on purple hair. His heart leapt as he found Zoe standing on a riser or makeshift platform of some kind. She was speaking passionately into a— karaoke machine?

For a moment, he was transported back to senior year at CNY College. Zoe didn't have a microphone back then, but the crowd had been so small, they'd had no problem hearing her.

Today, there had to be at least sixty people standing behind Zoe, with more joining them. They held protest signs that read:

ASIAN STORIES ARE UNIVERSAL STORIES

NOT YOUR MODEL MINORITY

PROUD TO BE ASIAN

And his favorite: LOVE OUR PEOPLE LIKE YOU LOVE OUR FOOD.

All his friends were out there, risking their jobs in order to stand up for his musical. But it wasn't just his musical. It belonged to all of them. Goose bumps spread across his arms. He'd been unable to stand behind her in college, but she'd given him an opportunity for a do-over.

Derek rushed outside as news vans pulled up. The camera people and reporters scrambled for positions next to the people who were already live streaming from their phones.

"This could be the first musical on Broadway with an all-Asian creative team and cast. Yet a white man wants us to strip all the Vietnamese from it because he claims they can't sell tickets that way," Zoe announced.

The crowd booed.

"The artistic director demanded that we dumb down this show for non-Asian audiences. He thinks you're not smart enough to understand it," Zoe continued.

"He's the dumb one," someone in front of Derek yelled.

"Why aren't we allowed to tell our stories the way we want to and not how Greg A. Powers thinks they should be told?" Zoe had the crowd on edge. "Our voices matter. Our stories matter!"

The actors began chanting, "Love our people like you love our food."

Wait, was that Zoe's brother chanting with them? And there were faces he'd seen cleaning up at Eden Center. Even their elders had come out to protest. Derek's heart swelled. He thought he'd have to face Greg alone this morning, but he had an entire community behind him. He needed to talk to Zoe. He needed to stand with her the way he hadn't in college.

"Zoe!" he yelled through the crowd, but she didn't hear him.

He gently pushed his way past people of all backgrounds who had joined them. Before he could get there, Greg appeared in front of Zoe.

"Look who's here! Greg A. Powers, artistic director of Prestige Repertory!" Zoe waved at the man, whose face was beet red with anger.

Greg turned to Derek, who'd finally made it to the center of the crowd. "Did you put your girlfriend up to this?"

"No, but I wish I'd been a part of this." Derek climbed the makeshift platform to stand next to Zoe.

"You don't have to do this," she whispered to him.

"I have to. I want to," he responded and grabbed her hand.

She squeezed his hand and nodded. Relief flooded his body. At least for this moment, they were in it together. He would apologize later and hope that she'd give him another chance to be her boyfriend.

"I called the cops. You need to leave right now." Greg waved his finger at Zoe and everyone behind her.

"The sidewalk is public property, so you can't make us." Zoe smirked.

"This is my theater. I'm in charge!" spat Greg. "I should've never allowed Derek to hire you."

"You told me I had final say on everything about *The Brocaded Slipper*," Derek countered.

"As long as you did what I wanted," the man shot back.

"We're changing everything back to the way it was originally written," Derek demanded. He should've stood up to the man much, much sooner.

"This is all your fault. You poisoned him against me," Greg accused Zoe. "If only you'd come to my office after hours like I suggested, we could've avoided all this."

"Wait, what?" Derek turned to Zoe. "He sexually harassed you?" Derek's hands balled into fists, ready to punch Greg.

"He's not worth it." Zoe pulled him back.

"He came on to me, too," Katie Mai cried out as she stepped forward. "He told me if I didn't get 'cozy' with him, he'd make up a reason for Derek to fire me. I don't even like men."

Katie Mai pulled Thảo in for a deep kiss. The crowd tittered.

"He tried the same with me," said another actress and then another.

"Did you catch that everyone?" Zoe asked the reporters and people live streaming.

"Loud and clear!" replied a Black woman standing next to them as she kept her phone camera on Greg.

"Lies!" Greg sputtered. "They came on to me because they wanted preferential treatment."

Derek's nostrils flared as he unclenched his hands and clenched them back into fists. Hitting a white man in front of so many witnesses was never a good idea. Not that Derek wanted to resort to violence. He could put up with Greg's numerous microaggressions disguised as feedback for the musical. But now the man had harassed his friends *and* the woman he loved.

Enough. He'd let the artistic director get away with too much already. His resolve to undo Greg's suggestions were now cemented. Derek wouldn't compromise on anything the man asked.

"How dare you accuse me of this nonsense," Greg continued as spit flew out of his mouth. His face was purple with rage as he pointed to the women who had spoken up about what he'd done to them.

"Shut up, Greg!" Derek commanded.

All the stress and anxiety that had been weighing him down dissipated with those words. He stood taller. He would no longer allow this man to bully him or anyone he cared for.

CHAPTER 49

Zoe's heart pounded in her chest. She'd never heard Derek sound so definitive, so sure of himself.

"For a man who loves to hear himself talk, you're not very smart," Derek continued. "You publicly admitted to sexually harassing my friends *and* my girlfriend."

Derek was standing up for her—in front of what must be at least a hundred people now. She grabbed his hand and pulled him closer to her. He smiled wryly at her.

"I hope you'll be my girlfriend again," he whispered. "I'm sorry it took so long for me to stand up to Greg."

"You're doing it now and that's what matters." Zoe handed him the microphone. "Keep going."

Derek nodded and squared his shoulders as if ready for battle.

"It's time that the community knows you for the bully you are," Derek said as he turned to the crowd.

Greg's red face had lost all color. He shook his head at Derek, as if daring him to continue. Derek glared back at him until Greg looked away. Zoe smirked at the artistic director's discomfort. Finally he was getting a taste of what he'd given to her and probably everyone he'd ever worked with.

"This man was supposed to be my mentor. Instead he sabotaged rehearsals of *The Brocaded Slipper*. I changed all the Vietnamese to English only because Greg threatened to fire me and take over if I didn't." Derek swallowed hard. "I couldn't let him ruin what we've worked so hard for."

Zoe gasped along with everyone else. Greg had been overbearing, but to take away Derek's dream show from him was even more villainous than she could have imagined.

"Why didn't you tell me?" she asked. Everything about the night she broke up with him made sense now. He had been trying to protect her and save the show.

"I was scared to lose everything I've worked for." Derek met her eyes and caressed her cheek. She leaned into his touch. "I thought I could fix things without taking you down with me."

"You idiot," she said affectionately. "We're in this together. All of us."

Everyone working on the production murmured in agreement.

"You were under so much stress that I didn't want to make it worse. You hired your boutique staff to help with the costumes. I didn't want to let you down."

"No, I let you down by assuming you didn't care about the show the same way I did," said Zoe. "I'm sorry, Derek."

Her stomach swirled with anxiety and regret. She shouldn't have given him an ultimatum when all he'd tried to do was to keep *The Brocaded Slipper* from Greg's grubby hands.

"I should've said something sooner. I tried to save the musical by myself but instead I lost the people I love most, especially you." Derek's eyes shimmered with unshed tears.

"You love me?" Zoe whispered. "Like more than best friends?"

"Now who's being an idiot?" Derek chuckled. "I've been in agony since you walked out that night. How shall I regain my heart that you've won from me?"

"Stop misquoting Sondheim," Thảo called out. "Just tell her, dummy."

Zoe laughed. How could she have forgotten they were surrounded by friends *and* strangers.

"I love you, Zoe," Derek declared. "I know I have to work on our communication skills, but will you have me back?"

"You've changed. You're daring. You're different at a protest," Zoe sang shyly with her own version of "It Takes Two" from *Into the Woods*.

"Seriously?" Thảo said loudly behind them. Everyone laughed.

"I love you, too, Derek." She put her arm around his waist. "I don't want to be apart from you anymore."

"I'm going to kiss you in front of all these people," Derek whispered.

Zoe wrapped her arms around his neck and their lips reunited. Electricity buzzed through her body as he kissed away all the harsh words between them.

The crowd cheered and applauded. She laughed into his mouth before she pulled away.

"To be continued at my place," she whispered in his ear. It was more than an invitation. It was a promise.

Derek grinned and nodded.

"Oh, for fuck's sake," cried out Greg. "Get your disgusting public display of affection away from my theater!"

Before either of them could respond, a Latino man in his fifties stepped onto the platform. He was wearing a navy suit and carried a very somber expression.

"Your theater?" A Hispanic man stepped onto the platform. "I'm Moises Perez, president of the Prestige's board and have something to say about that. May I?"

The man gestured at the microphone. Derek eagerly handed it over and raised his hand up to silence the crowd.

"My fellow board members and I conducted an emergency

meeting mere moments ago." The man cleared his throat. "Effective immediately, Gregory Powers is no longer employed by Prestige Repertory."

The crowd broke out in applause and cheers.

"How dare you! You'll be hearing from my lawyer," Greg yelled.

"I look forward to it," replied the board president.

Greg opened his mouth but was at a loss for words. A first since Zoe had met him.

"Go home, Greg," Derek shouted.

The crowd roared as if Derek had made a three-point basket to beat the buzzer. Soon chants of "Go home, Greg!" chased the man away from the platform. He tried to disappear into the crowd, but the news crews ran after him.

"We did it," Thảo said as she hugged Katie Mai. "It worked!"

Zoe grinned. When she'd suggested the walkout, it was a shot in the dark. But seeing Greg run away with his tail between his legs had been icing on the cake.

"Hey, you," she whispered to Derek as their friends high-fived and hugged one another, "Kiss me again."

CHAPTER 50

Zoe stifled a yawn as she threaded her needle. The adrenaline rush from the morning's protest had had worn off hours ago.

She smiled to herself as she pinned a custom appliqué onto Tấm's final costume, which was softer and more feminine than her previous ones. The creamy orange chiffon hinted at the persimmon tree where the Emperor completed his third and last quest to prove his love to her.

Derek had also completed a quest by standing up for himself, her, and *The Brocaded Slipper*. After the crowd outside had broken up, he and Thảo went straight to work to undo Greg's damage to the show. He'd tried to send the cast home, but they insisted on staying to rehearse their choreography.

He'd promised to come downstairs when he had a break. They had so much to discuss without an audience following their every word.

"You should take a nap," TJ suggested from his worktable next to her. "Shawn set up cots in the extra fitting room."

With all the late work hours due to their shortened timeline, the costume shop manager had instituted a no-questions asked nap policy. Sleep deprivation made operating the industrial sewing machines and extra-hot steam irons dangerous, so Shawn encouraged power naps.

Zoe filed the idea way for Something Cheeky. Her sewists didn't pull late nights often, but it might be a possibility once she launched her Asian-inspired formal-wear collection. She hadn't told anyone about her decision, but she was ready.

"I'm almost done attaching the last persimmon appliqué— ouch!" Zoe had stabbed her thumb with the needle.

She immediately dropped everything on the table and stepped back. Blood was the most difficult stain to remove from fabric, especially from a delicate fabric that couldn't handle a lot of scrubbing, like chiffon.

"Zoe, are you okay?" Derek called out from the costume shop door.

His forehead wrinkled with concern as he handed Shawn the large paper bags in his hands before rushing over to Zoe.

"What happened? Are you hurt?" he asked.

"I'm fine." Zoe laughed as she held out her thumb, where a tiny red bead of blood appeared. "It shocked me more than hurt. I only jumped back because I didn't want to mess up the costume."

"Chill, Derek. She's not going to sleep for a hundred years," TJ teased as he handed Zoe an antibacterial wipe and a bandage.

"Wrong fairy tale." Zoe rolled her eyes at TJ but smiled anyway.

"Let me," Derek offered and took the first-aid supplies from her. He cleaned her thumb and gently bandaged it as if she were made of glass.

"That was proof you needed a nap." TJ tsked disapprovingly. "Or to go home."

"What I need is caffeine. And to rethread my needle."

"I thought you might, since it's the midafternoon lull." Derek jumped in before Zoe could remind TJ that opening night was in less than a week. "I brought coffee, sodas, energy drinks, *and* snacks for the costume shop as a thank-you for your hard work."

"He's a keeper," TJ whispered loudly to Zoe. "Oooh, are those shrimp chips?"

TJ pointed to a familiar pink and red bag sticking out of the brown grocery bags.

"That's very thoughtful of you," she said to Derek. "Everyone could use a pick-me-up."

"I need some sunlight while we still got some. And fresh air," TJ announced. "Anyone want to join me?"

Zoe chuckled at TJ's not-so-subtle way of clearing the costume shop to give her and Derek privacy.

"Great idea," agreed Shawn as he winked at her. "Let's take a fifteen-minute break and stretch our legs."

The staff murmured thanks to Derek as they grabbed refreshments and followed TJ and Shawn upstairs. The costume shop was silent without the rhythmic whir of sewing machines and the steam hissing from the irons.

It was also the first time she had been alone with Derek after their breakup. Here was their chance to talk without an audience, yet Zoe didn't know how to start. She bit her bottom lip as she spread the costume out on the table to keep the chiffon from wrinkling.

"I brought you this." Derek smiled awkwardly as he dug out a large thermos.

"What is it?" Zoe asked as shyness overcame her.

How in the world could she feel this way with a man who had seen her naked multiple times in the past several weeks *and* made her cry out in pleasure in more ways than she'd thought possible.

"It's cà phê sữa đá," he spoke the Vietnamese haltingly. The ice clanged inside as he shook the container.

"I will never turn down iced coffee," she said a little too loudly for the now quiet room. "Hey, that was good!"

"Thanks. I've been watching videos online to work on my Viet pronunciation." He blushed.

"That's really smart, Derek. But you don't have to learn it for me." She dug through the pile of snacks that TJ had dumped onto the counter. "Almond chocolate Pocky! I didn't know there was a place near Prestige that sold it."

"I'm learning for myself," he admitted. "I had them delivered from H Mart. After this morning's excitement, we could bond over some childhood snacks. I got a bunch for the cast, too."

"I love that you're always thinking of others," she said as she glanced at the clock. The staff would return from their break soon. "But I'm done sharing you with others for a while. Let's go somewhere we can talk in private."

"Fitting room?" he said the same time she did. They laughed.

Those two words conjured flashes of their various afternoon "meetings." They'd only been apart for a week, but it might as well have been a month. She hadn't realized how much she needed Derek in her life and in her arms until he wasn't.

"This time we won't be interrupted," Zoe added in a husky voice.

His eyes darkened and he grabbed her hand. "Let's go."

As SOON AS Derek turned the lock to the spare dressing room, Zoe pinned him against the door. She grabbed his hair as his lips crashed into hers. He was as hungry for her as she was for him.

She deepened their kiss as she pressed her breasts against his chest. He groaned, grabbing her ass and pulling her impossibly closer. Heat flared through her torso as her body reawakened to his touch.

For six days—at least 144 hours—she'd deprived herself of everything Derek. She'd avoided looking at his handsome face, laughing at his jokes, and feeling the heat of his naked body in her bed. They had lost time to make up starting now.

"I'm sorry for making you choose," Zoe said as she broke their kiss to catch her breath.

"You're not a mind reader. I should've told you how bad things had gotten," replied Derek as he swept her hair back to drop kisses on her neck.

She shivered as tiny jolts zipped across her back. Her eyes closed as she sighed in pleasure.

"You were so hot this morning when you took charge," she whispered. She rubbed her cheek against his jaw, allowing his stubble to tickle her. He smelled of coffee and cinnamon.

"You're the one who was sexy in the spotlight," he said as his thumb drew circles around her nipple through her top.

"I'm usually a behind-the-scenes person." Zoe's mouth went slack as she reveled in the delicious sensations his thumb created.

"Zoe, I wish you could see how beautiful you are right now." His eyes widened. "I have an idea."

He turned off the fluorescent lights and flicked the switch for the bulbs that framed the vanity's mirror. A soft, warm glow filled the small room.

"What are you doing?" Zoe laughed. "I'm not putting on makeup or costumes. I'd rather rip your clothes off and do unspeakable things to you."

"Fuck, yes." Derek's voice deepened. "But first, I want you to see how beautiful you are when you come. Trust me?"

Things had gone sour between them when she'd stopped believing that he'd support her. She vowed to never make that mistake again.

Zoe answered with a slow, deep kiss. He began undressing her until all that was left were her bra and panties. She was very glad that she'd taken care to match her undergarments today.

"Your turn."

Her costuming skills made quick work of the buttons on his shirt. Soon his clothes were a pile on the floor except for his black boxers. The thin fabric couldn't hide the thickness of his hard cock.

He walked her backward to the vanity and turned her around so that she faced the large mirror. Standing behind her, he met her eyes in the mirror and cocked his head as if to ask *Are you ready?*

Zoe bit her lip and nodded as her body tingled in anticipation.

"Relax into my arms," he said as he wrapped his arm around her waist.

"Yes, Director," she murmured as she readjusted her feet to do as he asked. She sighed as her almost bare back rested on his naked chest. Heat surged between her thighs as she imagined all the ways he might touch her in this position.

"Open your eyes and see how I see you." He lifted her chin up.

Her eyelids fluttered open. Zoe's breath hitched. The woman in the mirror with flushed cheeks and swollen lips was stunning. Was this how she looked to him whenever they made love?

"How have I missed thee? Let me count the ways," Derek said as he met her eyes in the mirror.

"My favorite sonnet?" Zoe arched her eyebrows in surprise. He'd remembered her love for Elizabeth Barrett Browning. "You're such a romantic."

"But this is my own version. For your ears only." He stroked her shoulder as he continued. "I miss the way your eyes light up whenever you get a new design idea."

She turned her head to face him as much as she could without leaving the strength of his chest. He kissed her hard and deeply, his hot tongue thrusting into her mouth and claiming her as his. She moaned into his mouth as she eagerly returned his kiss. When he finally pulled away, she grumbled impatiently.

"How have I missed thee?" Zoe said as she tried to catch her breath. A sonnet could be a duet. "I miss the way you bite your bottom lip when you're super-focused. It's so cute."

Derek's eyes were dark as he unhooked her bra. She lifted her arms one at a time so he could slip it off. She sighed as her breasts hung heavy and ready for his attention.

"I miss your silky breasts." He cupped both breasts in his hands. "And hard nipples."

He reached up and rolled her nipples between his thumbs and forefingers. Groaning as they tightened, she forced herself to keep her eyes open. He continued until he was satisfied with the hardness of her nipples.

"How do I love thee? Let me count the ways." He rubbed his palms across her sensitive nipples. "I love your courage to try new things on your own—and succeed at opening your own boutique."

Zoe sighed as tiny jolts zipped through her body. She was weak in the knees, but she knew that Derek would keep her steady. He'd be there to support her like he always promised.

"How do I love thee?" Zoe murmured softly. "I love the way you envision a future that puts our people in the spotlight."

Her entire body tensed with anticipation as she followed his reflection. He caressed her hip and then her ass. She held her breath waiting for him to touch her even more intimately.

"You're the only person in my spotlight, Zoe."

Derek tucked his fingers into the lace and pulled down her panties. He helped her step out of them. The cool air on her thighs and pussy only intensified the heat growing inside her. He ran his fingers between her lips, grazing her clit to send sparks through her. But it wasn't enough.

"Please," she begged his reflection as she pushed her ass out to meet his hand. "Touch my clit."

He met her eyes in the mirror and grinned. "How do I love thee? I love how you're always ready to stand up for your values and yourself. It's so fucking sexy."

Derek emphasized his words as his fingers found her most sensitive spot. He caressed it with the pads of his fingers, adding the right amount of pressure to make her moan. Zoe's eyes rolled back as the waves of pleasure pulsed through her body. Her hips bucked against his hands. She needed more than his fingers.

"Abso-fucking-lutely beautiful," he whispered. "See how you've bloomed, Zoe."

With effort, she blinked her eyes open to meet his in the mirror. He smiled encouragingly and gestured for her to watch herself. The woman in the mirror was incredibly sexy as she undulated in time with her boyfriend's hand. That woman was her.

And then there was Derek. His eyes were slightly unfocused behind his glasses. He bit his bottom lip as he concentrated on giving her pleasure. Zoe swallowed a sob. He truly loved her and would do anything to make her happy. It didn't matter what she chose to do next. She knew that he'd support her completely.

Zoe loved him so much that she thought her chest could burst. She'd been a fool not to have seen it sooner. It'd taken her too many years to recognize how she'd felt about it.

"I love the way you found your voice this morning," she panted. "I promise to never give you ultimatums again."

"You won't have to because I'm never keeping secrets from you again." He nibbled her neck as she bucked into his hand.

"I love you, Derek," she cried hoarsely. "Now fuck me."

"As you wish."

He quickly ditched his boxers and grabbed a condom from his wallet to slide onto his cock. She smiled hungrily at his hard-on before meeting his eyes in the mirror. Derek gently bent her over the vanity table but tapped her chin to remind her to keep her eyes open. He groaned as he slid into her.

"How have I missed thee? I've missed your cock." Zoe's laugh turned into a grunt as he thrust into her. She held on to the table as their bodies reunited again and again. Her eyes threatened to roll back but she'd promised him to keep her eyes on the mirror.

Derek's eyes bore into hers in the mirror. Together, they watched as the other came and shattered into a million pieces. Zoe knew that he'd always be there to hold her up. And her him.

CHAPTER 51

Zoe washed her hands and straightened the neckline on her dress. She could spare a few seconds for a quick check in the bathroom mirror before heading out to the opening-night reception. The actors had received a five-minute-long standing ovation at curtain call, which had given her a chance to beat the crowd to the bathroom. Downing a large iced coffee to calm her nerves before the show had been a mistake.

"Excuse me," a petite Asian woman a couple of sinks down asked. She was wearing what had to be a custom dress, because it fit her perfectly. "Are you Zoe Tran, the costume designer?"

"Yes, I am," Zoe said proudly. This was the first stranger who'd recognized her from the program.

"Is that your design, too?" She gestured to Zoe's deep purple satin dress. "It's stunning."

Zoe nodded. She'd kept the classic áo dài silhouette, but she'd skipped the high collar. She'd draped the fabric to create a dramatic asymmetrical off-the-shoulder neckline. Underneath she wore matching straight-legged satin pants pressed with a sharp crease.

"It's my take on a modern áo dài. I didn't catch your name."

"I'm Lan Hoang." She shook Zoe's hand. "I'm a stylist and have some high-profile clients who would love your work. I know Kelly Marie would love your designs."

Zoe's mouth dropped.

"As in *the* Kelly Marie Tran?"

Lan winked. "And many others."

"Wow. That would be amazing." Zoe tried to play it cool but a giant grin spread across her face.

"Can I see your phone?" She tapped on Zoe's phone and then Lan's phone vibrated. "There. Now we have each other's numbers. I'll reach out to you next week."

"I look forward to it," Zoe said calmly, even though she wanted to jump up and down in excitement.

"I'll see you at the reception." She nodded and exited Zoe's life as quickly as she'd entered it.

If Lan's confident stride in the three-inch heels was any indication of the woman's ambition, Zoe would be foolish to pass up this opportunity. She couldn't wait to find Derek to share the good news.

An impromptu receiving line had formed next to the lobby bar. Derek grinned ear-to-ear as people shuffled through to offer their congratulations. Zoe could tell that Derek's eyes were beginning to glaze over and a tick was starting in his cheek from smiling too long.

"Excuse me," Zoe interrupted as she sidled up to Derek. She batted her eyes at the gray-haired man still shaking Derek's hand. "I need to borrow Mr. Director for a bit."

"Apologies. Please enjoy the opening reception and bar." Derek bowed and waved his arm toward the bar.

"I needed a break. Thank you," he whispered in relief as she tucked her arm into his elbow and led him toward a quiet corner of the lobby.

She grabbed two glasses of champagne off a tray from the nearest waitstaff. The caterer had transformed the large atrium with several stations of tiny hors d'oeuvres and desserts. All Vietnamese-inspired, obviously.

"Once again, I'm here to save my damsel in distress," she teased.

"I could've stepped away whenever I wanted." Derek pressed his lips together and shook his head. "Yeah, you saved me lots of small talk."

Zoe laughed and handed him a glass for a toast. "Congrats, babe. You did it!"

"No, we all did it." Derek wrapped an arm around her waist and pulled her in for a kiss.

Zoe sighed happily in his embrace. It was freeing to hold him and kiss him publicly without worrying about a certain former artistic director being around.

"There you are!" A familiar feminine voice called out to them.

Derek groaned and broke off their kiss. Zoe blinked her eyes open to find his mother waving at them. Zoe's mom was right behind her. Their moms had met for the first time the day before and—to no one's surprise—hit it off immediately.

"We've been looking for you two, but you're hiding back here making out," her mom said a little too loudly.

"Mom!" Zoe blushed. "Keep your voice down, please."

"All this kissing will lead to grandbabies," her mother said in a marginally lower voice as she nodded in approval.

"Not yet Co Hồng," Derek's mother tugged on Hồng's arm. "They need to get married first."

"Yes, Chị Linh, we should meet with the fortune teller to find an auspicious date," replied her mom. "I know just the person."

"Will you two stop!" Zoe laughed. "Let us enjoy tonight first."

Both moms tsked at them. Suddenly, they were planning their wedding as if Derek and Zoe weren't standing next to them.

"They're not going to stop," Derek mock-whispered. "Are you hungry?"

"There are some adorable bánh mì sliders calling my name."

Zoe pointed at a table across the lobby. "Think we can make it over there without being stopped?"

"Mission accepted." Derek winked. "I'll make us a plate. You grab some drinks and meet me on the balcony."

Five minutes later, they were finally alone, outside in the warm summer air. This late at night, Southwest was fairly quiet except for a few cars and a couple of folks walking their dogs. She'd sweet-talked TJ into grabbing a bottle of champagne from behind the bar.

"I didn't realize how loud it was inside until we came out here." Zoe tore off the foil from the bottle. "Too bad we can't see the Potomac River from here now that the high-rises are up."

"I've got the perfect view from here," Derek said, looking directly at her.

"Kiss up." She laughed.

"You read my mind." Derek pulled her in for a deep kiss.

Kissing him under the stars was all she needed right now. Tech and dress rehearsals had kept them busy. This moment was the first time they'd been alone and too exhausted for more than a peck on the lips before passing out.

"How about we skip the reception and sneak back to my apartment," suggested Derek. His hand ran lazy circles around her back, leaving tingles in its path.

"As tempting as that sounds, our moms would kill us." Zoe chuckled as she imagined the two women storming the lobby to find them as they called out both their names.

"By the time we go back inside, they'll have names picked out for our future kids," Derek joked. "I'd rather stay out here with you."

"Me, too." She leaned against his shoulder. They swayed to the muffled music coming from inside. Zoe wasn't ready to discuss how they'd handle their relationship once Derek returned to New York. His contract was technically fulfilled tonight.

"Mr. Perez wants me to make a speech later," he said as he glanced at the glass doors.

"Then we should eat before you return to your duties. I'm starved." Zoe studied the two plates that he'd loaded with food. "Look how adorable these tiny egg rolls are."

She bit into the crispy outer wrapper and murmured in appreciation. They were almost as good as the ones from her parents' restaurant. Almost.

"I have news," Derek blurted.

His cheeks were flushed, but it wasn't due to nervousness or anxiety. He had a little bounce of excitement. It didn't feel like bad news.

"I have something, too. You first," she said encouragingly.

"Mr. Perez pulled me aside after the preshow donor dinner."

She was supposed to be his date, but Katie Mai's persimmon dress had snagged on a set piece during sound check. Even though she and TJ had worked as quickly as they could to fix it, Zoe had barely made it to her seat next to Derek before the house lights went down.

"Everything okay?" Zoe held her breath.

"He introduced me to Mike Chen, who's a new board member and donor."

"*The* Mike Chen, tech millionaire?" Zoe exclaimed. She'd never met him but knew he was a private partner of Hazel's Kitchen.

"Mike thinks he can get enough people to produce the show on Broadway."

"Are you serious?" Zoe yelled and immediately clapped her hand over her mouth.

"I couldn't believe it either, but our musical might go big-time." He ran his hand through his hair. "Our dream is coming true."

"Another toast then." Zoe filled their glasses.

"There's something else," Derek added before taking a long sip.

Zoe's entire body tensed while she waited for him to drop the news that he would return to New York and ask her to move with him. She didn't want to choose between her career and him.

"The board asked me to be the next artistic director for Prestige Rep."

"No way!" She blew out a breath in relief. "And?"

"I'm taking it. We're meeting next week to hash out details." Derek beamed.

"You're staying in DC?!" Zoe threw her arms around him in a giant bear hug.

"I was hoping we could move in together. If Mr. Bobbins will have me."

"I get the final vote, but he might appreciate some tuna-flavored bribes."

"I can do that." Derek laughed. "I haven't told my mom yet, but I'm hoping she'll move down here, too. It would be good to have her close by again."

"If you can't convince her, I'm sure my mom can."

"Those two together will be trouble!" Derek exclaimed dramatically. "What's your news?"

Zoe told him about her run-in with the celebrity stylist in the bathroom.

"Does this mean you're done with theater?"

"For now. It's time for me to launch my new formal-wear line. I used *The Brocaded Slipper* as an excuse to delay it because I was scared. But I'm ready now." The more she said it out loud, the more confident she felt about her decision.

"I don't want to take time away from your new fashion collection, but will you help us bring the show to New York?"

"Are you kidding? I'm not letting anyone mess up my designs." She huffed at the thought. "I'll come out of retirement only for you."

The music suddenly sounded clearer and louder. They turned to see Heather with her head out of the lobby door. "Derek, it's almost speech time."

"Be right there," he replied.

"Five minutes." Heather held up a hand to emphasize. "You're on after Mr. Perez introduces Mike Chen."

"Thank you, five," Derek said automatically.

Heather gave him a thumbs-up and disappeared.

"Well, Mr. Artistic Director, are you ready for your adoring fans?" Zoe asked as she straightened his collar.

"As long as I have you, all the other fans don't matter."

"You're so sappy, but you're *my* sap," she teased. Her tone grew serious as she looked into his eyes. "I love you, Derek."

"I love you, Zoe, too." He brushed her cheek.

"We have three more minutes out here." Zoe tiptoed up to meet his lips. "Kiss me again."

AUTHOR'S NOTE

When I first created Zoe Tran in my first book, *Happy Endings*, I didn't know she was demisexual. It was only during my work on this novel that her sexual orientation became important. I enjoy reading friends-to-lovers romances, but struggled with Zoe and Derek's best friends to lovers arc. Why couldn't they get together sooner? I always want my characters to bang as soon as possible, but that didn't work for their story.

Prior to writing *Something Cheeky*, I'd begun to explore how my sexuality didn't fit into the neat little heterosexual label I'd always worn. The more I explored the asexuality spectrum and specifically demisexuality, the more things clicked for me. I never had celebrity crushes—though I did pretend that Jordan was my favorite NKOTB boyfriend back in middle school. As an adult, I chose Idris Elba as the movie star I had the hots for. Yet, it was all a lie. I chose them to fit in and be able to join conversations about book boyfriends and sexy celebrities.

Now that I've embraced my demisexuality, I'm comfortable admitting that I don't have crushes on actors and actresses. I hope reading about Zoe will help other demis be more confident in their sexuality, too.

Looking at the story I'd plotted for Zoe and Derek, it made complete sense that Zoe is demisexual. She already had a deep, emotional connection with Derek. All she needed was to take him out of the friend zone. Perhaps Zoe was already demi in the beginning of my first draft and I didn't see it. It took understanding this part of myself in order to fully articulate it in her character.

Representing Zoe's asexuality was subconscious at first, but I purposely wanted her to be fat aka plus-sized. As someone who's never been skinny, I couldn't relate to waif-like heroines who were easily carried by their heroes. Or don their partner's large (to them) shirts. Olivia Dade's novels were some of the first romances I read where her heroines were unapologetically fat.

Similar to how my Vietnamese characters' heritage wasn't a conflict in their relationships, I wanted the same for Zoe with her body size. Not only that, I wanted Zoe to love her body and help other fat women feel great in their bodies. Perhaps in a parallel universe, I'm running a lingerie boutique similar to Something Cheeky.

Now that this novel has cemented my status as a theater nerd, let's discuss how much (and how little) theater has changed since I worked as a costume designer and costumer for the stage. During one of my professional summer jobs, I was deeply encouraged to teach white actors how to do their makeup in order to look "more Asian" for a production of *South Pacific*. After my shock wore off, I refused. Unlike Zoe, I didn't face any repercussions because helping actors with their stage makeup wasn't part of my job.

While *Hamilton* has demonstrated how color-blind casting (hiring actors for roles regardless of the characters' and actors' race) can be successful, we have a long way to go with equity and inclusion in theatre.

Even now, when AAPI folks are writing our own movies and musicals, we're criticized for being unrelatable (see Disney Pixar's *Red*) or not having enough English (see *K-Pop the Musical*). The pushback that Derek received is not new and not uncommon in creative industries. We're held to a higher standard when it comes to our work.

Yes, romances are supposed to be fun and escapist. However, it's important for me to show real-world struggles, such as racism and gentrification in my novels because BIPOC folks experience all these things and still find joy and love in their lives.

I encourage you to support work from BIPOC creators by buying their work, telling all your friends about work you've enjoyed, and leaving reviews for them. We need more voices telling our different experiences and stories.

Thanks for reading *Something Cheeky*. If you're a fellow theater nerd, hit me up on social media!

ABOUT THE AUTHOR

THIEN-KIM LAM writes stories about Vietnamese characters who smash stereotypes and find their happy endings. A recovering Type-Asian, she guzzles cà phê sữa đá, makes art, and bakes her feelings to stay sane. Thien-Kim is also a certified sex educator and the founder of Bawdy Bookworms, a subscription box that pairs spicy sexy romances with erotic toys. She's been featured on Jezebel, Bustle, *Entertainment Weekly*, and Oprah Daily.

thienkimlam.com